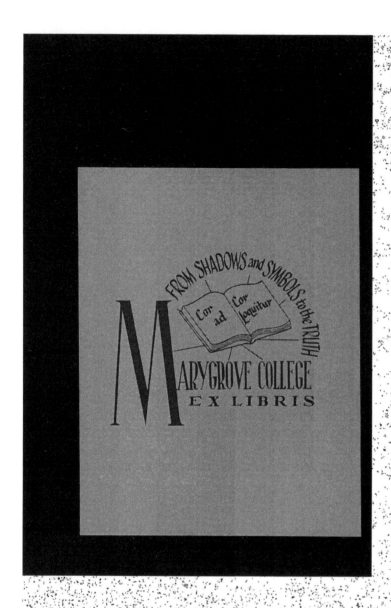

BINODINI

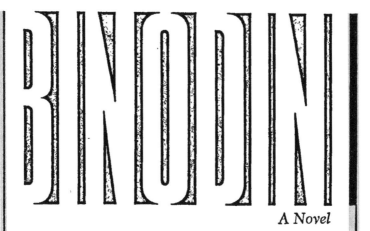

BINODINI

A Novel

by Rabindranath TAGORE

Translated by Krishna Kripalani
with sketches by Marilyn King

Published by

EAST-WEST CENTER PRESS, Honolulu

In co-operation with Sahitya Akademi, New Delhi

TRANSLATOR'S FOREWORD

This novel, which in the original Bengali is known as *Chokher Bali* (*lit.*, "Eyesore"), was first published in 1902. It is the first modern novel in Bengali—and, one might say, in Indian literature, for the modern movement in Indian literature was first registered in Bengali and was later carried to other Indian languages. This is not to say that no novels were written in Bengali or other Indian languages before it. The credit of being the first great novelist in modern Indian literature must belong to Tagore's predecessor, Bankim Chandra Chatterji, whose novels laid the foundation of this form of literature in modern India. Tagore himself had written two earlier novels in the 'eighties of the last century in which Bankim's influence is clearly discernible. But these novels, whether Tagore's or Bankim's, can hardly be called modern in any true sense of the word. They are historical romances or social melodramas or a mixture of both, and, while they can be still read with delight, they have little to do with life as commonly lived in contemporary India.

Though primarily a poet, it was Rabindranath Tagore who paved the way for the truly modern novel in India, whether realistic or psychological or concerned with social problems. And he began it with *Chokher Bali*.

The story is simple and is simply told. It centres round the problem of human relationship and tells of what happens behind the staid façade of a well-to-do, middle-class Bengali home of the period, where a widowed mother lives with her only son, on whom she dotes. One would imagine that nothing much ever happens in a home like that, and in fact nothing happens that may not happen in any Indian home. And yet passions, heroic and savage, are roused within hearts seemingly lowly, and battles rage until the home is nearly burnt down without flame or smoke being visible to the outside eye.

There are only six characters in the novel—the fond mother devoted and jealous, the pampered son vain and self-centred, the simple untutored wife whom intense suffering alone could turn into a woman, the pious aunt who finds refuge in religion, the loyal friend so virtuous and noble that he seems somewhat of a prig, and the beautiful and vivacious widow who gives the name to the book. Of all women characters created by Tagore in his many novels, Binodini is the most real, convincing, and full-blooded. In her frustrations and suffering is summed up the author's ironic acceptance of the orthodox Hindu society of the day.

A beautiful, talented, and well-educated girl cannot get a husband because the parents have spent what little they had on her education and could not save enough for the dowry. In panic—since an unmarried girl over twelve years of age is a social disgrace to a respectable Hindu family of the day—she is married off to a poor and sickly nobody who dies soon after, leaving her stranded in an unsympathetic village. Conscious of her beauty and wit, she rebels against the unjust privations of a bleak and humiliating existence to which as a widow she is condemned for life and asserts her right to love and happiness. She burns her fingers and nearly burns up a home. If in the end she retires from the contest it is not because she is crushed but because she disdains a victory achieved at too sordid a cost. Her tragedy is a lasting shame to the Hindu conscience.

Tagore wrote several other novels some of which are better known than *Chokher Bali* and as literary masterpieces far surpass it. In them his poetic imagination, the range and play of his intellect, his intuitive understanding of human nature, and his inimitable flair for style found more mature scope. But in no other work of his—the short stories excepted—is he a better storyteller. In no other novel has he watched the human drama with such gentle and calm irony, without the intrusion of poetic rhapsodies or intellectual dissertations. In no other novel has he accepted the kinship between love and sex with such frank sympathy—the white lotus of love rooted in the slime of desire.

Needless to say, much of the literary flavour of the original is lost in the translation. As Tagore himself once put it, whatever else a translation may retain, the vitamins are inevitably destroyed in the process. This is all the more so in the case of a novel which is concerned with intimate domestic relations in a typical Hindu family with its complicated pattern of values and sentiments utterly alien to the idiom of the English tongue. Between the two alternatives of taking liberties with the original in order to make the reading smooth for the reader and of rendering it faithfully even at the risk of some obscurity and of inviting the charge that the translation is in places un-English, the translator has chosen the latter, in the hope that the intelligent reader would prefer grappling with the authentic to being entertained by the spurious.

The translator's liberty in changing the title of the book may be excused if it is recalled that in the first synopsis of the story jotted down by the author in his note book the title originally conceived and given by him was "Binodini."

Main Characters in the Book

RAJLAKSHMI

A rich widow who dotes on her only son, Mahendra, and succeeds in spoiling him.

ANNAPURNA

Rajlakshmi's widowed sister-in-law and Mahendra's aunt on father's side who lives in the same house on sufferance. A good and pious lady.

MAHENDRA

Spoiled darling of a foolish mother. Main character in the novel, although anything but heroic.

BIHARI

Mahendra's friend from childhood. A true friend, able, honest and generous, but like most good people a bit too self-righteous.

ASHA

Annapurna's niece, later married to Mahendra. Illiterate and inexperienced, she is ill-equipped for the conflicts of a society in transition. Her utter innocence and sweetness of disposition are at once her asset and her handicap.

BINODINI

A young and attractive widow who rebels against the social injustice which deprives her of her woman's right to love and happiness. More sinned against than sinning, she is the real heroine of the story and one of the most authentic characters in Tagore's fiction.

viii

1

BINODINI'S MOTHER HARIMATI importuned Mahendra's mother Rajlakshmi for her son's hand. The two ladies had been brought up in the same village and had played together as children. Rajlakshmi pleaded with Mahendra.

"Mahin, my son, we must come to the rescue of the poor woman. I hear the girl is very pretty and was tutored by an English lady. She's just what you modern young people look for in a bride."

"But, mother, there are lots of modern young men besides myself."

"That's the trouble with you, Mahin. You won't even listen to a proposal."

"No great crime, mother. There are plenty of subjects left to talk about."

Having lost his father in infancy, Mahendra's ways with his mother were not what one would expect in a young man of twenty-two who had taken his M.A. degree and was now studying medicine. He was petulant and wayward and had constantly to be humoured and fussed over by his mother. Eating or resting, at work or at leisure, he needed his mother to hover round him. Like a kangaroo cub he continued to nestle in the maternal pouch long after he had been released from the womb.

This time when Rajlakshmi pressed him hard, Mahendra at last relented.

"Let's have a look at the girl," he said. But on the day fixed for the visit, he suddenly declared, "What's the use of my seeing her? Since I must marry to please you, why this farce of looking before the leap?"

There was a touch of resentment in the words, but the mother hardly took note of it, knowing that the resentment would turn into tenderness when he saw the bride for the first time on the wedding day. He would then wholeheartedly endorse the mother's choice.

And so with a light heart she fixed the wedding day. But as the day drew nearer, Mahendra became more nervous. Two or three days before the wedding he flatly announced, "No, mother, I can't go through with it."

Born with a silver spoon in his mouth and pampered since childhood, Mahendra was used to having his own way. The idea that he was being hustled to the altar to suit some-one else's wish had worked on his mind till it had become insufferable.

Mahendra's best friend was Bihari. He addressed Mahendra as Dada or elder brother and Rajlakshmi as mother. The mother looked upon him as a necessary and serviceable adjunct to her son, a sort of barge towed by her son's steamboat, and was accordingly and in a way fond of him. In her predicament she went to him and said, "My son, you must now marry the girl or else the poor thing. . . ."

"Please, forgive me," interrupted Bihari with folded hands, "this is more than I can do. I have often let you feed me with sweets which Mahendra did not care to touch, but while I don't mind being a dumping ground for left-over sweetmeats, where a girl is concerned . . . . no, it's too much."

Rajlakshmi was amused. She believed that Bihari was reluctant to marry because his world was centred in Mahendra and had no room in it for a bride. Flattered by such devotion, her affection for Bihari, largely compounded of pity, increased.

Though Binodini's father was not a rich man he did not stint where the education of his only daughter was concerned and had engaged a missionary lady as a private tutor. That his daughter was growing past the prescribed age of marriage seemed to have escaped him altogether. When he died, his widow was left with a grown-up daughter and hardly any money for dowry. The widowed mother was beside herself, frantically looking for a bridegroom. At length Rajlakshmi succeeded in getting Binodini married to a distant cousin of hers in her native village, Barashat. Soon after, the girl became a widow. Mahendra laughed. "Lucky I was not the bridegroom. With my wife a widow, where should I be?"

2

Three years passed. One day the mother and son resumed the old topic.

"I am being unnecessarily maligned, my son," complained Rajlakshmi.

"Why, mother, what havoc have you caused?"

"They say I am deliberately not letting you marry—lest I lose you to the bride."

"A very legitimate fear," said Mahendra. "Were I a mother, I should never take the risk, let people say what they will."

Rajlakshmi laughed. "What a thing to say!"

"The bride will monopolise the son," went on Mahendra. "Then what's to become of the dear, devoted mother? You may not mind it, but I—I hate the prospect."

Rajlakshmi was inwardly thrilled. Addressing her widowed sister-in-law who had just entered, she said: "Did you hear, Mejo-bou,* what Mahin said? He won't marry for fear I be ousted by the bride. Have you ever heard a thing so absurd?"

"That's too bad, my boy," replied Mahendra's aunt turning to him. "What is attractive at one age is ludicrous at another. It's time you let go your mother's apron and set

* Lit., second sister-in-law. In Bengal members of a family are addressed by terms denoting the exact relationship.

up a home of your own. It's shameful to see you behave like a little boy."

Rajlakshmi was not pleased at these words and what she said by way of retort was also more plain than pleasant. "If my son," she said, "loves his mother more than sons normally do, why need it seem shameful to you? Had you a son of your own, you would know what it means."

She is jealous of my good fortune, this widow with no child of her own, thought Rajlakshmi.

"It's you, sister, who broached the subject of a bride in the house," replied the sister-in-law, "otherwise what business have I?"

"If my son does not want a bride, what is it to you that you resent it so? If I could bring up my son all these years, I can still look after him—by myself. I need no one's help!"

Tears in her eyes, the sister-in-law hurried away without another word. The scene pained Mahendra and weighed on his mind. Returning early from college he went straight to his aunt's room. He knew well enough that what his aunt had said had no other motive save her affectionate concern for him. He also knew that she had a young niece, her deceased sister's daughter, an orphan, whom she would like him to marry, so that she might have the orphaned niece near her and see her happy. This sentiment of his aunt's seemed to him natural and very touching, despite his personal aversion to marriage.

There was not much of daylight left when Mahendra entered the room. His aunt Annapurna was sitting by the window, her head resting against the bars, her face drawn and pale. In the adjoining room lay her covered plate of rice, still untouched.

Mahendra was always easily moved to tears. At the sight of his aunt's face they welled up to his eyes. Coming closer he called affectionately, "Kakima!" *

* Auntie.

4

Forcing a wan smile, Annapurna murmured, "Come and sit down, Mahin."

"I'm very hungry," said Mahendra. "Won't you let me have some *prasad?*" *

Annapurna understood Mahendra's trick and forcing back her tears partook of her meal and helped Mahendra to some. By the time the meal was over Mahendra was so overcome with sentiment that wishing to please auntie he blurted out in a fit of effusion, "Kaki, will you not let me see your niece—of whom you have talked so often?"

No sooner had he uttered the words than his heart sank with fright. Annapurna smiled.

"Why, Mahin! . . . . are you planning marriage?"

"No, no," hurriedly explained Mahendra. "It's not of me I am thinking but of Bihari. So why not fix a date?"

"Bihari!" murmured Annapurna pensively. "Could the girl be so lucky as to have a husband like Bihari!"

Coming out of the aunt's room, Mahendra found his mother at the door.

"Is that you, Mahendra?" she asked. "What were you two discussing?"

"Nothing particular," replied Mahendra. "I went in for a *pan*." †

"But your *pans* are ready in my room."

Without replying Mahendra hurried away. Rajlakshmi entered the room and seeing Annapurna's eyes swollen with tears put two and two together. "Well, dear sister-in-law," she hissed, "so you have taken to pestering the boy." Saying which she swept out of the room, not deigning to wait for a reply.

---

* Food consecrated by being offered to or tasted by a deity or a holy person. In this case it means that Annapurna herself must first eat before Mahendra could partake of it.
† Betel nut and spices wrapped in a betel leaf, which Indians love to chew, especially after meals.

3

Mahendra had almost forgotten about the date. Annapurna had not. She wrote to the uncle who was her niece's guardian and fixed a date for the young men to see the girl.

"Why this undue haste, Kaki?" Mahendra protested when he heard of it, "I haven't yet spoken to Bihari."

"It can't be helped now," replied Annapurna. "What will they think of us if you fail to go to see the girl?"

Mahendra sent for Bihari and told him everything. "In any case let us see the girl," he added. "If you don't like her, no one can force her on you."

"I don't know about that," replied Bihari. "I wouldn't have the heart to say that Kaki's niece was not good enough for me."

"Excellent sentiment," said Mahendra.

"But it was wrong of you, Mahinda," * went on Bihari, "to foist obligations on others, evading yours. It is now very difficult for me. How can I hurt Kaki's feelings?"

Mahendra was embarrassed. "What then do you propose doing?" he asked coldly.

"Since you have assured her on my behalf, I shall marry the girl. No need of this farce of going to see her."

Bihari was devoted to Annapurna; his regard for her almost amounted to veneration. When Annapurna heard what Bihari had said, she sent for him and pleaded: "How can that be, my son? I can't let you marry a girl whom you have not seen. And if having seen her you do not like her, I swear you shall not consent to such a marriage."

* *Da* short for *dada*, elder brother. The suffix is also added to the name when addressing familiarly a friend senior in age. Feminine, *di* for *didi*.

On the day appointed for the visit, Mahendra as soon as he was back from college asked his mother for his silk kurta and his fine Dacca muslin dhoti.

"Why, where are you off to?" asked the mother.

"I'll tell you later," said Mahendra. "Please let me have them now."

Mahendra could not resist the temptation to put on his best—the youthful instinct to show off even when the girl to be seen was not for him.

The two friends set off on their mission. The girl's uncle, Anukul Babu of Shyambazar, lived in a three-storyed house that towered over the neighbourhood. After the death of his poverty-stricken brother, he had taken charge of the orphaned daughter. Annapurna had offered to keep the girl with herself, but though the offer was convenient to his purse, it did not suit his dignity. In fact so keen was his sense of social prestige that he did not once allow the girl to visit the aunt's house. The girl grew up to a marriageable age, but unfortunately the old Sanskrit adage, that the fruit of success depends on faith and earnestness, no longer works where the marriage of girls is concerned. Along with faith and earnestness not a little money is required. And whenever the question arose of providing a dowry for her, Anukul declared that he had daughters enough of his own and could not be expected to bear extra burden. And so the days passed and the girl remained unmarried. Such was the state of affairs when Mahendra well-groomed and perfumed arrived on the scene with his friend.

It was a day in April. The sun was about to set on the southern veranda of the second storey, floored with shining fancy tiles, where the friends were led up and seated at one end. In front of them were silver dishes piled with fruits and sweets and iced water in silver glasses frosted outside with dew. Mahendra and Bihari were feeling shy and embarrassed as they partook of refreshments. Down below in the garden the mali was sprinkling water over the plants. The south breeze laden with the cool fragrance of the moistened earth rustled against the loose ends of Mahendra's perfumed muslin scarf. Through the chinks in the doors and windows could be heard muffled whispers, giggles and the tinkling of ornaments.

After the refreshments Anukul Babu turned his glance in the direction of the inner apartment and called out, "Chuni, dear, let's have the *pans* please." In a little while one of the doors at the back was timidly opened and a young girl blushing all over came and stood beside the uncle, holding a casket of *pans* in her hand. "Why this shyness, little mother," * said the uncle. "Place the *pans* before the gentlemen." The girl bent down and with a trembling hand laid the casket on the floor near the guests. From the western end of the veranda the light of the setting sun cast its glow on her bashful face. In that instant Mahendra looked up and caught a glimpse of the sweet pathetic face of the shrinking maiden.

As the girl was about to leave Anukul Babu said, "Wait a minute, Chuni." Then turning to the guests he continued, "Bihari Babu, this is the daughter of my younger brother Apurba. He has passed away and she has now no one but me." He heaved a deep sigh.

Mahendra felt a tug of pity. He shot one more glance at the orphan girl. He wondered what her age was. The auntie had never mentioned her age. Only vague casual statements, "Must be twelve or thirteen"—which probably meant fourteen or fifteen. But having been brought up on sufferance, her timid, frightened air belied her years and bore evidence of a youth retarded.

Mahendra was moved. He asked, "What's your name?" Anukul Babu enthusiastically endorsed the guest's interest. "Do tell your name, little mother." Used to obedience to the

* Affectionate way of addressing a young girl.

8

uncle's commands, the girl murmured with bent head, "Ashalata." *

Asha! What a tender, pathetic name and how sweet the voice that uttered it! Orphaned Asha! Mahendra was deeply affected. When the two friends came out and were driving back in the carriage, Mahendra said, "Bihari, don't let go this girl."

Without giving a direct reply, Bihari said. "She reminds one of her aunt. Her nature must be equally sweet."

"I hope the burden which I have thrust on your shoulders does not weigh very heavy now?" asked Mahendra.

"Indeed, no. I dare say I can bear it."

"Why strain yourself? Let me take over the burden. What do you say?"

Bihari looked at Mahendra. His voice was grave as he spoke. "Are you serious, Mahendra? Please make up your mind while there's yet time. If you marry her, Auntie will be far more pleased. She can then have the niece always by her."

"Are you crazy?" laughed Mahendra. "Had I wanted it, it would have happened long ago."

Bihari did not say anything more and took his leave. Mahendra did not reach home directly. He made a long detour and slowly retraced his way home, arriving at a very late hour. His mother was still busy in the kitchen and Kakima had not yet returned from her niece's house; Mahendra went up to the roof terrace which was deserted and spreading a mat lay down. Silently the half-moon spread its eerie radiance over the city's house-tops. The mother came up to announce the dinner. Mahendra responded lazily. "I'm too cozy to get up, mother."

"Let me fetch the dinner here," offered the mother.

"I don't feel like eating. I've had enough."

"Where did you eat?" asked the mother.

* *Asha* literally means hope, and *lata*, creeper.

9

"That's a long story. I'll tell you later."

Rajlakshmi was hurt at this unusual behaviour on her son's part and turned to leave without a word. Recovering himself and feeling guilty, Mahendra called, "All right, mother, let me have the food here."

"What's the use if you have no appetite?"

After a few more passages between the hurt mother and her reticent pet, Mahendra had to sit down to another meal.

4

Mahendra could not sleep well that night. Early in the morning he repaired to Bihari's house and said, "I've been thinking, old chap. Kakima really wants me to marry her niece."

"It needed no thinking to discover that fact," replied Bihari. "She has expressed the desire in a hundred ways."

"That's why I say that if I don't marry Asha, Kakima will have a lasting disappointment."

"Possibly."

"It would be very wrong of me to cause her disappointment. Won't it?"

There was a forced warmth in Bihari's voice as he suddenly exclaimed, "Excellent. What could be better than that you should consent to this! Only—it would have been better if your conscience had functioned a little earlier."

"A day's delay needn't matter."

Having given rein to his imagination on the prospect of marriage, Mahendra could contain himself no longer. He was impatient to see it through without any more ado. As soon as he returned home, he said to his mother, "Very well, mother, I'll do as you wish. I am agreeable to marriage."

Then Rajlakshmi understood why Mahendra had taken such pains to dress up the previous day and recalled that her sister-in-law had also gone that evening to see her niece. So

Annapurna's scheming had succeeded where her own persuasion had failed! Everything, the whole world had conspired against her. Controlling her resentment, she said, "Very well, I'll look out for a suitable girl."

"The girl has been found."

"She won't do, my child. Let me tell you plainly."

"But why, mother, what's wrong with her?" Mahendra too restrained his rising temper.

"Why, indeed! An orphan with no connections. What happiness can such a marriage bring to your family?"

"I don't mind if there are no connections. I like the girl."

Mahendra's determination only added fuel to the fire. Rajlakshmi went straight to Annapurna and flared up. "You devil! How dare you conspire to rob me of my only son by marrying him to that unlucky orphaned wretch!"

Annapurna burst into tears. "Believe me," she pleaded, "I haven't spoken a word to Mahendra about marriage. I don't even know what he has been telling you."

Rajlakshmi refused to believe a word of it. Then Annapurna sent for Bihari and with tears in her eyes said, "It was with *you* that the whole thing had been fixed. Why then have you upset everything? Please do not back out, I beg of you. If you do not stand by me, I shall be in a very embarrassing position. I assure you, the girl is good in every respect. You won't regret it."

"Your assurances, Kakima, are unnecessary. There's no question of my not wanting it when it concerns your own niece. But Mahinda. . . ."

"No, my son, she can never be Mahin's bride. Believe me when I say that I shall be most satisfied if she is your bride. In fact, I do not approve of her match with Mahin."

"If that is so, Kakima," said Bihari, "there need be no difficulty about it."

So Bihari went up to Rajlakshmi straight away and announced, "Mother, I am engaged to be married to Kakima's niece. Unfortunately, none of my female relatives is in town. I have therefore to be shameless enough to break the news to you myself."

"How wonderful, Bihari!" said Rajlakshmi warmly. "I'm so glad. She is a fine girl, worthy of you in every respect. Don't you let go of her."

"Why should I let go of her? Mahinda himself chose her for me and fixed it all up."

Mahendra was chagrined. This new obstacle only made the sore more inflamed. He was angry with both his mother and aunt and left the house and took a room in a dingy students' hostel. Rajlakshmi was beside herself with apprehension. She went into Annapurna's room and cried. "Save my child, sister dear. I fear he may leave us for good and turn an ascetic."

"Take it easy, sister," consoled Annapurna. "He'll cool down in a couple of days."

"You don't know him," wailed Rajlakshmi. "If he doesn't get what he wants, he is capable of going to any length. You must somehow arrange the match . . . ."

"How's that possible, sister?" said Annapurna. "The match with Bihari has been more or less confirmed."

"Shouldn't take long to break," said Rajlakshmi.

She sent for Bihari and said, "My son, I myself shall look out for a suitable bride for you. This girl you must give up. She's no good for you."

"Excuse me, mother, but that is out of the question. I've given my word."

Baffled, Rajlakshmi went back to Annapurna. "I beg of you, sister," she pleaded, "please send for Bihari and talk him out of it. You alone can prevail on him."

So Annapurna called Bihari and said, "I don't know how to put it to you, Bihari, but what can I do? Personally I should like nothing better than that Asha should be yours— but you know how things are."

"I understand, Kakima," replied Bihari. "Whatever you say shall be done. But don't ever again talk to me of marriage."

So saying Bihari left. Annapurna's eyes filled with tears. She hastily wiped them away lest tears bode ill for Mahendra. She consoled herself by repeating over and over again, "Everything is for the best."

And so the wedding day was fixed. A silent tension of hurt pride and resentment aggravated by looks of reproach and counter-reproach persisted between Rajlakshmi, Annapurna and Mahendra. But there was no lack of outer manifestations of pomp and gaiety. A thousand lamps were lit, the *sanai* played its sweet and plaintive music and sweets galore were distributed.

Asha stepped into her new world, a graceful figure charmingly attired, her sweet face suffused with a bashful radiance. Her timid, innocent spirit had no foreboding of the thorns in the path ahead. In fact, the prospect of going into a home where she would be near her beloved aunt filled her with a joy and confidence in which there was no room for any apprehension.

Soon after the wedding Rajlakshmi called Mahendra and said, "I think the Bouma * had better stay at her uncle's for a few days."

"But why, mother?" asked Mahendra.

"Well, your examination is nearing. You might be distracted in your studies."

"Am I a baby," flared up Mahendra, "that I can't be trusted to take care of myself?"

"What does it matter?" persisted the mother. "It's only a matter of one year."

"Well, if her parents had been living, I might have let her

* *Lit.*, little bride-mother. The usual affectionate term for the daughter-in-law.

13

stay on with them for a while, but I am afraid I can't send her back to her uncle's house."

"Heaven help us!" said Rajlakshmi to herself. "Already he's behaving like the master of the house. And I . . . . I'm nobody. What solicitude for the bride . . . . come only yesterday! We also were newly wed brides once . . . . but our husbands never behaved in this shameless, hen-pecked manner!"

Mahendra tried to console her by what he imagined was an emphatic assurance: "Don't you worry, mother. My studies shall not suffer."

5

Rajlakshmi displayed unbounded zeal in training the daughter-in-law in the intricacies of domestic economy. Between the pantry, kitchen and the household shrine, Asha's day passed in an endless round of duties. At night Rajlakshmi would call the daughter-in-law and make her sleep beside her . . . . a maternal gesture to make up for the loss of her parents. Annapurna wisely kept herself at a safe distance.

Mahendra felt like a hungry child who watches in helpless despair his hefty guardian munch away the entire length of sugar-cane and suck in the last ounce of juice. Before his very eyes the loveliness of his youthful bride was being drained away in domestic drudgery. It was more than he could bear. He went up to Annapurna and complained, "The way mother is working the poor girl to death is scandalous . . . . intolerable."

Annapurna knew that Rajlakshmi was overdoing it. Nevertheless she replied, "Why, Mahendra, what's wrong with teaching the bride how to be a good housewife? Would you rather have her as a modern girl, lazily lounging about the whole day, reading novels or doing fancy knitting, waited upon by others?"

"A modern girl must be modern," said Mahendra with vehemence, "whether it be good or bad. If my wife were to enjoy novels as I do, what would there be to regret or ridicule about it?"

The high-pitched voice reached Rajlakshmi's ears who putting all work aside hastened to Annapurna's room. "What consultations are going on here?" she asked sharply. "Let me hear."

"No consultations," replied Mahendra defiantly. "It's merely that I won't allow my wife to be treated like a servant."

Restraining her anger Rajlakshmi asked sarcastically, "How's the princess to be treated then?"

"I shall teach her to read and write," replied Mahendra.

Without another word Rajlakshmi left the room hurriedly and almost immediately returned dragging Asha by the hand. "Here, take your bride," she said. "Teach her what you like."

Then turning to Annapurna she added with folded hands: "Forgive me, honoured sister-in-law, for having failed to realise the dignity of your niece and for letting her delicate hands be soiled with turmeric. Take her back now, cleanse her of all stains of household duties, dress her up as a lady and place her hand in Mahin's. Let her loll at ease as befits her dignity and toy with books. I shall do the maid's work." Saying which Rajlakshmi hurried back to her room banging the door.

Annapurna remained seated on the floor like one stunned. Asha unable to understand the reason of this sudden domestic crisis went pale with fear and concern. Mahendra was furious and decided: "No more of this nonsense. Henceforth I must be responsible for my wife. I owe it to her."

And so duty and pleasure were combined. The combination was as effective as when the wind fans the fire. Forgotten were the college, the impending examination, the other friends and obligations. The zeal to improve his wife's mind

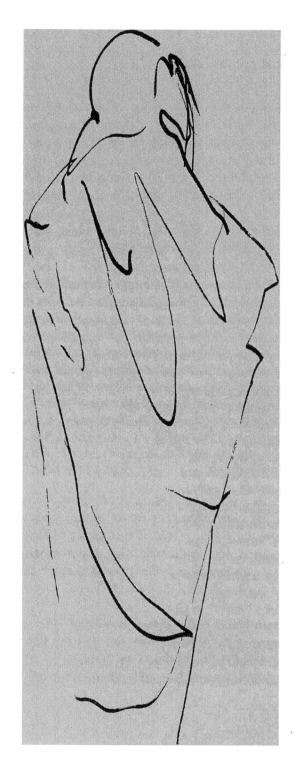

16

kept Mahendra and his pupil secluded in the bedroom. He hardly bothered as to what happened to his own studies or what others thought of it.

Rajlakshmi was left to nurse her wounded pride. She said to herself, "Were Mahin and his bride to come and fall at my feet begging for forgiveness, I would still not look at them. Let me see how long he can carry on like this—without his mother."

The days passed but there was no sign of the repentant couple waiting at her door. Rajlakshmi decided that if now Mahendra came and begged forgiveness, she would generously forgive him—otherwise the poor boy would be heartbroken. But still no pleading voice reached her ears. At last she made up her mind that it was her duty to announce her forgiveness to them. How can a mother bear to see her son unhappy, pining for forgiveness!

At one end of the terrace on the second floor was a small room which Mahendra had turned into a bedroom-cum-study. All these days the mother had neglected her wonted routine of setting her son's room in order, making his bed and putting his day's clothes out. This sudden disuse of her ever-active maternal solicitude was as painful as when a mother, her breasts bursting with milk, is prevented from suckling her babe. And so in the afternoon when Mahendra was supposed to be at college she decided to go up and tidy his room. When he returned from college he would recognise at a glance his mother's touch on everything. She went up the stairs and found the door of Mahendra's room open. As she neared the door she suddenly stopped with a start as though pricked by a thorn. She saw that Mahendra was asleep on his bed on the floor and Asha, her back turned to the door, was gently massaging his feet. Rajlakshmi was shocked at this shameless spectacle of marital tenderness enacted in broad daylight. With a contemptuous frown on her face she silently crept downstairs.

As the dry, wilted stalks of the cornfield, when after a

temporary drought the rains descend, suddenly turn green and shoot up vigorously, confidently, almost defiantly as though eager to make up for the long bleak days of fast—so Asha blossomed into womanhood. In the uncle's house where she had passed her maidenhood she had had almost no rights; in the new home which she entered as a stranger she found herself the darling of a devoted husband. The neglected orphan was suddenly seated on the throne as the queen of her husband's domain. Naturally and gracefully, without any hesitation, she assumed the new role assigned to her and casting aside the bashful timidity of a new bride she took her rightful place by her husband's side in the proud dignity of a beloved wife.

Rajlakshmi found it difficult to forget the sight she had witnessed that afternoon when she had gone up to Mahendra's room and seen this newcomer from a strange home seated by her son's side in a pose of confident intimacy as though exercising a long-enjoyed monopoly. She had immediately retraced her steps, burning with anger at this shameless impertinence. Eager to scorch Annapurna with the flame that was consuming her she hurried to her sister-in-law's room and hissed: "Please go up and have a look at your darling niece. See the ways of her ladyship learnt in her lordly parental home. Were Mahendra's father alive . . . ."

"Didi," replied Annapurna in a gentle, pained tone, "she is your daughter-in-law. You may guide her, punish her, as you like. Why bring me in?"

"My daughter-in-law!" snapped Rajlakshmi. "Why would she bother about me when you are there to advise, guide and minister to her?"

Goaded by this taunt, Annapurna rushed upstairs warning the couple of her approach by deliberately loud footsteps. Without any preamble she thundered at Asha: "How long must I hang down my head in shame at your scandalous behaviour? Idling away shamelessly here while the aged mother-in-law has to drudge in household slavery! An evil day for me when I brought you into this house!"

She burst into tears as she spoke. Asha stood before her dumbly, with bent head, tears trickling from her eyes, her fingers mechanically fiddling with the loose end of her sari. Mahendra intervened. "Why, Kakima, why must you rail at her unnecessarily? It's I who am responsible for keeping her here."

"And why need you have done so?" said Annapurna. "This poor child whom her mother left an orphan before she could teach her anything—she does not know what is good for her and what is bad. And what can *you* teach her?"

"Why, don't you see this slate, this notebook, this primer! I've brought them for her lessons. I shall see to it that she learns—whether you like it or not and whatever the gossips may say."

"But lessons needn't drag on the whole day," protested Annapurna. "An hour in the evening should be enough."

"Not so easy, Kakima. Learning takes time."

Annapurna left the room in disgust. Asha was about to follow her when Mahendra closed the door and stood in the way, unmindful of her pleading, tearful eyes. "Wait," said he. "We must make up for the time lost in sleep."

Lest a serious, simple-minded reader imagine that Mahendra did really waste his time in sleep, it is necessary to state that Mahendra's principles and practice of teaching were so original that no Inspector of Schools would have approved of them.

Asha had implicit faith in her husband. Although she knew that it would not be easy for her, for various reasons, to learn to read and write at her age, yet she felt that it was her bounden duty to carry out her husband's wishes. And so she did her best to discipline her restless, wandering thoughts. Seated demurely on one side of the mat spread on the floor, she would bend over the book, her head moving in a slow rhythmic motion. At the other end of the bedroom sat the teacher at a table with medical manuals spread in front of him. Occasionally he shoots a glance from the corner of his eye at his pupil. Suddenly he shuts the medical manual and calls, "Chunil"—the pet name by which Asha is known. The startled pupil raises her head. "Let me see how much you have done," says Mahendra. "Please bring the book."

Asha is frightened lest Mahendra test her progress, for she has made none. The more she pored over the primer the more the words assumed the appearance of innumerable black ants crawling and recrawling in front of her. Nervously she picks up the book and comes and stands timidly by Mahendra's chair. Putting his arm around her waist and drawing her close, Mahendra takes the primer with the other hand and says gravely, "Now let me see how much you have read today." Asha points out the few lines she had been able to read. "So much!" exclaims Mahendra in an aggrieved tone. "Would you like to see how much I have been able to read during the time?" He points to the heading of one chapter in the medical manual. "Only that much?" asks Asha, her eyes wide with amazement. "What then were you doing all this while?"

"I was thinking of someone," replies Mahendra holding up her chin with his hand. "But that someone was herself so heartless as to be absorbed in her primer."

Asha could truthfully retort that that was not so, but being shy she quietly accepts her defeat in love's competition. It should be obvious from this instance that Mahendra's system of teaching could hardly have worked in any other school, public or private.

Maybe, another day Mahendra is out. Asha sits down with her primer determined to concentrate on her lesson. Suddenly two hands are clasped over her eyes from behind and a teasing voice whispers in her ear, "What cruel indifference! Can't you think of me when you are alone instead of reading?"

"Would you rather I remained illiterate?"

"What about me? Have I made any progress in my studies since you came?"

Asha suddenly feels guilty. "How do I come in the way of your studies?" she asks as she turns to go. Mahendra catches hold of her hand. "How can you understand?" he teases. "It's easy enough for you to prefer the book to me. Not so easy for me to think of anything but you."

Asha bursts into tears at this accusation—but like an autumn shower the tears soon dissolve and the sunshine of their conjugal happiness seems all the fresher and brighter for the shower.

And so, with the teacher as the chief distraction, Asha continued to fumble in the wilderness of learning. Now and again her aunt's bitter taunt came back to her mind reminding her that the lessons were merely an excuse for the shameless pleasures of love. If by chance she caught sight of her mother-in-law, she blushed with shame. The mother-in-law obstinately refrained from assigning any household task to her or from even saying anything to her. One day Asha went up to her of her own accord and tried timidly to assist her but the mother-in-law cried out in mock dismay: "Oh no, please don't waste your valuable time. You have to study so hard."

Unable to contain herself, Annapurna again chided Asha. "It is easy enough to see how much *you* are learning—but won't you let poor Mahin pass his examination?"

Asha was deeply mortified. She said to Mahendra: "Your studies are suffering, let me go and stay in Mashima's room downstairs." Tears filled her eyes and her lips trembled as she announced her austere resolve.

"Very well," replied Mahendra. "Let's move into Kakima's room, if you prefer that. She can come up into our room."

Asha was annoyed by this light-hearted reaction to her earnest gesture of self-effacement.

"It would be far more effective," went on Mahendra, "if you took the matter in your hands and stood guard on me day and night to see that I don't neglect my studies."

Asha readily agreed. How well she discharged her responsibility was made evident when the examination results announced that Mahendra had failed. Asha's own progress in her studies could be gauged from the fact that she did not yet know what a cuttle-fish was, although *Charu Path*, the Bengali primer she was supposed to be reading, had a long lesson on the various kinds of *purubhuj* or polypus.

Nor was the process of mutual tutoring as uninterrupted as the lovers would have wished. Now and again Bihari butted in, shouting "Mahinda! Mahinda!" and insisted on dragging Mahendra out of his sanctuary. He would reproach Mahendra for neglecting his studies and would taunt Asha: "Bouthan, * it's no use swallowing too much at a time. It causes indigestion."

"Don't you listen to him, Chuni," interrupted Mahendra. "He's jealous of our happiness."

"Well, then, don't provoke jealousy," rejoined Bihari. "Enjoy your happiness soberly so as not to cause envy."

"Ah, but others' envy is sweet. It adds to our enjoyment," said Mahendra. "Do you know, Chuni, I was about to let you fall into Bihari's hands? What an ass I would have been!"

"Shut up," whispered Bihari flushing red.

Incidents such as this only irritated Asha and strengthened her prejudice against Bihari. The fact that at one time she was almost engaged to him made her self-conscious in his presence. She resented his company—a fact which pleased Mahendra all the more. Bihari saw and understood what was happening.

* Bouthan, Boudidi or Boudi are terms of address for elder brother's or friend's wife.

Rajlakshmi sent for Bihari to confide her woes. Bihari sympathised and said, "The grub is safe only as long as it is in cocoon—once it has come out, you can't lure it back."

When the news of Mahendra's failure in the examination reached Rajlakshmi's ears she flared up like a forest fire. Unfortunately, the only victim at hand was poor Annapurna who took the full impact of this heat.

6

The evening sky was overcast with clouds and the season's first shower had descended on the parched earth. Flaunting a thickly woven jasmin garland on his neck and a fine muslin wrap on his shoulders, Mahendra tiptoed into his bedroom in a thrill of expectancy, hoping to take Asha unawares. As he peeped inside he found the room in darkness. The eastern window was wide open, the rain-laden wind was sweeping into the room, the lamp had gone out and Asha was lying on the floor, her body shaking with suppressed sobs. Rushing to her side and kneeling, Mahendra asked, "What's the matter, Chuni?"

No reply—only the sobbing increased and became more vehement. After a great deal of petting and cajoling, Mahendra was told that Annapurna, unable to bear the humiliation any longer, had left the house and shifted to her cousin's. Mahendra was annoyed. Why couldn't Kakima choose some other day to leave the house? Why spoil this first beautiful day of the rainy season? Gradually the rising anger was transferred to the mother. She was at the root of all this trouble. "We'll also go where Kakima has gone," he announced. "Let's see what mother does now."

He started shouting for the servants and noisily packing his things. Rajlakshmi understood what was happening. She came up to Mahendra and asked gently, "Where are you going?"

Mahendra at first refused to reply. After the mother had repeated the question several times, he replied, "To Kakima."

"You don't have to take the trouble," said Rajlakshmi. "I'll go and fetch her here for you."

She immediately ordered the palanquin and went to where Annapurna had shifted. Holding the shoulder-ends of her sari in folded palms she begged, "Be pleased to forgive me, dear sister-in-law."

Overcome with embarrassment Annapurna hurriedly bent down and touched Rajlakshmi's feet. "Why must you put me to shame, Didi?" she said. "I'll do whatever you command."

"Because you have left the house, my son and daughter-in-law threaten to do the same." Saying so Rajlakshmi burst into tears—tears of anger, humiliation and self-pity.

The sisters-in-law returned home together. It was still raining. When Annapurna went up to Mahendra's room Asha's tears had dried and Mahendra was trying his best to make her smile. Judging from the scene it was obvious that the romantic possibilities of the cloudy evening had not been entirely wasted. Annapurna went up to Asha and said in a stern voice, "Chuni, you've made my life a hell. I can neither stay here in peace nor go elsewhere."

Asha was dumbfounded. She continued to stare at her aunt like a stricken deer.

"Why, Kakima, what has Chuni done?" asked Mahendra bitterly.

"I left the house," replied Annapurna, "because I couldn't bear to see her shameless complacence. And now she makes her mother-in-law come weeping to drag me back. The brazen hussy!"

What a nuisance these aunts and mothers are in the romance of life, thought Mahendra.

24

Next day Rajlakshmi sent for Bihari. "Bihari, my son, please persuade Mahin to let me go for a few days to my village home. I haven't been there for years."

"Since you have done without it for so many years, you may as well continue to do so," replied Bihari. "However, I shall speak to Mahin about it, though I doubt very much if he will agree to let you go."

But Mahendra readily agreed. "It's but natural," he said, "that she should like to visit her native village. But she had better not stay there too long—the place is not healthy during the rains."

Bihari was annoyed at this ready compliance. He said, "How can she go alone? Who will look after her?" He added with a smile, "Why not let Bouthan go with her?"

The taunt went home. Mahendra retorted, "You think I can't do that?" But the argument made no further progress. Asha was even more annoyed at this indiscretion. Her resentment against Bihari hardened. Bihari sensed this and seemed deliberately to provoke her as though he derived a secret amusement from it.

Needless to say, Rajlakshmi was by no means keen to visit her ancestral village. As the boatman in summer, when the river becomes shallow, has constantly to dip the measuring rod in the water to gauge its depth, so Rajlakshmi was always devising new tests to discover how much her son still cared for her. She had not expected that Mahendra would so readily and so willingly agree to her proposed visit to Barashat. Sorely disappointed she said to herself, "When Annapurna leaves the house, so much fuss is made, but if I leave the house, it hardly matters. Such is the difference between a sorceress and a mere mother. It's time I left."

Annapurna understood that the situation was delicate. She told Mahendra, "If Didi goes away, I can't stay here." So Mahendra went up to his mother and said, "Have you heard, mother? If you go away, Kakima too will do the same. Who will then look after us?"

Controlling her rising tide of anger and jealousy, Rajlakshmi turned to Annapurna and said, "Please, Mejo-bou, you mustn't leave the house. How can the household run without you? You must stay on."

This was the last straw on the camel's back. Rajlakshmi prepared to leave the next morning. Every one expected that Mahendra himself would escort and take her to the ancestral village, but when the time came to depart it was found that Mahendra had deputed the steward and one gate-keeper to accompany her.

"Mahinda," asked Bihari, "aren't you going?"

Embarrassed Mahendra mumbled, "I . . . er . . . there's college. . . . ."

"Never mind," interrupted Bihari. "I'll go and take mother."

Mahendra was annoyed and told Asha later, "Bihari is trying to show that his concern for mother is greater than mine. He's becoming insufferable."

Annapurna was obliged to stay on, but she made no secret of the fact that she was ashamed, humiliated and disgusted. Her contemptuous aloofness irritated Mahendra and pained Asha.

7

Bihari was to take Rajlakshmi to her village home and return immediately to Calcutta. But when they reached the village and saw the conditions there he did not have the heart to leave Rajlakshmi behind alone. A couple of decrepit old widows were living in Rajlakshmi's ancestral house. All around were thick jungle and clusters of bamboo; the stagnant pool in the grounds was coated over with a thick green slime; day and night one could hear the jackals cry. It was a most depressing sight.

"Not every native place," said Bihari, "is a 'heaven on earth'—certainly not this one. Come, let's go back to Calcutta. I can't possibly leave you behind in this wilderness. Criminal of me if I did."

Rajlakshmi too felt depressed and suffocated and might have yielded to the persuasion if Binodini had not turned up in the nick of time.

Binodini has already been introduced to the reader. At one time her hand had been offered to Mahendra and failing Mahendra to Bihari. Finally she was married off to a gentleman in this same village whose only claim to distinction was his excessively enlarged liver. Soon after marriage, he passed away. The widow continued to live in the village after her husband's death, a lone garden-creeper in a jungle, a pathetic glory in a joyless wilderness. Seeing her mother's old friend come to the village, the orphaned widow welcomed her with genuine feeling and looked after her with singular devotion.

Rajlakshmi was charmed and deeply moved. What a girl! Whatever she did was superb, her cooking, her ways, her speech. Tireless in her devotion, she was busy in her endless round of voluntary duty. Rajlakshmi pleaded with her, "Come now, little mother, have a bite yourself." But no— not until she has fed Rajlakshmi and fanned her to sleep. "But you'll fall ill if you continue like this, dear," Rajlakshmi would protest. Binodini laughed. "Hardship and suffering have made my body immune to sickness, mother," she said. "My only regret is that I have so little to offer you here."

Bihari soon became the leading figure in the village. A continuous stream of visitors waited on him, the sick for medicine, the litigants for legal advice, fathers asking for jobs in Calcutta for their sons, the illiterate begging him to draft petitions on their behalf. Bihari was not only versatile but was sociable, good-natured and generous. He mixed freely with all, joined the elders at their game of cards, the lower castes at their drinking and merrymaking. Every one felt at home with him and yet one and all respected him.

Binodini felt sorry for this youth from Calcutta trapped in exile and did her best to lighten his hardship, keeping herself unseen and hidden in the inner apartment. Whenever Bihari returned from his village round he was surprised to find his room done and everything neatly and tidily arranged, fresh flowers and leaves in a brass vase and some volumes of Bankim and Dinabandhu placed near his bed. On the fly-leaf was inscribed 'Binodini' in a mature but feminine hand.

This was indeed much more than one would expect of village hospitality. When Bihari said so to Rajlakshmi, she replied, "She's the same girl you both had spurned."

"I admit I was wrong," laughed Bihari. "And yet it is better to lose by not marrying than to lose by marrying wrongly."

Rajlakshmi could not get over her regret: "If only Binodini had been my daughter-in-law! Oh, why did it not so happen?" Whenever she broached the subject of her return to Calcutta, Binodini's eyes filled with tears and she would say, "Why did you ever come, Pishima,* if you had to go back? My life somehow dragged on before you came into it, but now how will I live without you?" Deeply moved Rajlakshmi cried, "Why didn't I have you as my daughter-in-law? How I would have cherished you, kept you always clasped to my heart!" Binodini blushed deeply and inventing some excuse ran away.

Rajlakshmi waited anxiously for a letter from Calcutta begging her to return. Her Mahin had never stayed without her for so long. He must naturally miss her and be impatient for her return: his letter would be full of affectionate reproaches. Her heart yearned for such a letter.

At last a letter came for Bihari. Mahendra wrote: "I hope mother is enjoying her stay there."

"Poor boy," said Rajlakshmi. "It's obvious he is missing me and has written out of hurt pride. 'Enjoying her stay'

* Aunt, on the father's side.

indeed! Can a mother ever enjoy her stay away from the son?" Then turning to Bihari she asked, "What else has Mahin written? Please let me hear."

"Nothing much," replied Bihari, crumpling the letter in his hand. He put the crumpled paper inside a book and threw the book inside his room. This only sharpened Rajlakshmi's curiosity. She felt sure that Bihari was unwilling to read out the letter to her for fear she would feel pained to hear Mahendra's tale of woe and reproaches. The more angry she imagined the reproaches, the more her heart dissolved in tenderness, like the cow that yields more readily both milk and affection the more roughly and painfully the hungry calf pulls at the teat. She forgave Mahendra completely. "Let him be happy with his wife," she said. "Let him do what he likes—only let him be happy. I shall never again come in his way. Poor boy, he is hurt because his mother has left him. No wonder, he is angry." She kept on crying and wiping her eyes and at the same time pressing Bihari to go for his bath. "Do go and have your bath, Bihari. You're getting careless these days." Bihari was in no mood for a bath.

"Let-me remain shabby, mother," he said. "Vagabonds like me are better off when neglected."

"No, my son," persisted Rajlakshmi, "Please go and get ready."

At last Bihari was obliged to get up. The moment he had gone Rajlakshmi hurried inside the room and came out with the crumpled letter in her hand. Handing it to Binodini, she said, "Please read out to me, dear, what Mahin has written to Bihari."

Binodini began to read aloud. At the outset Mahendra had written about his mother—but it was a bare reference only, not more than what Bihari had read out. After that it was all about Asha and Asha only. Mahendra had written like a lover in frenzy. Binodini had hardly read a few lines when she blushed and stopped. "No need to read any more, Pishima."

Rajlakshmi's face which a moment ago was beaming with

tenderness had hardened like a stone. She sat staring dumbly for a while, then said, "Enough!" and without taking the letter back got up and went away.

Binodini took the letter and went inside her room. She locked the door and lay down in her bed reading the letter. What thrill she derived from reading it, she alone knew. But it was not the thrill of curiosity. She read and re-read the letter and as she read her eyes gleamed like sands in the midday sun, her breath hissed like hot wind in the desert. What sort of a person is Mahendra, what is Asha like, what is the nature and form of their love—these questions kept on revolving in her mind, setting her imagination aflame. She lay in her bed a long time, her head resting against the wall, the letter in her lap, her eyes staring blankly.

In the afternoon of the same day Annapurna suddenly arrived. Fearing ill news about her son, Rajlakshmi's heart sank at the sight of her sister-in-law's sudden appearance. She dared not ask any questions. She merely stared dumbly at Annapurna pale with fright. Annapurna herself volunteered, "Didi, all is well in Calcutta."

"Why then are you here?" asked Rajlakshmi.

"Didi," said Annapurna, "please go back to your house. I am no longer able to attend to worldly duties. I've made up my mind to retire to Kashi * and spend my remaining days in devotion. In fact, I am on my way there and have come here to ask your blessing and to beg you to forgive me for whatever wrong I may have done, knowingly or unknowingly." The tears swam into her eyes and fell down one by one as she continued. "As for your daughter-in-law, she is still a child—motherless. Whatever her shortcoming she now belongs to you." Her voice broke down and she could speak no further.

Not knowing what else to do Rajlakshmi busied herself arranging her sister-in-law's bath and food. Bihari rushed back from the village as soon as the news reached him. Touching

* Old name of Banaras, the holy city of the Hindus.

Annapurna's feet he said, "How can you leave us like this Kakima?"

Swallowing her tears Annapurna said, "Bihari dear, do not please try to hold me back. May you all be happy! My going away will make no difference."

Bihari was silent. After a little while he said, "Unlucky Mahendra to let you go like this!"

"Please don't say such a thing," said Annapurna with a shiver. "I've no grievance whatsoever against Mahin. In fact, I feel that my going away is necessary for their family peace and happiness."

Bihari said nothing. He remained seated with a faraway look in his eyes. Annapurna unfolded a knot in the loose end of her sari and took out a pair of thick gold bangles.

"Keep these, my son," she said. "When the bride comes, put them on her with my blessings."

Taking the bangles in his hands Bihari raised them to his forehead and controlling his tears hurried to an adjacent room.

At the time of her departure Annapurna said to Bihari, "Please- look after my Mahin and Asha." Then turning to Rajlakshmi she put a piece of paper in her hand and said, "I have transferred by this document my share of family property to Mahin's name. He need only send me fifteen rupees a month."

Bending low she touched Rajlakshmi's feet and started on her pilgrimage.

8

A nameless fear seized Asha. First mother-in-law and then auntie left the house, one by one. Where would all this lead to? Their conjugal happiness was driving others out of the house. Would her turn come next? It seemed to her unseemly and inauspicious that their marital romance should have the bleak setting of an empty, deserted house.

Love severed from the hard realities of life is like a plucked flower in splendid isolation; its limited sap cannot sustain it for long. Gradually the petals fade and drop. Asha soon began to feel the weariness of ceaseless lovemaking. Love's embrace seemed to wilt and loosen. Without the stimulus of the rough and varied jolts of the struggle of living, love's embrace needs artificial props to keep it going which become increasingly less and less adequate. If love fails to strike roots in the workaday world, its enjoyment is neither complete nor steady.

Mahendra had tried, in open defiance of family and convention, to taste to the full the bliss of conjugal love, burning all the candles in one burst of splendour and filling the ominous emptiness of the house with the glamour of reckless enjoyment. He taunted Asha: "What is the matter with you, Chuni? Why must you go about moping with a long face because Mashi * has gone? Is not our love adequate to fill your life?"

Poor Asha felt pained and wondered if her love was really wanting. "That's why I cannot forget Mashi and am frightened that my mother-in-law has gone away." She tried with all her heart to forget everything else and rise to what she believed was expected of her love.

The household was in a mess. The servants were negligent and shirked their tasks. The maid did not turn up and sent word that she was indisposed. The cook took to drinking and no one knew where he was. Mahendra laughed. "What fun!" he said. "Let's do our own cooking today."

He sent for a carriage and drove to New Market to do the household shopping. Not knowing what was needed and in what quantity, he collected a pyramid of purchases and returned home in great glee. Asha too was no adept at housekeeping and did not know what to do with all these pur-

* Aunt, on mother's side.

chases. Finally, late in the afternoon, some sort of lunch was got ready and Mahendra hugely enjoyed eating what he had never eaten before and what was perhaps not easy to eat either. Asha could not share this enjoyment. Painfully conscious of her ineptitude she blushed with shame and embarrassment.

All the rooms in the house were in disorder. It was difficult to find anything when required. The surgical instruments on Mahendra's table found their way into the kitchen where they were used for cutting vegetables until they finally disappeared no one knew where. Mahendra's medical notebook served as a hand-fan for lighting the kitchen fire and was soon reduced to ashes. These mishaps gave endless amusement to Mahendra, but Asha felt more and more crestfallen. To float merrily on the wanton wreck of their own household seemed to the poor girl a joke too perverse and sinister for enjoyment.

One evening the lovers were reclining in their bed which was laid in a covered veranda overlooking the roof-terrace. The rain had stopped. As far as the eye could reach, the tops of Calcutta mansions were flooded with moonlight. Asha was making a garland of *bakul* flowers freshly plucked from the garden and still wet with the rain. Mahendra was impishly tugging at it and trying to tease and provoke her by little affectionate pranks. Asha protested and began to chide when Mahendra suddenly put his arm round her, clamping his hand on her mouth. Just then the pet *koel* from the neighbouring house began to call. Automatically their eyes turned upward to where their own pet *koel* was wont to rock in a cage hung from the ceiling. Whenever the neighbour's *koel* called, their own pet responded. Today it was silent. Asha asked anxiously, "What is the matter with the bird today?"

"Your voice has shamed it into silence," replied Mahendra facetiously.

"Please, it's no matter for joke," said Asha in a pleading, agitated tone. "Do get up and see what's happened to it."

Mahendra got up, unhooked the cage and brought it down. The bird had died of starvation. After Annapurna's departure the bearer had gone on leave and no one had bothered to feed it.

Asha went pale at the sight. Her fingers were numbed, the garland remained uncompleted, the flowers lay in a heap. Mahendra too was grieved but for fear of spoiling the evening's romance tried to be light-hearted. "So much the better," he said. "The wretched thing would have pestered you with its cooing in my absence." Putting his arms round Asha he tried to press her close to him, but Asha gently withdrew from the embrace and flinging the flowers aside, said, "Please, no more of this. What a shame! For God's sake go immediately and fetch your mother back."

9

Just then some one called out from the lower floor, "Mahinda! Mahinda!"

"Come in, come right up," shouted back Mahendra. Bihari's voice came as a boon to Mahendra at this critical moment. Before Bihari had been an impediment to the rapture of their honeymoon; now suddenly he seemed a godsend. Asha too felt relieved at this intrusion. As she got up, lifting the end of her sari over her head, Mahendra said, "Where are you off to? It's only Bihari."

"Let me go and get some refreshments for Thakurpo," * replied Asha. It was good to have some work to do. Asha's depression lessened. She lingered, with her head covered, in the hope of hearing news of her mother-in-law. She had not yet overcome her shyness before Bihari and was not used to speaking directly to him.

* A term of address for husband's younger brother.

34

Entering the veranda Bihari exclaimed in mock surprise, "Good Heavens! Have I intruded on a romantic scene? Don't be afraid, Bouthan. Please be seated. I'll be off in a minute."

Asha looked at Mahendra. Mahendra inquired, "What news of mother, Bihari?"

"Why this concern about such a prosaic old thing like mother? There's plenty of time to talk about her," said Bihari, adding in English, "Such a night was not made for sleep, nor for mothers and aunts!"

He made as if to beat a retreat when Mahendra caught hold of him and made him sit down. "Please note, Bouthan," said Bihari turning to Asha, "he is forcing me to stay. Don't curse *me* for a sin which is *his* doing."

Unable to make an effective retort, Asha was irritated. She understood that Bihari was deliberately mocking her.

"It's easy to see how beautifully the house is running," went on Bihari, "nevertheless, isn't it time mother returned?"

"Indeed, she should," replied Mahendra. "We are expecting her all the time."

"If you would only let her know that," replied Bihari. "It'll take you a couple of minutes to scribble a line to her. She will be overjoyed. Will you, Bouthan, be pleased to spare Mahinda for a couple of minutes so that he may scribble the line?"

Asha left the veranda, deeply mortified, the tears trickling down her cheeks.

Mahendra said: "What an auspicious moment it was when you two first saw each other! Always mocking and bickering—never friendly!"

"Your mother spared no pains to spoil you," replied Bihari. "Now your wife has taken over the job. It's because I find it insufferable that I have a dig at her whenever I get a chance."

"And what is the result?" asked Mahendra.

"Nil so far as you are concerned. As for me—somewhat bitter."

Bihari stayed on till Mahendra had written the letter. He took the letter himself and left the next day to bring Rajlakshmi back. Rajlakshmi understood quite well that the letter had been written at Bihari's instance; nevertheless, she could not stay back any longer. Binodini came with her.

When Rajlakshmi saw what a disorderly and dirty mess her house had fallen into, her prejudice against Asha deepened. But what a change had come over her daughter-in-law! She now followed her mother-in-law like a shadow and was always eager to assist her even without being asked and, in fact, despite the latter's snubs. "Please leave it alone. You'll only make a mess of it. Why poke your finger in what you do not understand?"

Rajlakshmi attributed the change-for-the-better in Asha to Annapurna's departure. But she was afraid that Mahendra might imagine that while he was happy with his bride during Annapurna's regime, the mother's return had spoiled everything. He might take it as a proof that Annapurna was his well-wisher and his mother an obstacle. This would only make matters worse. She was therefore chary of encouraging Asha in her new zeal, though she was secretly pleased and flattered by it.

Now if Mahendra sent for Asha during the day Asha would hesitate to go until Rajlakshmi almost bullied her into compliance. "Can't you hear that Mahin is calling you? How dare you ignore him! This is what comes of too much petting and indulgence. Go to him at once. You needn't bother about cutting the vegetables."

Again the same old farce with the slate, pencil and primer —love's make-believe of fault-finding and hurt pride, the endless wrangling as to whose love is more absolute, the turning of the rainy day into night and the moonlit night into day, the artificial postponing of love's ennui and weariness, the forced nourishing of the illusion that one can't do without the other even for a minute, though the others' presence has long ceased to inspire. The eternal curse of love that its embrace turns so soon into a bondage!

10

One day Binodini came up to Asha and putting her arm round her said, "May your happiness last for ever, sister—but why need you ignore this unhappy creature?"

Because Asha had been brought up by her relatives as an orphan and made to feel she had no rights, she had developed a complex which made her unduly shy before strangers, as though she was constantly on guard against a possible rebuff. When she had first seen Binodini, she was so overawed by her beauty and grace and the piercing intelligence of her eyes that she lacked the courage to make an effort towards better acquaintance. She was further impressed when she noticed how free and easy were Binodini's ways with Rajlakshmi and how the latter made much of her. Rajlakshmi in fact missed no opportunity of rubbing into Asha how superior and wonderful Binodini was. Asha could also see for herself how skilled and efficient Binodini was in every detail of household-management, how easily and naturally she exercised authority, how well she controlled the servants, getting work out of them and pulling them up when necessary. The more Asha watched Binodini the more inferior she felt to her and thus kept away from her.

When this paragon of beauty and virtue herself made the first advance to court her affection, the young and inexperienced Asha was overwhelmed with joy and responded with all her heart. Like the magician's tree, their friendship took root, sprouted and blossomed forth, all in a day.

Asha said, "Let us call each other by a special pet name."

"What would you suggest?" asked Binodini.

Asha mentioned several names of beautiful things, from the Ganges water to a *bakul* flower.

"They are all worn-out and hackneyed," commented Binodini. "A loving name hardly connotes love any more."

"What then would you prefer?" asked Asha.

"Eyesore!" laughed Binodini.

"Well, then, Eyesore!" exclaimed Asha as she clasped her arms round Binodini's neck and burst out laughing. She would have preferred a sweet-sounding name but so greatly was she charmed by Binodini that love's abuse sounded sweet to her.

Asha was in sore need of a friend. Love's festivity is incomplete if the lovers have no companions to feed on vicarious thrills. Binodini, starved of love, listened to the young bride's experiences of first love with the avidity of a drunkard thirsting for the fiery wine. Her head reeled with the warm pulsations of blood set on fire.

In the still summer afternoon when the mother-in-law was having her siesta and the bearers and maids had retired for a rest and Mahendra had been obliged by Bihari's taunts to put in an appearance at the college, when an occasional, faint cry of the kite could be heard from the distant blue of the sky, Binodini and Asha were closeted in the lonely bedroom, Asha reclining with her loose hair overspreading the pillow and Binodini lying beside her, face downwards, her breasts pressing against the pillow underneath her, listening like one intoxicated to her companion's whispered confidences. As she listened her ears flushed red to the tips and her breathing became heavy and fast. She would ask questions and draw out of her companion small intimate details; she would listen to the same description over and over again and would even imagine hypothetical scenes and ask, "What would you or he do in such and such situations?" Thus she would drag on and prolong the sweet confidences by sketching all sorts of imaginary and unimaginable scenes.

Binodini said, "Supposing, dear Eyesore, you had married Bihari!"

"No, dear Eyesore, please don't even utter such a thing," Asha pleaded. "The very thought makes me sick with shame. But—how nice it would have been if you had married him! In fact, there was at one time some such proposal."

"There were several such proposals—all still-born. However, just as well. I am best as I am."

Asha would remonstrate. How can a widowed state be better than a married state? She would persist, "Well, then, let's suppose, my sweet one, that you had married my husband! You know, it could easily have happened."

Indeed, it could. Why didn't it happen? This chamber, this bed would then have been hers. Binodini looked round the room and at the bed with a painful, frustrated longing. Why was she denied her place in this house? Today she was a mere guest who would and must depart soon.

In the afternoon Binodini would herself with her matchless skill do Asha's hair and help her to dress for the evening rendezvous with her husband. Her inflamed fancy surreptitiously followed the decked-out bride on her way to the impassioned lover waiting anxiously. Sometimes, on the other hand, she perversely detained Asha, remonstrating: "Wait a while, dear. Your husband won't run away in the meantime. He's not a wild deer of the forest, he's a well domesticated pet." Thus by cajoling and teasing she would detain Asha—much to the annoyance of Mahendra who flared up when Asha finally turned up.

"What a nuisance this friend of yours! She won't budge. When will she go back home?"

"Please don't be angry with my Eyesore," Asha pleaded anxiously. "You don't know how much she loves to hear about you and with what care and skill she helps me to dress for your sake."

Though Rajlakshmi was reluctant to assign any household duties to Asha, Binodini managed to overcome her objection. She herself was a tireless worker and was busy with some task or other from morning till night. She kept Asha by her side, engaging her in some task in such a way that poor Asha could find no loophole for escape. The fact that Asha's husband was fidgeting impatiently in the bedroom on the terrace upstairs seemed to excite Binodini's imagination and provide her with an inexhaustible fund of secret amusement. She would inwardly chuckle as Asha pleaded anxiously, "Please, let me go now, dear Eyesore. He will get angry."

"Just a moment," Binodini would say hurriedly. "Let's finish this—it won't take long."

After a few minutes Asha would fidget and again plead, "Please let me go now. He's sure to get angry."

"What if he does?" Binodini teased. "Love without outbursts of jealous anger is insipid—like a vegetable dish without chilli and spice."

What the chilli-and-spice part of love was like, was all that Binodini could taste. The main vegetable dish was outside her reach. Her nerves tingled as though scorched by a flame. Her eyes shot sparks of fire. "This happiness, this passionate ardour of the husband was my due and should have been mine," she said to herself. "I could have ruled this house like a queen, could have made the husband into a slave and transformed both the household and the husband into something wonderful from the present shabby, silly state. What I was denied and deprived of now belongs to this slip of a girl, this little playdoll!"

But actually she flung her arms round Asha's neck and said, "Do tell me, dearest Eyesore, what you said to each other last night. Did you say what I had coached you to say? It makes me so happy to hear of the love between you two."

11

Mahendra was fed up and told his mother, "It's hardly proper to have a young widow, a stranger, hanging round the house. It's a responsibility which I don't think we ought to take upon ourselves. Who knows what scandal it may give rise to, one of these days!"

"A stranger did you say? She's our Bipin's widow and not a stranger."

"Whatever she be, it's no good her sticking on here. I don't like it."

It was not easy for Rajlakshmi to ignore Mahendra's wishes. So she sent for Bihari.

"Bihari, dear," she pleaded, "please make Mahin understand what a relief it is to me in this old age to have Bipin's widow in the house. She does most of the work and I get a little respite from drudgery. Whether she is a blood relation or not, no one else has ever done so much for me."

Bihari did not say anything to Rajlakshmi but went upstairs and spoke to Mahendra. "Mahinda, have you thought about Binodini?"

"Thought about Binodini?" Mahendra laughed. "I can't sleep at night for fear of her. Why not ask your Bouthan? She will tell you what an obsession Binodini has become for me!"

From beneath her veil Asha tried silently to remonstrate with Mahendra.

"Indeed!" laughed Bihari. "A second Poison Tree!" *

* Reference to Bankim Chatterji's famous novel of that name (*Visha Vriksha*) in which a young widow is the cause of the ruin of a happy family.

41

"Almost that," said Mahendra. "That's why Chuni is so anxious to get rid of her."

Again a silent protest issued from behind the veil. Asha's eyes burnt with anger at this mockery.

"Even if you get rid of her now," said Bihari, "it won't take her long to return. There's only one remedy—get the widow remarried. That will remove the poison fang altogether."

"Kundan * too had been married off," commented Mahendra.

"Never mind. Enough of this simile. I have given some thought to Binodini's case. She can't stay on here with you for long. On the other hand it is hard for her to be sentenced for life to that God-forsaken wilderness where she was living. I have seen the place. It's terrible."

Though Binodini lived in the same house she had not yet appeared before Mahendra. But Bihari had seen her and knew that such a girl could not possibly be condemned to spend her days in a wilderness. He also knew that the same flame that lights a home can also burn it down. Mahendra teased Bihari for his obvious concern for Binodini and though Bihari met this raillery with light-hearted repartees, he was worried in his mind, for he knew that Binodini was not a girl to be either trifled with or ignored.

Rajlakshmi warned Binodini. "Be careful, my child. Do not overdo your friendship with Asha. You were married into a village home and do not know the ways of these modern young people. You are a wise girl and should watch your step."

After this admonition Binodini kept away from Asha and made her deliberate aloofness very obvious. She said to Asha,

* Name of the young widow in the novel, *Visha Vriksha*, referred to earlier.

"After all, what am I, dear sister? If we poor creatures are not careful, we may only invite snubs."

Asha wept and remonstrated but Binodini was adamant. She would not listen to Asha though the latter was bursting to pour out her heart.

Meanwhile Mahendra was getting bored and restive; love's embrace had become limp and eyes erstwhile infatuated now drooped with fatigue. The disorderly, off-handed routine which had previously seemed so amusing was now beginning to be a painful strain. Asha's ineptitude as a housewife irritated him, though he said nothing. Nevertheless Asha could sense that the glory of love had faded in the heat of prolonged indulgence. Overstrain and false notes had put their married bliss out of tune.

The only remedy in such cases is to run away from each other. So Asha, impelled by her feminine instinct, did her best to keep away from Mahendra. But where could she go except to Binodini?

As for Mahendra, having gradually awakened from the torpor of infatuation, he began to be aware that he had neglected his studies and his other normal obligations. He succeeded in rescuing his medical books from all sorts of impossible places where they had been thrown and began to dust them. His coat and trousers which were his college dress and which had been long in disuse had also to be taken out and put in the sun to dry.

12

Having failed to win back Binodini's confidence, Asha thought of a stratagem. She said to Binodini, "How is it, dear Eyesore, that you never appear before my husband? Why need you avoid and run away from him?"

"For shame!" protested Binodini in mock modesty.

"Why, what's wrong about it? I've heard mother say that you belong to the family."

"In this world," replied Binodini gravely, "no one belongs to any one. Those who care can make others their own; those who do not care are strangers even though blood relations."

Asha was impressed and said to herself, "What she says cannot be disputed. It is indeed true that my husband has been unjust to her and has resented her presence as a stranger."

In the evening Asha tried to cajole and plead with her husband.

"You must meet my Eyesore."

"How very brave of you!"

"Why, what's there to fear?"

"From what you say of her beauty, it doesn't seem so very safe."

"Never mind, I shall cope with the danger. Now stop teasing and tell me—will you see her or no?"

It was not that Mahendra was not curious to see Binodini; in fact, at times his curiosity took on the edge of eagerness. But he feared this eagerness which seemed to him unseemly. He flattered himself on his high code of love. Previously he had refused to entertain a proposal of marriage for fear of disturbing his mother's monopoly over his attention. Now he was equally anxious to preserve Asha's monopoly and was therefore reluctant to admit even to himself his curiosity about any other woman. He prided himself on being fastidious and steadfast in love.

It was the same with his friendship for Bihari. Its loyalty permitted no room for any other friend. If any one else made a friendly advance to him he made a virtue of repulsing it and then boasted about it to Bihari, reviling and mocking the unfortunate fellow and flaunting his distaste for the company of the ordinary and vulgar persons. If Bihari remonstrated he would reply, "You may stand them, Bihari—

44

indeed, you make friends wherever you go: but for me, I can't make a friend of every Tom, Dick and Harry."

When this same Mahendra found his steadfast mind troubled again and again by curiosity and impatience for a sight of the unknown lady, he felt ashamed before himself for letting down his own ideal. Hence he had worked himself into a righteous annoyance and pestered his mother to send Binodini away.

So now when Asha pleaded with him, he replied, "Why bother, Chuni? Where have I the time for your Eyesore? The working hours are for studies, the leisure for you. Where's the gap in between for your friend?"

"Very well," said Asha, "I won't ask you to spare time from your studies, but from the time reserved for me I shall give a portion to my Eyesore."

"You may," laughed Mahendra. "But why should I?"

Mahendra had often taunted Asha that her love for Binodini was evidence that her love for her husband was not all-sufficing. He would boast that no one could love so exclusively as he. Asha would challenge his claim, would try to refute his allegation, would argue, quarrel and weep but could never win the debate. Mahendra's boast that in his love for Asha there was not even a needle-space to accommodate any one else used to irritate and provoke Asha, but today she was willing to yield that claim.

"Very well," she said, "not for her sake but for my sake be pleased to make my friend's acquaintance."

Having established the superiority and single-mindedness of his love, Mahendra condescended to accede to Asha's importunity. "All right, I'll see her—but please see that I am not unduly pestered."

Early next morning Asha went up to Binodini while the latter was still in bed.

"How strange," exclaimed Binodini when Ashta told her,

* Feminine of *chakor*, a bird said to be in love with the moon and to live on its rays.

45

"that the *chakori* * should neglect the moon and court the cloud!"

"These poetic metaphors, dear sister, are beyond me," said Asha. "Why cast pearls into the wilderness? Come and talk to one who can appreciate and pay back in the same coin."

"And who is this bright wit?" asked Binodini.

"Your brother-in-law—my husband," replied Asha. "No, I'm not joking. He's very anxious to make your acquaintance."

Binodini understood that Mahendra's anxiety was of Asha's engineering. She was not to be caught so easily. She saw through the game and flatly declined to meet Mahendra. Asha felt humiliated before her husband. Mahendra was angry. His vanity was stung. How dare this woman decline to make his acquaintance! Did she regard him as one of the common herd? Didn't she realise that had Mahendra been like any other man he would have made advances to her long ago? The fact that he disdained to do so should be evidence enough of his superior calibre. If only she came to know him she would understand how different he was from other men.

Binodini too nursed a secret grievance against Mahendra. She had been in the house for such a long time and he had never made an attempt to see her! After all it wasn't so very difficult. When she sat chatting with Rajlakshmi he could easily enter his mother's room on some pretext or other. Why this indifference? As though she was a piece of furniture! Wasn't she human, wasn't she a woman? If only he came to know her he would see the vast difference between her and his pet Chuni.

At last Asha hit upon a stratagem. She said to her husband, "I'll tell Binodini that you have gone to college and will bring her along to my room and then you suddenly come into the room from outside. She'll be nicely trapped."

"What has she done," asked Mahendra, "to deserve such severe chastisement?"

"This time I'm really angry with her," replied Asha. "She

won't even see you! What cheek! I shall break her pride and won't rest till then."

"I am not dying to see your friend," said Mahendra. "Why then should I sneak in like a thief?"

Asha caught hold of Mahendra's hand and pleaded, "Please, for my sake, you must do this. Let's humble her pride once. After that you may do as you like."

Mahendra was silent. Asha renewed her pleading, "Please be a darling and do this for me."

Mahendra's own curiosity was getting the better of him. He therefore allowed himself to be persuaded, after a couple of half-hearted protests.

The autumn afternoon was clear and still. Binodini sat in Asha's room teaching her how to knit bedroom slippers. Asha was absent-minded, her glance kept on straying towards the door, the number of mistakes she made in counting the stitches was incredible. Binodini lost patience. Snatching the slipper from Asha's hand she flung in on the ground and said, "No, you'll never learn. Let me go. I've other work to do."

"Please give me one more chance," begged Asha. "I won't make any more mistakes."

She resumed the stitching. From the door to her back Mahendra stealthily tiptoed into the room and stood behind Binodini. Asha did not raise her head but a smile played on her lips.

"What's amusing you?" asked Binodini. Asha could restrain herself no longer and burst out laughing. She threw the slipper into Binodini's lap and said, "You're right, dear sister. I'm no good at this work." Then putting her arms round Binodini's neck she burst into a renewed fit of laughter.

Binodini had all along understood what was happening. She

had seen through Asha's fidgeting and meaningful glances and was fully aware that Mahendra stood at her back. It suited her to seem naïve and to be taken unawares.

"Why should this poor fellow be excluded from the cause of this merriment?" asked Mahendra as he came forward.

Binodini gave a start and hurriedly drawing her sari-end over her head got up to leave. Asha caught her hand.

"Please," said Mahendra, "either let me go away or let's both sit down."

Unlike the average girl, Binodini made no unnecessary fuss or scene to flaunt her shocked modesty. She replied very simply, "I shall respect your wish and stay—but please don't curse me in your heart for doing so."

"My curse shall be—may you remain immobile for long," said Mahendra.

"I fear no such curse, for your 'long' will not be very long." Saying so Binodini again made as if to get up. Asha caught her hand and begged, "Please stay a while—for my sake."

13

Asha asked her husband, "Tell me truthfully, how did you like my Eyesore?"

"Not bad," mumbled Mahendra.

Asha was annoyed.

"No one is good enough for you," she said petulantly.

"Except one," smiled Mahendra.

"Well, let the acquaintance ripen. Then we shall see whether you like her or not."

"Ripen?" exclaimed Mahendra. "Do you mean this pestering will continue?"

"After all there's such a thing as politeness," said Asha. "Having made her acquaintance if you now cut her, what will she think? You're too fastidious, I must say. Any other man would have been only too eager to cultivate a girl like that. You behave as though a gargoyle has been foisted on you!"

Mahendra was flattered by this contrast with other men. He said, "Very well, we shall see. There's no need to make any fuss about it. I can't run away from the house, nor is your friend showing any signs of budging. So it is inevitable that occasionally we shall run into each other and when we do, rest assured that your husband will not fail in politeness. He has that much sense."

Mahendra took it for granted that henceforth Binodini would contrive occasions for showing herself. He was mistaken. Binodini kept her aloofness and avoided crossing his path even by accident. Mahendra dared not talk of Binodini with Asha lest his interest in her should become obvious. He suppressed his eagerness for her company and the more he suppressed and concealed it the worse it became. Binodini's indifference only added fuel to the fire.

The day after his meeting with Binodini he asked Asha in a casual tone of disinterested amusement, "Well, what did your Eyesore think of your unworthy husband?"

He had fondly hoped that Asha would of her own accord tell him everything with her usual enthusiasm. But when the expectation bore no fruit he was obliged to ask the question himself, pretending that is was by way of a joke. Asha was embarrassed, for her friend had made no reference whatsoever to the event. Asha felt a legitimate grievance against her Eyesore. To her husband she replied, "Wait, let the acquaintance grow a little. It's too early for her to know what she thinks. After all she saw you only for a minute and hardly exchanged a few words."

Mahendra was disappointed and found it difficult to keep up his pose of indifference. Just then Bihari turned up.

"Hallo Mahinda," he shouted. "What are you two arguing about?"

"Just think of it," replied Mahendra. "Your sister-in-law

goes and makes friends with Kumudini or Pramodini or whatever her name is and they call each other by a special pet name, Hair Knot or Fish Bone or God knows what—and now I'm being pestered to exchange a pet name with her, Cheroot Ash or some such absurdity. Is it fair?"

Asha flushed red with anger behind her veil. Bihari looked at Mahendra and said nothing for a while. Then he smiled and said, "Bouthan, the signs are ominous. This frantic protest is a bluff. I've seen your Eyesore. I can swear that to see such a face again and again will never seem a misfortune. So when Mahinda protests so much, it does seem highly suspicious."

Asha was more than ever convinced that her husband was made of different stuff—altogether superior to Bihari.

Mahendra suddenly developed an interest in photography. Previously he had tried to fiddle with a camera but had soon given it up. Now he had the camera repaired, brought some rolls of film and began taking snaps of every one in the household, including the servants.

"You must take a snap of my Eyesore," insisted Asha.

"Very well," replied Mahendra without wasting words.

But the Eyesore replied even more briefly, "No."

Asha had once again to resort to a stratagem and, as before, Binodini was not unaware of it. The plan was that Asha would persuade Binodini to have the afternoon siesta in Asha's room and while she rested, Mahendra would come from behind and take a shot of her. The proud and obstinate beauty would thus be taught a lesson.

The wonder of it was that Binodini who never slept during the day readily stretched herself on Asha's bed and seemed overcome by languor. Her eyes closed, heavy with sleep. Her face turned towards the window, a red shawl spread over her, she seemed so beautiful in her repose that Mahendra felt as if she was specially posing for a picture. He tiptoed into the room, camera in hand. He gazed at her for a long time, from various angles—ostensibly to fix a suitable position for the camera. He even found it necessary, in the interest of art, to shift her loose strands of hair from one place to another and not finding the effect satisfactory to restore them to their original position. He whispered to Asha, "Shift the shawl a little to the left of her feet."

"I'm afraid I won't do it well and might wake her up," whispered back the incompetent wife. "Better do it yourself."

Mahendra did so. Finally he took his position and fixed the film into the camera. Suddenly, as though wakened by a sound, Binodini heaved a sigh, turned on her side and sat up. Asha burst into a shriek of laughter. Binodini was red with anger. She turned her sparkling, fiery eyes on Mahendra and snapped, "How wrong of you!"

"No doubt, it was wrong of me," replied Mahendra. "But look at my misfortune. I lost the goods almost as soon as I stole them. I am neither here nor there. Please at least let the wrong be accomplished before you punish me."

Asha too pleaded and pestered Binodini until she agreed to have her photograph taken. The first exposure went wrong and so a second sitting had to be arranged the following day at the insistence of the photographer-artist. Then he proposed that the two girl-friends should be snapped together as a souvenir of their everlasting friendship. Binodini could not say no to it, but she insisted that that would be the last. Fearing that she meant what she said Mahendra went on spoiling one exposure after another. Thus repeated sittings enabled the acquaintance to ripen.

14

As the smoldering embers when prodded can be made to yield a second flame, so the languishing romance of the newlyweds revived under the impact of a fresh impulse from outside. Asha was a poor conversationalist but Binodini had an inexhaustible gift of the gab which Asha looked upon as a blessing. She had no difficulty now in keeping Mahendra amused and entertained.

In the first infatuation of married love the young couple had almost squandered their capital and were now faced with the prospect of endless boredom. The hang-over of drunken revelry can be cured by another spell of drunkenness. But Asha's resources had dried up. Where was the wherewithal for the second spell of revelry? At this critical moment Binodini came with a bowlful of wine and placed it in Asha's hands. Asha was relieved to see her husband once more gay and happy.

From now on Asha ceased to draw on her own resources. When Mahendra and Binodini indulged in playful repartee she merely listened and giggled to her heart's content. When Mahendra cheated her at cards she would turn to Binodini and appeal to her fair judgment. If Mahendra ragged her or said something provoking she would look to Binodini for an effective repartee. Thus the three of them carried on merrily.

Binodini did not, however, neglect any of her duties in the household. She joined the company only after she had attended to all her duties in the house including looking after Rajlakshmi's comfort. Mahendra would grow impatient.

"You'll only spoil the servants and make them lazy," he grumbled.

"Better than spoiling oneself by indulging in laziness," replied Binodini. "Now get up and get ready for college," she added.

"It's such a lovely, cloudy morning—"

"No, that won't do," interrupted Binodini. "The carriage is waiting outside to take you to college."

"But I had told the driver that the carriage won't be required!" exclaimed Mahendra.

"I told him it would be," said Binodini tersely, as she laid out his clothes.

"You should have been born in a Rajput family," commented Mahendra. "You would have hastened the warrior to the battlefield and helped him with his armour."

Thus Binodini put her foot down and did not allow Mahendra to miss college or neglect his studies on any pretext. No dalliance was permitted during the day with the result that the evening rendezvous became very much more romantic and desirable. Mahendra's day was spent in longing for the day to close.

Previously it had often happened that the morning meal was not ready in time, which had served as a ready excuse for Mahendra to miss his classes. Nowadays Binodini saw to it that his meal was always punctual. As soon as the meal was over he received intimation that the carriage was waiting for him at the door. His change of dress was always neatly laid out. Formerly not only were his clothes never laid out but it was difficult to find them. They were either with the dhobi or were mislaid in some out-of-the-way shelf or corner.

At first Binodini teased Asha in Mahendra's hearing for these lapses. Mahendra too would join in this raillery and laughter. Gradually, however, Binodini took over the responsibility of looking after Asha's portion of the household—ostensibly to oblige her friend. Everything was now well-regulated. The previous disorder and shabbiness were replaced by neatness and beauty.

A button has fallen off Mahendra's coat. Poor Asha doesn't know what to do. Binodini snatches the coat from her hands and fixes the button in no time. One day the cat pounced on the food before Mahendra could sit down to eat. Asha was in a panic, not knowing what to do. Binodini hastened to the kitchen and soon brought back a trayful of enough to tide over the crisis. Asha was speechless with surprise.

Thus in every detail of the day's routine, whether it concerned his food or his wardrobe, his work or his leisure, Mahendra felt the touch of Binodini's solicitude. The home-slippers he wore had been knitted by her and so was the woollen scarf which was wrapped round his neck like a tender caress. Even in Asha when she came up to him in the evening, fresh from her bath, beautifully dressed and delicately perfumed, he could sense Binodini's touch. It was as though Asha's beauty was only half hers, the other half was the reflection of some one else's loveliness. Like the waters of the Ganges and the Jamuna the two women had mingled their charms into one overwhelming seduction.

Bihari had ceased to be a welcome guest. He was now hardly ever invited to a meal. So one day he wrote to Mahendra inviting himself to lunch on the following day which happened to be Sunday. Fearing that the day's romance would be spoiled by Bihari's intrusion, Mahendra hurriedly wrote back to say that an urgent piece of business necessitated his absence from home on that day. In spite of it Bihari turned up after lunch. Learning from the bearer that Mahendra had not left the house at all, he hurried upstairs shouting "Mahinda!" Mahendra was embarrassed and pleading the excuse of a severe headache hurriedly lay down on the bed, his head propped up by a pillow. Hearing her husband complain suddenly of headache and seeing his face change colour, Asha was scared. She did not know what to do and looked helplessly at Binodini for guidance. Binodini understood that nothing was really the matter, nevertheless she said anxiously, "You've sat up too long. Better lie down and rest for a while. Let me go and fetch eau-de-cologne."

"Please don't bother," mumbled Mahendra.

Binodini did not listen and hurried out. She soon returned with eau-de-cologne mixed in iced water. She gave the soaked handkerchief to Asha and said, "Please keep it on Mahendra Babu's forehead."

Mahendra kept on murmuring, "It's not necessary—not

54

necessary." Bihari watched the drama with undisguised amusement. Mahendra said to himself with pride, "Let him see how much they care for me."

Asha was shy and nervous in Bihari's presence. Her hand shook and a drop or two of eau-de-cologne dripped into Mahendra's eye. Binodini took the handkerchief from Asha's trembling hand and herself fixed it on Mahendra's forehead. She took another piece of soaked cotton and began dripping it gently on the wet handkerchief. Asha pulled the veil down her face and began fanning Mahendra.

"Are you feeling better, Mahendra Babu?" asked Binodini tenderly, as she threw a quick glance at Bihari. She saw that Bihari's eyes were laughing with amusement as though he was witnessing a farce. She understood that here was someone not easy to fool.

"Binod-bouthan," said Bihari laughing, "such nursing will not cure the sickness. It'll only make it worse."

"Is it so indeed?" said Binodini innocently. "How are we ignorant girls to know what is right! All this is no doubt written in your medical books?"

"Indeed it is written. Seeing such nursing, my head too begins to ache. But unlucky heads like mine have to do without the luxury of such nursing. Mahinda is a lucky dog."

Binodini put the wet rag down. "You had better treat your own friend," she said.

Though amused, Bihari was no less secretly irritated by what he had witnessed. He had of late been busy with his studies and had not realised that meanwhile the other three had involved themselves in such a tangle. He looked at Binodini and seemed for the first time to take her measure. Binodini too took his. To Binodini's remark he replied sharply, "You're right. A friend should look after a friend. I had brought about the headache and I shall take it away with me. Don't waste eau-de-cologne unnecessarily."

Turning to Asha he added, "Bouthan, prevention is always better than cure."

15

Bihari said to himself, "This won't do. I must not leave them to themselves and let things drift. Somehow I must get into their midst even if they don't like it."

And so without waiting to be invited and ignoring all snubs, Bihari began to penetrate into Mahendra's stronghold. He said to Binodini, "Binod-bouthan, this young man was petted and spoiled by his mother and by his friends. His wife is continuing the process. Please for God's sake, turn your attention elsewhere instead of aiding and abetting his downfall."

"That is. . . ." asked Mahendra.

"That is, to some one like myself whom no one ever bothers about," replied Bihari.

"So you wish to be spoiled!" said Mahendra. "The privilege of being spoiled, Bihari, is not easy to attain. It's not merely a question of applying for it."

Binodini laughed and said, "Moreover, to be capable of being spoiled is a talent by itself, Bihari Babu."

"Even if I lack the talent, your skill will make up for it," replied Bihari. "Why not try?"

"It doesn't work if one is already prepared for it. One must be caught unawares," smiled Binodini. "What say you, dear Eyesore? Why don't you take your brother-in-law in hand?"

By way of protest Asha nudged Binodini with her fingers. Bihari too did not relish the joke and remained silent. Binodini had observed that Bihari could not stand raillery at Asha's expense. She resented the fact that while he tried to make light of her, he had a deep regard for Asha. She turned again to Asha and said, "This brother-in-law of yours is hungry for your favours. He's really begging for them

56

though ostensibly addressing me. Do be kind to him, sister dear."

Asha burnt with annoyance. Bihari flushed red but he soon recovered and said laughing, "Why must you commission another in my case and yourself directly minister to Mahinda?"

Binodini understood that Bihari was all set to ruin her game. She must be well-armed to meet his menace.

Mahendra was annoyed. The charm of poetry is marred by calling a spade a spade. He said somewhat sharply, "Bihari, your Mahinda does not trade in anything. He is content with what he has."

"He may not go out of his way to trade," rejoined Bihari, "but as luck would have it, the trade blows profit into your lap from outside."

"You may seem empty-handed at the moment," interposed Binodini, "nevertheless, a wind is blowing in from somewhere." She nudged Asha with a roguish twinkle in her eyes.

Asha was furious and left the room. Bihari chafed in silence, knowing himself worsted. He was about to get up to leave when Binodini said, "Don't go away heartbroken, Bihari Babu. I'll send back my Eyesore right away."

Saying this Binodini left the room. Mahendra was vexed at this disruption of his court and showed it in the frown of his face. Bihari could contain himself no longer and burst out, "Mahinda, if you must go to the dogs, do so by all means. Your previous training has consistently helped you to it. But don't blast the life of the simple, true-hearted wife who is clinging to you so trustfully." Bihari's voice was thick with emotion.

"I don't understand what you're saying," replied Mahendra coldly. "Leave off riddles and say it plainly."

"Indeed I will," rejoined Bihari. "Binodini is deliberately trying to seduce you and you like a fool are playing into her hands."

"It's a lie," thundered Mahendra. "If you can impute such base motives to a decent lady, you don't deserve access to the inner apartments." *

Just then Binodini re-entered with a plateful of sweets which she smilingly placed before Bihari.

"Why all this!" he exclaimed. "I've no appetite."

"That won't do," said Binodini. "You must sweeten your mouth before you leave."

"So my petition is granted!" laughed Bihari. "The pampering has begun."

"A brother-in-law doesn't have to petition," replied Binodini with an arch smile. "Why beg when the right is there? The affection is there for you to grasp. Isn't that so, Mahendra Babu?"

Mahendra was speechless with surprise. Binodini went on. "What's the matter, Bihari Babu? Why don't you eat? Is it shyness or anger? Would you like me to call someone else?"

"Not necessary," replied Bihari. "What I've received is ample."

"Still bantering? What a wag you are! Even the sweets failed to shut your mouth!"

At night when Asha and Mahendra were alone, Asha gave vent to her resentment against Bihari. Unlike previous occasions, Mahendra did not make light of it but wholeheartedly joined in the tirade. Next morning he got up early and went to Bihari's house.

"Bihari," he said, "I am afraid Binodini resents your familiarity. After all, she is not a member of the family and you are a stranger to her."

"Is that so?" exclaimed Bihari. "I'm sorry I did the wrong thing. I needn't see her if she objects to my presence."

Mahendra was relieved. He had not anticipated such easy

* Part of the house reserved for ladies where no males except near relatives and intimate friends of the family are allowed access.

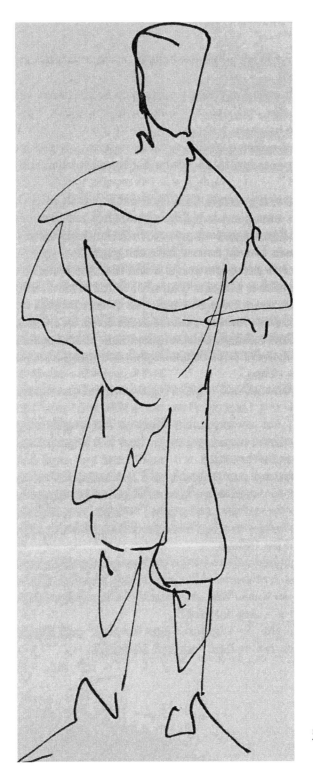

59

success in his unpleasant mission. He was secretly afraid of Bihari.

That very day Bihari turned up in the inner apartments and said to Binodini, "Binod-bouthan, please forgive me."

"Why, what's happened, Bihari Babu?" asked Binodini.

"Mahendra has told me that you resent my presence in the inner apartments. So I came to beg your pardon and take my leave."

"But how absurd, Bihari Babu!" exclaimed Binodini. "I'm a mere guest in this house—for a few days only. Why should you depart on my account? Had I suspected I'd cause this mess, I would never have come here."

Her face lost colour as she said this. She made an effort to hold back her tears and hurriedly left the room. Bihari's first reaction was a sense of regret that he had perhaps unjustly accused Binodini and wounded her feelings for nothing.

In the evening Rajlakshmi came up to Mahendra and said in a dejected tone, "Mahin, Bipin's widow insists on leaving for her village."

"Why, mother?" asked Mahendra. "Is she uncomfortable here?"

"No, not uncomfortable. She says that people will gossip even without cause if a young widow like her stays on indefinitely in this house."

"But this is no stranger's house!" protested Mahendra, as he shot a contemptuous glance at Bihari who happened to be sitting there. Bihari felt guilty. "Perhaps I was unjust in my insinuations yesterday," thought Bihari. "I have unnecessarily hurt her feelings."

Both husband and wife made a great grievance of their injured sentiments. Asha reproached Binodini, "So we are strangers to you!" He complained, "After all these days we're nobodies—mere outsiders!"

"But you can't keep me here for ever!" said Binodini.

"How can we dare!" rejoined Mahendra.

"Why then did you steal our hearts?" wailed Asha.

"No, my friends," replied Binodini, as she turned a pathetic, soulful glance at Mahendra, "it's no use encouraging brief attachments."

Nothing was decided that day. The following day Bihari came up to her and said, "Binod-bouthan, why must you talk of leaving? Have I done some wrong for which you are punishing me?"

"No question of your wrong," said Binodini turning her face aside. "It's my fate that is wrong."

"If you go away I shall never cease to feel guilty that you left in resentment on my account."

Binodini looked up at Bihari. Her eyes were sad and pleading. She asked, "It wouldn't be proper for me to stay, would it?"

Bihari was in a dilemma. How could he admit that it would be proper for her to stay on? He replied, "No doubt, sooner or later you must leave. But where's the hurry? Why not stay on for a few days at least?"

"Since you all insist on my staying," said Binodini with downcast eyes, "it is difficult for me to disregard your wishes. But let me tell you, it is not right."

From between her long eyelashes big drops of tears streamed down her face. Bihari was deeply moved by this endless flow of silent tears. He said, "In these few days you have so captured by your charming ways the hearts of all of us that no one wants to let you go. Please do not misunderstand, Binod-bouthan. Who can willingly part with such an angel?"

Asha who was sitting nearby, her face veiled, began furiously to wipe her eyes with the end of her sari.

After this episode Binodini ceased to talk of leaving.

16

To wipe out the traces of this tearful interlude Mahendra proposed a picnic to the Dum Dum garden on the following Sunday. Asha was enthusiastic but Binodini would not agree. Asha and Mahendra were greatly upset by this non-cooperation on Binodini's part and wondered why she was nowadays keeping aloof from them.

As soon as Bihari turned up in the evening Binodini complained: "Look, Bihari Babu, how unfair it is. Because I do not wish to join the picnic, both Mahin Babu and Asha are angry with me."

"Not at all unfair," replied Bihari. "If you don't accompany them their picnic will be such a mess that one would not wish one's enemy to suffer it." .

"Why don't you go, Bihari Babu?" pleaded Binodini. "If you go I shall come."

"Excellent proposal. But the house must run as the master wills it. What does the master say?"

Neither the master nor the mistress could help resenting this undue partiality for Bihari. At the prospect of Bihari joining the picnic, half Mahendra's enthusiasm evaporated. He had been at pains to rub into Bihari that his company was unwelcome to Binodini and now she goes out of her way to invite him herself. It would be impossible after this to control Bihari.

"That would be fine," he said outwardly. "But Bihari, you've a habit of provoking a scene wherever you go. I am afraid you'll either gather the village urchins around us or will pick a quarrel with a white skin."

Bihari understood what Mahendra was feeling and chuckled inwardly. "That's the fun of life," he rejoined. "You never know what's going to happen next, where the next rumpus will break out—Binod-bouthan we must start at day-break. I'll be here in time."

A third-class hackney coach for servants and the luggage and a second-class one for the family were duly ordered for the Sunday morning. Bihari arrived in good time with a huge picnic basket.

"What's that for?" asked Mahendra. "There's no room left in the servants' coach."

"Don't you get excited, Dada," replied Bihari. "I'll see to all that."

Asha and Binodini got into the coach. Mahendra hesitated, not knowing what to do about Bihari. Bihari quietly dumped the box on the top of the coach and himself jumped on to the box of the coach. Mahendra heaved a sigh of relief. He was afraid Bihari might take a seat inside. He was capable of anything. Binodini was worried. She said anxiously, "I hope he doesn't fall off."

Bihari heard the remark and said, "Please don't worry. I'm not in the habit of falling—either off or in a swoon."

After the carriage had started, Mahendra said petulantly, "If you're so worried about Bihari, let me go up on the box and send Bihari inside."

"No, no, you can't go," said Asha in a panic, seizing hold of his shawl.

"You're not used to roughing it," added Binodini. "You may topple down. No use taking the risk."

"Topple down?" shrieked Mahendra excitedly. "Never." He made as if to rise.

"You accused Bihari Babu of making scenes," said Binodini. "You seem to be an adept at making them yourself."

"Very well," sulked Mahendra. "Let me engage a separate coach and let Bihari come and sit with you people."

"In that case I shall come with you," said Asha.

"And I would be expected to jump out of the coach!" said Binodini with acerbity.

After this outburst the party lapsed into silence. Mahendra

wore a heavy frown all the way until the coach reached the Dum Dum garden. The servants' coach which had started much earlier had not yet arrived.

The autumn morning was exceedingly beautiful. Though the dew on the ground had dried in the rising sun, the trees and shrubs still glistened in the clear, soft light. Along the garden wall was a row of *sephali* trees whose scattered blossoms had carpeted the ground underneath, filling the air with glad perfume.

Asha freed from the brick-and-mortar prison of Calcutta felt elated with joy and frisked about like a wild gazelle. She took hold of Binodini and gathered heaps of flowers, plucked ripe custard apples and sat and ate them under the tree. The two friends jumped into the pool and stayed in the water for a long time. Their simple, spontaneous joy filled the landscape with delight and seemed to be reflected in the play of light and shade under the trees and on the water and in the gentle dance of stalks laden with flowers.

When the two friends returned after their swim they found that the servants' coach had not yet arrived. Mahendra was sitting on a chair in the veranda reading a foreign advertisement and looking a picture of dejection.

"Where's Bihari Babu?" asked Binodini.

"Don't know," was the curt reply.

"Let's go and find him," said Binodini.

"There's hardly any danger of his being stolen," remarked Mahendra. "He'll turn up without any search."

"Maybe he's frantically looking for you, fearing that the precious jewel is lost. It's necessary to set his mind at rest."

They found Bihari under a huge banyan tree beside a pond. Round the trunk of the tree was a built platform where he had unpacked his box and was heating water on a kerosene stove. He welcomed the party and made them sit on the platform. Very soon he served each with a hot cup of tea and a plateful of sweets. Binodini remarked again and again, "Thank God that Bihari Babu had the foresight to

65

come so well equipped. What would Mahendra Babu have done without tea?"

In fact the cup of tea did revive Mahendra. Nevertheless he said, "Bihari is always overdoing things, trying to be dramatic. We came here for a simple picnic and there he is with all the usual elaborate paraphernalia. It spoils the fun."

"Very well, then," laughed Bihari. "Let's have that cup of tea back. You're welcome to have your fun—without the tea. We won't stand in the way."

The day advanced but the servants' coach did not arrive. Bihari opened his box and brought out all the provisions for a full-fledged lunch—rice, dal, vegetables, and finely ground spices in small bottles. Binodini stared in amazement and exclaimed, "Bihari Babu, you put us ladies to shame. You've no one at home—where did you learn all this?"

Bihari smiled. "Necessity has taught me. Having no one to look after me, I have to look after myself."

Though Bihari's tone was flippant, Binodini looked at him gravely, her eyes soft with pity and tenderness.

Bihari and Binodini busied themselves with cooking. Asha tried timidly to help but Bihari did not let her do so. Mahendra did not even offer to help. He reclined against the trunk of the tree, stretched one leg over the other and began to watch the dance of sunlight through the trembling leaves of the banyan.

When the cooking was almost done, Binodini called to him, "Mahin Babu, you won't be able to count all the leaves of the tree. Better get up and have a bath."

The servants' coach at last arrived. It had broken down on the way. It was past midday when it turned up.

After the meal some one proposed a game of cards in the shade of the tree. Mahendra, however, declined to join and very soon fell into a doze. Asha went inside the pavilion and lay down to rest. Binodini also made as if to rise and lifting the end of her sari over her head, said, "Let me also go inside."

"Why, where's the hurry?" said Bihari. "Please sit down and tell me about your village home."

Now and again gusts of warm afternoon breeze rustled through the overhanging leaves and the *koel* called from the *jam* tree on the water's edge. Binodini began the story of her childhood, of her parents and her early playmates. As she recaptured the memories of those days the half-drawn veil gradually slipped down from her head and the usually provocative sensuousness of her beauty seemed to soften and mellow. Her black velvet eyes normally sparkling with a playful, ironic look which the astute Bihari feared and mistrusted were now suffused with so gentle and calm a tenderness that Bihari felt he was looking at an altogether different person. Behind the glamour of her beauty a heart still throbbed with chaste feelings, the woman in her had not yet dried up in the insatiable heat of frivolous gaiety. All these days Bihari had never even for a moment pictured Binodini as a chaste and loving wife or as a mother tenderly clasping a babe to her breast—today for the first time it seemed as if the glamorous actress on the stage had vanished, revealing the woman in her simple, homely setting. Bihari was amazed—agreeably. Heaving a deep sigh he said to himself, "Binodini looks a gay butterfly but deep inside her burns the austere light of a pure and devoted woman. How little we know even of ourselves! We identify a person with that facet of his personality which a particular set of circumstances happens to reveal. The true being is known only to the Creator."

Keeping his thoughts to himself Bihari encouraged Binodini to continue her reminiscences by filling the pauses with well-timed questions. Binodini had never had such an audience before, she had never had an occasion to talk freely and without self-consciousness to a man. Absorbed in her own recital she shed all reserve and coquetry and spoke simply and naturally and with such sincerity that her own mind was purged of tension and felt clean, calm and content, like the parched earth after the new rains.

Having had to get up at dawn, Mahendra was so tired that he did not wake up from sleep till five in the afternoon.

"Let's make a move," he said gruffly as soon as he woke up.

"Why not wait till the sunset?" suggested Binodini.

"No," replied Mahendra curtly. "Why risk being accosted by a drunken white soldier!"

By the time everything was packed the dusk had descended. The servants came and reported that the coach had disappeared. A couple of white soldiers had forced the coachman to drive them to the railway station. So a servant was dispatched to look for another coach. Mahendra was impatient and could hardly conceal his irritation. "What a miserable day!" he kept on repeating to himself.

Gradually the moon extricated itself from the mesh of trees fringing the horizon and rose gracefully in the clear sky, casting its own net of light and shade over the garden, hushed and stilled. An awareness of this unearthly beauty lighted up for Binodini an altogether different facet of her being. In an overflow of affection untinged by affectation she and gave her a good hug. Asha noticed tears in Binodini's caught hold of Asha, as they stood under the *bithika* tree, eyes and asked anxiously, "Why are you crying, dear Eyesore?"

"It's nothing," smiled Binodini. "It's been a wonderful day."

"What was there so wonderful about it?"

"I feel as though I had died and am now in a different planet where everything can yet be mine."

This was beyond Asha. She felt bewildered and the reference to death pained her. "Please, dear Eyesore, don't ever talk of such things."

A coach was brought at last. Bihari took his seat on the coach box as before; Binodini did not speak during the drive and watched in silence the fleeting panorama of trees standing like shadowy sentinels of the moonlight. Asha fell asleep and Mahendra maintained his scowl.

68

17

Mahendra was anxious to recover the ground lost during that unfortunate picnic and to rehabilitate himself in Binodini's esteem. But Rajlakshmi was laid up with influenza the very next day and though the attack was not very virulent she suffered much from weakness and discomfort. Binodini nursed her day and night.

"If you go on like this night and day without respite, you'll take to your bed yourself," protested Mahendra. "Let me engage a nurse."

"Don't be upset, Mahinda," broke in Bihari. "Let her do her duty as she likes. Who else can do it half as well?"

Mahendra kept on slipping into the invalid's room. The efficient Binodini had no patience with a person who fussed around without being of any use. More than once she snapped at him, "What good does your hovering around do, Mahin Babu? Please go to your college and don't miss your classes."

Though Binodini was flattered and pleased by Mahendra's attentions, the idea that he should so demean himself as to ogle hungrily at her by his sick mother's bed revolted her. When she took a task upon herself she did it with single-minded devotion, forgetting everything else. She was meticulous in her care of the patient, looking after every detail of nursing and feeding and brooked no distraction from outside.

Mahendra smarted under the rebuff and started attending college with a vengeance. His temper was in a chronic state of irritation which was considerably aggravated by the renewed disorder in his domestic regime. The food was no longer served in time, the coachman invariably disappeared when he was wanted, the holes in his socks grew wider and wider. This disorder which he had previously found so amusing was no longer so, since he had tasted in the meantime the luxury of every comfort being served to him on a silver platter as it were. Asha's ineptitude and clumsiness had now ceased to be a source of endless amusement and fun.

"How many times have I told you, Chuni," he burst out at last, "that my clothes must be laid out and the studs fixed in my shirt before I go for my bath? Not once has it been done so far. It takes me two hours looking for my clothes after my bath and trying to fix the studs."

Asha went pale with shame and remorse. "I had told the bearer to do so," she faltered.

"Told the bearer to do so!" mimicked Mahendra. "Couldn't you have done it yourself? Can't you make yourself useful in any way?"

Asha was dumbfounded. She had never been scolded like this before. It did not occur to her to retort, "It's you who would not let me learn." She had had no opportunity to realize that housekeeping, like other arts, is a matter of training and experience. She suffered from a complex that she was congenitally slow-witted and inept and incapable of doing anything smartly. Even on occasions when Mahendra had so far forgotten himself as to belittle her *vis-à-vis* Binodini, she had accepted the snub with humility and without any rancour.

Many a time Asha hovered around her invalid mother-in-law's room and would even linger shyly in the doorway, wanting desperately to make herself useful in some way. She was eager to show that she could do something, but no one wanted her assistance. She did not know how to insinuate or force her way in, how to claim her rightful place in the household and was condemned by her own diffidence to loiter outside the threshold. An undefined pain was growing and gnawing inside her, she could not tell what it was, she did not understand what she feared. She felt that everything was crumbling around her but what it was that was crumbling, how it was built up, how undone and how it might be remade, she could not understand. She only knew that she

70

longed to weep aloud and cry, "I am worthless, utterly useless and incredibly stupid!"

How wonderful were the old days when she and Mahendra sat side by side, hour after hour, sometimes chatting, sometimes silent, but always happy and absorbed in each other! Now Mahendra finds it hard to carry on a *tête-à-tête* in Binodini's absence and finds silence even more embarrassing.

"Whose letter is it?" asked Mahendra of the bearer.

"It's for Bihari Babu."

"Who gave it to you?"

"The young lady, Sir" (meaning Binodini).

"Let me see it."

Mahendra took the letter and was sorely tempted to tear open the cover and read it, but after turning it over half a dozen times, he tossed it back into the bearer's hand. Had he opened the cover he would have read inside: "Pishima flatly declines to have any more of barley water. Can I make her some pulse soup?" Binodini never consulted Mahendra about his mother's treatment or diet; she relied wholly on Bihari's advice.

After pacing the veranda for a while Mahendra went inside his room. His glance fell on a picture on the wall which hung awry, its string having nearly given way. He almost barked at Asha, "Nothing ever strikes your eye! This is how things are ruined."

The brass flower-vase still held the faded flowers brought from the Dum Dum garden on the day of the picnic and neatly arranged by Binodini. Normally Mahendra would not have bothered to notice it. Today he did and said caustically, "I suppose they will remain there until Binodini comes and throws them out." He picked up the vase and flung it away on the landing from where it clanged merrily down the steps. "Why is Asha not as I want her to be? Why can't she do anything right?" thought Mahendra angrily. "Why can't she hold me fast to her instead of making me sick of this married life with her clumsiness and ineptitude?" As these thoughts were whirling in his brain, he noticed that Asha's face had gone pale as death, her lips were trembling and she was holding on to the bed-post, quivering all over. Suddenly she fled out of the room.

Mahendra came to himself and went down softly to retrieve the vase. Then he came and sat on the chair by his reading table and remained there a long time, his face hidden in his hands.

In the evening the lamps were lit but Asha was nowhere to be seen. Mahendra went up to the roof-terrace and began to pace up and down. It struck nine and yet Asha did not turn up. A ghostly silence as of midnight seemed to have settled on the deserted bedroom. At last he sent for Asha. She came and stood nervously at the doorway opening on to the terrace. Mahendra went up to her and clasped her to his heart. Asha burst into sobs, her head resting against her husband's breast; it seemed as though the sobs would never cease, the tears would never dry. Mahendra held her close, kissing her hair. Overhead the stars continued their silent vigil.

Later in the night when they were in bed, Mahendra said, "It's my turn for night-duty in the college hospital. I'm afraid I shall have to move into diggings near the college for some time." Asha wondered, "Is he still angry with me? What a miserable wretch I am to drive my husband out of his house! It's better I were dead."

But there was no trace of anger in Mahendra's behaviour that night. He held Asha's head in a silent embrace and gently played with her hair, loosening the knot at the back. Formerly when he played with her hair and ruffled it too much she would protest. Tonight she quivered with delight and said not a word. Suddenly she felt a tear drop on her forehead. Mahendra gently lifted up her face and whispered lovingly, "Chuni!" Asha stretched out her soft arms and without replying clung closer to her husband. Mahendra said, "I've done wrong, Chuni. Please forgive me."

"No, no, don't say such a thing," Asha whispered hurriedly, shutting his mouth with her hand. "You've done no wrong. It's I who am at fault. Please punish me as you will and make me worthy of you."

Early in the morning before leaving bed Mahendra whispered, "Chuni, my darling, my jewel, you will always be the first in my heart—no one can dislodge you from there."

Asha was so elated that she felt capable of any sacrifice. There was however one little request she had to make.

"Promise me that you'll write every day."

"And you too?" insisted Mahendra.

"You know I can't write," pleaded Asha.

"You can write better than even Akshay Kumar Dutta *— yours would make really pleasant reading," said Mahendra, tenderly pulling a wisp of hair over her ear.

"Don't be a tease," chided Asha affectionately.

Asha busied herself with packing Mahendra's portmanteau. It was not easy to fold the heavy winter garments so as to accommodate them in its very limited capacity, but somehow the husband and wife managed to tumble them in, filling two boxes where one would have been enough. Some pieces were still left over, which had to be wrapped up in several separate packages. Though Asha was embarrassed and felt humiliated by her lack of skill, she soon forgot all that in the excitement and thrill of pushing, teasing and laughing at each other. It was like old days. So elated and happy she was that she forgot altogether that his hilarious packing was a prelude to a painful parting. Several times the coachman sent

---

* Author of *Charu Path*, the children's reader which Mahendra was reading with Asha. The title literally means "Pleasant Reading," and hence the pun on the word.

word that the carriage was ready. Mahendra turned a deaf ear. Finally he lost patience and ordered the horse to be unharnessed.

The morning advanced into noon, the noon into evening. The lovers were still wrapped up in one another, each begging the other to look after his or her health and to write regularly, repeating the request again and again, till their hearts were too full for words. At last they parted.

Rajlakshmi had left her sick bed only two days before. She was feeling better and wrapped round in a thick shawl was playing cards with Binodini, when Mahendra suddenly entered the room in the evening. Without glancing at Binodini he said to his mother, "Mother, I've night duty in the college hospital and so will be away from home for a few days."

"Very well, my son," replied Rajlakshmi somewhat piqued. "You can't afford to neglect your studies."

Though she had by now fully recovered, she suddenly felt or imagined she felt very weak, and asking Binodini to fix her a pillow she lay down. Binodini gently massaged her feet. Mahendra touched his mother's forehead and tried to feel her pulse, but she pushed his hand away, murmuring petulantly, "What can you know from the pulse? I am all right, you don't have to worry." She turned and lay down on the other side, seeming very feeble.

Mahendra touched his mother's feet and left the room without taking any notice of Binodini.

18

Binodini wondered what the matter was. "Is it wounded pride or anger or just fear? Is he trying to show off that he doesn't care for me? Let's see how long he can stay away."

Nevertheless she was restive. Having lost the pastime of goading and provoking Mahendra, she now felt bored and listless. The house no longer held any interest for her and Asha without Mahendra seemed very insipid. Her love-hungry soul was now deprived of the vicarious thrill of watching and instigating the drama of conjugal love. Though the game was painful to watch—it roused her dormant, frustrated longings—it held a sinister fascination for her.

The nature of her own feelings towards Mahendra was not clear to her. She had not forgotten that he had spurned her hand in marriage and deprived her of her right to love and happiness. He had rejected her priceless gift and fallen for a silly, empty-headed girl like Asha. Did she hate him for it and seek to avenge her wrong, or did she love him and want to offer herself in self-surrender? All she knew was that she was being consumed by a passionate flame inside her, whether of hate or of love or of both, she could not say. She would smile bitterly at herself and say, "Was any woman ever in such a predicament? Do I wish to die or to destroy? Am I the hunter or the hunted? I wish I knew." But whether she wanted to destroy or be destroyed, this much she knew that she desperately needed Mahendra. Her flaming dart must strike him down sooner or later. There was no escape for him. He must come back to her.

Soon after leaving the house, Mahendra received a letter written in a familiar hand. He kept it in his breast pocket, not wishing to open it in the din and bustle of the day. While listening to a lecture or in course of his hospital rounds he had a delicious feeling as if the bird of love was quietly resting in the nest of his heart. Later in the day when he would wake it up, it would warble its sweet music in his ear.

In the evening when there was no one else about, he stretched himself comfortably in his chair, with a lamp by his side, and took from his pocket the letter warm with the heat of his body. For a long time he did not open it and kept on looking at the address on the envelope. He knew that there would not be much inside it, for poor Asha did not know how to express her feelings in words. His imagination would have to reconstruct her heart's speech from the unsteady scrawl of her childish hand. Looking at his own name on the envelope inscribed with much care in a childish scrawl, he felt he was listening to an unheard symphony whose exquisite music came from the heartbeats of a chaste and loving heart.

The brief separation from his wife had already relieved the nausea of love's surfeit and had revived the ardent memories of their early raptures. Forgotten was his irritation with Asha's clumsiness and ineptitude; he remembered only her sweet face radiant with a love that was innocent of all earthly demands. He opened the envelope very gently and pressed the letter with his forehead. A sudden waft of fragrance reached him like a passionate sigh, reminding him of his own gift of a perfume bottle to Asha. As he unfolded the letter and read it he was struck dumb with amazement. The immature handwriting was Asha's, but the language—no, it could never be hers! He read:

"Dearest, why need this letter inflict on you the memory of her to forget whom you have gone away? Why should the creeper which you tore apart and flung away raise its head from the dust and try shamelessly to cling to you again?

"And yet would it do you any harm if you did think of her for a brief moment? It would only be a passing thought. As for me, your indifference is like a thorn stuck in my side—whichever way I turn it pains, day and night, at work or at rest. Teach me, I beg of you, the art of forgetting which you know so well.

"Was it my fault that you once loved me? I had not dared to hope for such happiness—no, not even in a dream. Who was I? A mere nobody. If you had never deigned to look at me, if I had been a mere maid without wages in your house, I would have had no cause or right to complain. You yourself picked me up from the dust and raised me up so high—why,

76

I do not know. What was there in me that charmed you so? And if the thunderbolt had to fall from a cloudless sky, why did it merely scorch me, why did it not blast me, body and mind, to ashes, letting nothing survive?

"How much I have suffered and thought during these last two days! One thing I cannot understand: Could you not have stayed in the house ignoring me? Why need you have left the house on my account? Was I such a thorn in your side? Such a pest that I could not be allowed to remain in a corner of your house or even outside the door? Even if I were, I could have been driven out, sent far away. Why need you have exiled yourself? Like a floating wreck I had drifted into your life and like a floating wreck I would have drifted away."

What a letter! It was not difficult to understand whose language it was. Mahendra remained seated with the letter in hand, like one dazed. His mind for the last few days had been like a railway train speeding at full steam in a certain direction. He had not realised that the desired object of his destination too was moving from the opposite direction along the same lines. The sudden collision threw him completely off the rails and there he lay, an inert heap of benumbed consciousness.

He sat for a long time lost in thought. Then he re-read the letter two or three times. What was like a distant shadow was gradually assuming a concrete shape. The comet which had previously seemed like a dim speck in a corner of his life's horizon now blazed its fiery tail across the sky.

The letter was indeed Binodini's, though the simple-minded Asha had penned it as her own. Listening to Binodini's dictation she had actually begun to feel the sentiments expressed therein. It was as though the dumbness within her had become articulate. Binodini's words gave form to her own undefined pain, a pain she was conscious of but was unable to express. She said to herself, "What a wonderful

77

friend to guess the secret of my heart and to mirror it so faithfully and so well!" Her devotion to Binodini was doubled; she felt more than ever dependent on one who provided the vehicle to her inmost thoughts.

Mahendra rose from the chair. His brow was clouded. He tried to be angry with Binodini but the more he tried the more annoyed he became with Asha instead. "What a nitwit!" he chafed. "How trying for the husband!" He sank back into the chair and read the letter once again. Each time he read it he felt a secret thrill of pride and elation. He tried his best to imagine that what he was reading was Asha's but found it impossible to do so. As soon as he had read a couple of lines a delicious suspicion bubbled up like foaming wine, wiping out the image of Asha. He was intoxicated by the prospect of a love, at once hidden and articulate, forbidden and forthcoming, poisonous and sweet, a love that was both a surrender and a challenge. He wished he could strike himself with a knife or do something drastic to break the spell of this intoxication and to divert his mind elsewhere. He banged his fist on the table and jumping up from his chair exclaimed, "Hang it all, I'll burn the letter!" He brought the letter near the lamp but instead of burning it, re-read it once again.

When the servant cleaned the room the next morning, he found plenty of ashes lying about. They were not the relics of Asha's letter but of several unfinished replies which Mahendra had attempted at night!

19

Another letter arrived.

"Why have you not replied to my letter? Perhaps you did well. The truth cannot be told. I have understood what your reply would have been. When a devotee calls upon the Lord, he does not receive a reply in words. I take it that this unhappy creature's letter has at least found a resting place under your feet.

"If my worship has disturbed my Lord Shiva's * trance, do not, I pray you, be angry with me. You may or may not respond, you may or may not look at me, you may or may not even know what I suffer, I cannot but love as I do. Hence these few lines—although you, my stone-hearted beloved, will remain unmoved. . . ."

Mahendra tried again to reply. But as soon as he began to write, the words addressed to Asha made their way to Binodini. He lacked the skill to write subtly and ambiguously. Having torn up several drafts, he at last wrote a reply in the small hours of the night, but as he inscribed Asha's name on the envelope he suddenly winced as though a lash had struck his back and a voice hissed, "Hypocrite, how dare you deceive an innocent, trusting girl?" He tore up the letter in a hundred bits and spent the rest of the night seated at the table, his face hidden in his hands, as though hiding from himself.

The third letter:

"Can one love, utterly devoid of pride? Love, abject and self-debased, is hardly a gift worthy of offering.

"Maybe, I did not understand you and dared too much. When you left me, I made bold to write to you. When you were silent, I laid bare my heart. But if I mistook you, was it all my fault? Look back on the past and tell me truly if from the first to the last it was not you who led me to believe as I did.

"However, whether right or wrong, what I wrote cannot be unwritten, what I gave cannot be revoked—this is my regret, my incredible shame as a woman. But do not imagine that one who loves will for ever submit to love being trampled under dust. If my letters are not welcome I will not in-

* Reference to the well-known legend of Shiva's anger at being roused from his trance by Kama's (Cupid's) dart shot at the instigation of Parvati who was in love with him.

flict them on you. If you do not reply, this shall be my last letter."

Mahendra could stand it no longer. He felt he must return home and imagined he was doing so in righteous indignation. How dare Binodini assume that he had fled from the house on her account! He swore he would prove to her that she was mistaken and would snub her impertinence.

Just then Bihari entered the room. Seeing him Mahendra's elation doubled. He had of late felt suspicious and secretly jealous of Bihari. Their friendship had cooled. But the letters had flattered his pride and allayed his jealousy. He could afford to be friendly and generous. He welcomed his friend effusively, rushed forward to greet him, smacked him on the back and led him by his hand to a chair.

Bihari seemed depressed. No wonder, chuckled Mahendra. Binodini must have snubbed him. Poor fellow!

"Have you been to our place, Bihari?" asked Mahendra.

"I am coming straight from there," replied Bihari gravely.

Mahendra's pity for his jilted friend increased. He felt more elated than ever. "Poor chap!" he thought. "Always unlucky in love." He touched the letters in his breast pocket and was reassured by their rustling.

"How's everybody at home?" he asked.

"Why have you left the house and what are you doing here?" asked Bihari without answering his question.

"A lot of night duty in the hospital these days. Rather inconvenient to come all the way from home."

"There used to be night duty before also. But I don't remember your ever shifting here."

"Do you smell a rat?" asked Mahendra laughing.

"Don't try to be funny. Come, let's go home."

Mahendra was eager to return home but Bihari's entreaty gave him an excuse for showing off his assumed indifference.

"How can that be?" he asked. "I shall lose my year in the college."

"Don't try to bluff, Mahinda," said Bihari. "I've known you since we were children. You can't put me off like this. Let me tell you bluntly. You're doing a great wrong."

"And whom am I wronging, Mr. Judge?"

"Where is your heart whose noble sentiments you used to parade so much?"

"At the present moment it is in the hospital."

"You are trying to be funny here, Mahinda, while there in the house poor Asha is sobbing her heart out, wandering aimlessly from room to room."

The news of Asha's weeping struck Mahendra like a blow. It had not occurred to him, in his new intoxication, that there were other human beings in this world with their joys and sorrows. He was taken aback and asked, "What is she crying for?"

"Is it something I should know or you?" answered Bihari angrily.

"If you must be angry because your Mahinda is not all-knowing, then be angry with his Creator."

Mahendra was surprised at Bihari's passionate concern. He had always imagined that Bihari suffered from no such thing as a heart. But these symptoms! When did it happen? On the day the two friends had gone to see Asha in her uncle's house? Poor Bihari! Mahendra chuckled as he relished the luxury of feeling sorry for Bihari. Confident of Asha's single-minded devotion to him, he could afford to be generous. The thought that prizes, which others coveted ardently but could not get, yielded themselves so easily to him for good, made his breast swell with pride.

"Very well, let's go," he said to Bihari. "Will you fetch a carriage, please!"

20

Asha's fears evaporated like mist in the sun when she saw Mahendra's face on his return home. Recalling what she had written in the letters she felt so shy that she could hardly lift her face before him. But Mahendra rubbed it in.

"How could you make such accusations in your letters?" he asked reproachfully, as he brought out from his pocket the three much-read letters.

"Please tear them up, I beg of you," pleaded Asha anxiously. She tried to snatch them away but Mahendra evaded her and replaced them in his pocket.

"I went on duty," he continued, "but you misunderstood. You suspected me!"

Asha was in tears. "Please forgive me this once," she implored. "It'll never happen again."

"Never?"

"Never!"

Mahendra drew her to him and kissed her.

"Please let me have the letters," begged Asha. "I'll tear them up."

"No, let them be."

"He's keeping the letters," said Asha to herself, "to punish me."

She felt annoyed with Binodini and did not, as usual, hasten to her to share the joy at her husband's return. She even avoided her. Binodini noticed it and kept herself altogether at a distance, on the pretext of some work or other.

Mahendra was surprised. "How very strange!" he said to himself. "Here was I hoping to see a good deal of Binodini this time but what is happening is just the contrary. What then was the meaning of those letters?"

Mahendra had made up his mind to make no move on his part to reach a woman's heart. He had thought, "Even if Binodini makes advances, I shall remain aloof." Now he felt that this wouldn't do. A studied aloofness might seem as if there was really something the matter between him and Binodini. No, it would be better to keep up the normal, easy, pleasant relations with her so as to leave no room for misunderstanding or tension. He said to Asha, "It seems I am the real eyesore to your friend. One hardly sees her these days."

"God knows what's the matter with her," replied Asha indifferently.

Rajlakshmi was in tears. She came and complained to Mahendra, "It's impossible to hold back Bipin's widow any longer."

"Why, mother?"

"How can I tell, my son? She insists on leaving for her village home. You don't know how to look after a guest. Why should a well-bred lady stay on if she is not made to feel at home?"

Binodini was sitting in her room and sewing a bed cover.

"Eyesore!" called Mahendra as he entered.

"Come in, Mahendra Babu!" responded Binodini sitting up properly.

"Good Heavens! Since when have I become Mahendra Babu?"

"How else shall I address you?" asked Binodini, her eyes fixed on her sewing.

"As you address your friend—Eyesore."

Binodini refrained from making one of her usual witty repartees. She remained silent and continued her needlework.

"I suppose it is too apt an epithet to be used playfully?" asked Mahendra.

Binodini took time to bite off a piece of thread before replying, "You know best. I don't." And then as if to put an end to the trend of conversation she asked gravely, "How is it that you suddenly left your college rooms?"

"How long can one go on dissecting dead bodies?"

Binodini bit off another piece of thread.

"I suppose you're looking for live bodies now?" she asked without raising her head.

Mahendra had come determined to amuse and impress Binodini with witty and provoking badinage but he found himself so affected by the tension in the atmosphere that he was completely at a loss for a light-hearted reply. Binodini's reserve and aloofness had roused in him a violent desire to draw closer to her and break to pieces the barrier she seemed to have raised against him. Ignoring the sarcasm of Binodini's last remark he moved nearer to her and asked, "Why are you leaving us? What wrong have we done?"

Binodini edged back a little and raising her head from her work fixed her large, luminous eyes on Mahendra.

"Each one of us has his own sphere of obligations and duties," she said. "You had to move to the college rooms. Was it your or any one else's fault? I too have my work and must go."

Mahendra could not think of a suitable reply. After a little while he asked, "Is the call so urgent that you cannot but go?"

"Urgency is felt only in the mind," replied Binodini, carefully passing the thread through the needle. "How can I explain all that to you?"

For a long while Mahendra sat lost in thought staring gravely through the open window at the top of a distant coconut tree. Binodini continued her sewing silently. So hushed and still it was that the dropping of a needle on the ground could have been heard. Suddenly Mahendra spoke, breaking the spell of silence. Binodini started, the needle pricking her finger.

"Will no entreaty of ours persuade you to stay?"

Sucking the drop of blood on her finger Binodini replied, "Why all this entreaty? What does it matter whether I stay or leave! Why should it bother you!"

Her voice sounded heavy with feeling as she spoke. Her head was bent very low and she seemed to be fully occupied with her sewing: a tear glistened in a corner of her eyes. The winter afternoon was losing itself in the dusk.

Impulsively Mahendra caught hold of her hand and said in a voice choked with emotion, "If it does bother me, will you stay?"

Binodini snatched her hand away and shifted her seat further back. Mahendra's spell was broken. The echo of his last words beat against his ears like a cruel mockery. He bit his guilty tongue and lapsed into silence.

At this moment Asha entered breaking the tense stillness of the room. Immediately Binodini turned to Mahendra and said as if in response to an argument, "Since your friends make so much of me, I must also in return respect your wishes. I shall therefore stay on as long as you want me to."

Asha delighted at the success of her husband's mission flung her arms round Binodini and exclaimed, "Now that's a promise! Please confirm it by repeating thrice that as long as we want you here, you will stay, stay, stay!"

Binodini repeated it thrice. Asha said, "Eyesore dear, when you had to yield, why did you make us beg so hard? In the end you had to admit defeat before my husband."

"Tell me, Thakurpo," said Binodini laughing and turning to Mahendra, "is the defeat mine or yours?"

Mahendra had remained as one stunned. He felt the room reek with his sin, his own disdain envelop him. How could he talk easily and naturally to Asha as though nothing had happened! How to cloak his ugly erstwhile lapse behind the mask of an innocent, disarming smile! He lacked the ready cunning for such a wile.

"The defeat is mine," he said gravely and left the room. After a little while he came back and said to Binodini, "Please forgive me."

"Why, what's the matter, Thakurpo?"

"We have no right to force you to stay on here."

"Where was the force?" laughed Binodini. "I saw no evidence of it. In fact, you were rather affectionate about it. Is that what you call force? What say you, Eyesore dear? Are love and force the same thing?"

"Not at all!" replied Asha vehemently.

"Thakurpo," went on Binodini, "you want me to stay, you will miss me if I go away—this is *my* good fortune. How rare to find such friends in this world who will share one's pain and joy! And having found them, how can one leave them, dear Eyesore!"

Seeing her husband stupefied and speechless, Asha was touched. She said to Binodini, "Who can outwit you in argument, dear sister? My husband has already confessed his defeat. Please now stop rubbing it in."

Mahendra once more hurriedly left the room. Bihari had been sitting with Rajlakshmi and had just left her to look for Mahendra when he ran into him outside Binodini's door. Thrown off his guard by this sudden encounter, Mahendra exclaimed, "Oh what a cursed humbug I am, Bihari!" So excited he was that his words reached inside the room.

"Bihari Thakurpo!" someone called from inside the room.

"Coming in a minute, Binod-bouthan," replied Bihari.

"Please, now—only a word," said the voice from inside.

Bihari entered the room and immediately looked at Asha. From what he could see behind the veil there was no suggestion of sorrow or pain in her face. Asha tried to get up and leave but Binodini pulled her down, saying, "Are you two such bitter rivals, Bihari-Thakurpo, that the moment my Eyesore sees you she wants to run away?"

Asha blushed hot and pinched Binodini.

Bihari laughed and replied, "Not that. Rather because Nature failed to make me sufficiently attractive."

"See, dear sister, how tactful he is! Instead of finding fault with your taste, he blames Nature. It's your misfortune that you can't appreciate the worth of such a Lakshmana*-like brother-in-law."

"I would have no regret, Binod-bouthan, if that earned me your pity," said Bihari.

"All the rivers of the world," replied Binodini, "cannot quench the thirst of a *chatak* † who must still yearn for the raindrop."

Asha would not stay any longer and snatching away her hand from Binodini's she left the room. Bihari too was about to leave when Binodini asked, "Thakurpo, what is the matter with Mahendra Babu?"

Startled, Bihari turned round and stood still.

"I don't know," he replied. "Has anything happened?"

"How can I tell, Thakurpo? I don't like the look of things."

Bihari sat-down in the chair and stared anxiously at Binodini hoping to hear something more. Binodini said nothing and went on with her sewing, seemingly absorbed in her work.

"Is there anything particular you have noticed about Mahinda?" asked Bihari after a while.

"I don't know, Thakurpo," replied Binodini very simply and naturally. "All the same I don't like it. I keep on worrying on my Eyesore's account."

She heaved a long sigh and laying down her sewing made as if to leave.

"Please stay a while," begged Bihari as he rose from his chair and sat down again.

* Younger brother of Rama in *Ramayana* who left his home to accompany his brother and sister-in-law in exile.
† A bird supposed to live on raindrops.

Binodini got up and opened wide the door and windows of the room. She raised the wick of the kerosene lamp a little higher and took her seat at the far end of the bed, resuming her sewing.

"I can't stay on here for ever, Thakurpo," she said. "But when I am gone, please keep an eye on my Eyesore and see that she's not unhappy."

She turned her face and looked the other way as if trying to pull herself together.

"No, you mustn't leave, Binod-bouthan," cried Bihari. "You have no one else to look after—please watch over the welfare of this innocent, helpless girl. Who will come to her rescue if you desert her?"

"You know how things are, Thakurpo. How could I stay on indefinitely? What will people say?"

"Let them say what they will. Turn a deaf ear. You are an angel—you alone can save this vulnerable child from the harsh buffets of this world. Forgive me, Bouthan, for having failed to recognise you at first. I, too, like the common, ungenerous crowd, had misjudged you in the beginning and imputed base motives to you. I had even suspected that you were jealous of Asha's happiness, as if—no, it's a sin to utter such thoughts even. Now that I know what an angel you are, my admiration for you compels me to confess the wrong I did you."

Binodini shivered with a thrill of delight. Although she knew she was playing a part she was deeply moved by Bihari's tribute. She had never received the like of it from any one else. For a moment she was lifted out of herself and felt as the pure, high-souled angel of Bihari's imagination. Tears of an undefined tenderness for Asha swam into her eyes. She did not try to hide them from Bihari. She let the tears flow down her face, comforted by the delusion of magnanimity which they helped to sustain.

Seeing Binodini's tears Bihari with difficulty controlled his own and left the room. He went up to Mahendra's room, curious to find out why the latter had accused himself so loudly of humbug. He did not find Mahendra in the room and was told that he had gone out. It was unlike Mahendra to go out without a strong enough reason, for he felt uncomfortable and ill at ease everywhere except at home, amid familiar faces. Bihari was worried and slowly turned his steps towards his own house.

Binodini went and brought Asha into her room and clasping her to her heart said with tearful eyes, "Eyesore dear, I am very unlucky, ill-starred."

Asha greatly moved flung her arms round her and said feelingly, "Why need you say such things, darling!"

Binodini hid her face on Asha's breast and sobbed like a child.

"I bring ill-luck wherever I go," she said. "Please let me go away, dear sister—let me return to my own wilderness."

"Don't talk like that, darling," coaxed Asha putting her hand under Binodini's chin and lifting her face up. "I shan't be able to live without you. Tell me, what has happened to make you talk like this?"

In the meanwhile Bihari had retraced his steps before he could reach home. Having failed to find Mahendra he was anxious, on some excuse or other, to see Binodini once more, in order to understand why she feared estrangement between Mahendra and Asha. He hit upon the excuse of leaving a message with Binodini for Mahendra inviting him to dinner the following day. As he called out, "Binod-bouthan!", he saw from outside the door the two girls locked in each other's embrace, their eyes glistening with tears, clearly visible in the light of the kerosene lamp. He stood still.

It occurred to Asha that Bihari must have maligned her Eyesore or said something nasty to her to cause this sudden reaction in Binodini. What an odious fellow this Bihari is! What a nasty mind! Asha was indignant with Bihari as she left the room. Bihari too hurriedly beat a retreat, deeply moved by what he had seen, his admiration for Binodini greatly enhanced.

The same night Mahendra announced, "Chuni, I am leaving tomorrow for Kashi by the morning passenger."

Asha's heart missed a beat. "Why?" she asked.

"Haven't seen Kakima for a long time," replied Mahendra.

Asha felt very ashamed. She should have thought of it earlier. Obsessed with her personal problems, she had neglected her loving aunt while Mahendra had not forgotten the pilgrim in exile. She reproached herself for her callous selfishness.

"She went away leaving her only treasure on this earth in my care," continued Mahendra. "I can't rest until I see her once again."

His voice broke as he spoke. His right hand strayed to Asha's forehead, gently caressing it as if in a mute, loving benediction. Asha could not understand the secret of this sudden overflow of tenderness, but she was deeply moved and the tears streamed down her cheeks. She recalled the unaccountable outburst of affection and solicitude on Binodini's part that very evening. Whether the two manifestations were connected in any way was more than she could understand. She vaguely sensed the imminence of something, whether good or bad, she did not know.

She was frightened and clung to Mahendra in a tight embrace. Mahendra felt the sudden tremor of her fright and said, "Don't you be afraid, Chuni. The blessings of your pious aunt are with you. She renounced the world for your good—nothing ill can ever befall you. You need have no fear, none at all."

Pulling herself together Asha firmly thrust all fear away, trusting her husband's benediction as an indestructible amulet. Repeatedly she bowed before the holy image of her aunt in her mind, praying, "Mother, may your blessings ever shield my husband!"

Mahendra left the next morning without saying goodbye to Binodini.

"How virtuous!" thought Binodini contemptuously. "He does the wrong and quarrels with me for it! Such virtue does not last very long."

21

When Annapurna in her seclusion saw Mahendra suddenly arrive she was overjoyed. At the same time she was afraid that Mahendra had probably again quarrelled with his mother on Asha's account and had come to her to vent his grievances and to find consolation. It was Mahendra's habit since childhood to run to his aunt whenever he was in pain or in trouble. She used to pacify him when he flew into a rage, would teach him to bear pain when he was suffering. But after Mahendra's marriage she had ceased to be his refuge, his solace and his teacher. In fact she soon realised that whatever she did, however she intervened, she only made the confusion in his domestic life worse confounded. When she realised that, she went into voluntary exile and seclusion. As when a sick child cries for water which the physician has forbidden and the unhappy mother unable to bear the sight rushes into another room, so Annapurna had left the house. Exiled in her distant pilgrimage she had, by her absorption in the daily ritual of prayer and offerings, succeeded largely in forgetting her old world of personal attachments when Mahendra suddenly appeared. She was afraid he might revive the memories of old feuds and reopen the wound that was more or less healed.

But Mahendra said not a word about his mother *vis-à-vis* Asha. Then Annapurna's fears assumed another shape. How is it that Mahendra who wouldn't attend his college because he couldn't bear to be away from Asha had come all the way to Kashi to see his aunt? Is he drifting away from her? She asked Mahendra somewhat anxiously, "Mahin dear, please tell me the truth, I implore you, how is my Chuni?"

"She's fine, Kakima."

"How does she spend her time, Mahin? Are you two still fooling about with each other or have you begun to take your life and work seriously?"

"Fooling about has completely stopped. The root of all mischief was that *Charu Path*. Fortunately the book has disappeared. No fear of recovering it. Were you there now, you would be delighted to see Chuni's complete indifference to learning—in the good old traditional woman's way expected of her."

"What news of Bihari, Mahin?"

"Busy as usual with every one else's business save his own. His steward looks after his land and property—with an eye to his master's welfare or his own, I cannot say. But Bihari was always like that—others look after his affairs, he looks after others' affairs."

"Won't he marry at all, Mahin?"

"I see no move in that direction," laughed Mahendra.

A deep pain stabbed Annapurna's mind. She recalled how once Bihari had been willing to marry her niece and how cruelly his enthusiasm had been rebuffed. He had then said, "Please, Kakima, don't ever again talk to me of marriage." These words of wounded pride now rang in her ears again and again. The memory of her dear, devoted Bihari left behind, dejected and downcast, haunted her. She had failed to console him. She wondered gloomily and half scared, "Is he still in love with Asha?"

Half seriously, half jokingly, Mahendra gave his aunt all the latest news of the house. He refrained, however, from mentioning Binodini.

His college in Calcutta was open and he could ill afford to spend many days in Kashi. But he went on postponing his departure, prolonging the luxury of being looked after by

Annapurna which was like the luxury of convalescence after a severe illness. The inner conflict which had begun its ravage in Calcutta gradually receded. The soothing presence of his pious and loving aunt calmed his troubled nerves and watching her at work he was surprised to see how simple and joyous the daily routine of living could be. His previous anxieties and fears seemed to him ludicrous. Binodini was nothing. He could not even recall her features very clearly. He felt braced and said to himself, "No one can dislodge Asha from my heart even by a hair's breadth."

At last he prepared to take leave of Annapurna. "Kakima," he said, "I shouldn't be absent from the college any longer. Please permit me to leave. Although you have cut off all earthly attachments and have retired into seclusion, nevertheless please allow me the privilege of paying my respects to you from time to time."

When Mahendra returned home he handed over to Asha her aunt's gift, a little case for vermilion powder * and a jar of inlaid white stone. Deeply moved, the tears streamed out of Asha's eyes as she received the gift and recalled how much that gentle, patient and loving aunt of hers had had to put up with, on her account, from her mother-in-law. She said to her husband, "I should love to go to Mashima once, to seek her blessings and to beg her forgiveness for all she suffered on my account. Do you think I could go?"

Mahendra understood Asha's feelings and agreed to her spending a few days with her aunt. The only difficulty was his reluctance to absent himself from college again in order to take her there. But Asha assured him that it would not be necessary for him to go, since she could easily accompany her eldest aunt who was shortly to go to Kashi. Mahendra ac-

---

* In Bengal Hindu married women apply vermilion powder at the parting of their hair on the forehead as an auspicious symbol of their married state.

93

cordingly told his mother that Asha proposed to go to her aunt in Kashi.

"Certainly," replied Rajlakshmi in a biting tone. "If your wife wishes to go she must. Go and take her there."

She had not liked the idea of Mahendra visiting his aunt and the proposal of his repeating the visit with his wife only irritated her further.

"I am afraid I can't accompany her on account of my college. She will go with her eldest aunt."

"How very nice," said Rajlakshmi, "that she should want to go with that aunt of hers who disdains even to look at us!"

The mother's sarcasm only hardened Mahendra's mind. He went away without another word, more determined than before to send Asha to Kashi.

When Bihari came to see Rajlakshmi, she said to him, "Do you know, Bihari, our Bouma wishes to go to Kashi?"

"Is that so? But Mahinda will again have to miss his classes."

"Not at all. Why should Mahin accompany her? That would be too old-fashioned. Mahin will remain here while his wife will go to Kashi with her eldest aunt. That's the way of *sahebs* and *memsahebs!*"

Bihari was worried—not over the modern ways of *sahebs* and *memsahebs*. He wondered what the matter was between Mahendra and Asha that when one went away the other remained behind. The signs were ominous. Must he, their friend and well-wisher, remain a passive witness to this widening gulf between them?

Incensed by his mother's attitude Mahendra sat gloomily in his room. Binodini had not been to see him since his return. She was in the adjoining room and Asha was trying to persuade her to come and cheer Mahendra up, when Bihari entered the latter's room and asked, "Is Asha going to Kashi?"

94

Mahendra flared up. "Why should she not go?" he barked. "What's there to prevent her?"

"Who's talking of preventing her?" replied Bahari. "I merely wanted to know what put the idea in her mind."

"A mere wish to see her aunt, concern for an exiled relative—such sentiments do afflict human nature sometimes."

"Are you accompanying her?"

As soon as he heard this, Mahendra suspected that Bihari had been sent to raise the question of the propriety of sending Asha with her snobbish aunt. To avoid argument which might inflame his rising temper, he answered briefly, "No."

Bihari knew Mahendra well enough to understand that his temper was rising and that any remonstrance would only serve to harden his obstinacy. He therefore refrained from any argument and said to himself, "If poor Asha has to leave with a heavy heart, it might help to cheer her if Binodini went with her." He therefore suggested gently, "Why not let Binodini accompany her?"

Mahendra lost his patience.

"Why don't you speak out what's in your mind?" he shouted. "You don't have to be diplomatic with me. I know you suspect that I am in love with Binodini. It's a baseless suspicion. I'm not in love. I don't care for her. You don't have to spy around in order to save me. Better save yourself. Had you been a loyal friend you would have confessed your feelings long ago and kept away from the house. Let me at least be blunt and tell you to your face that you are in love with Asha."

As a wounded creature blindly rushes forward to fling itself against the assailant, so Bihari, hurt to the very quick, sprang from his seat, livid with rage, and advanced towards Mahendra. However, he immediately recovered himself and said, uttering each word painfully and with great difficulty, "May God forgive you! Goodbye."

As he reeled out of the room, Binodini hurried out of hers and called, "Bihari Thakurpo!"

Stopping and leaning against the wall for support, Bihari tried to smile.

"Yes, Binod-bouthan?"

"Thakurpo, I will accompany Eyesore to Kashi."

"No, no, you mustn't do that. I beg of you, Bouthan, do nothing because of what I said. I'm nobody here and have no desire to interfere in anything. It's no good, it'll only make matters worse. You are an angel and will do what you consider proper. Goodbye!"

Bowing politely he hurried away.

"Please listen, Thakurpo!" called Binodini. "I'm no angel, I tell you. Your going away like this won't do good to any one. Don't blame me hereafter for what may happen."

Bihari gave no heed and went away. Mahendra remained seated where he was like one thunderstruck. Binodini, her eyes blazing like balls of fire, threw a contemptuous glance at him and went back into her room, where Asha sat crushed under a load of shame. Hearing her husband shout and accuse Bihari of being in love with her, she felt so ashamed that she could hardly lift up her face. But Binodini felt no pity for her. Had Asha looked up she would have been frightened by the hard, cruel gleam in Binodini's eyes. A mocking, defiant fury against the whole world raged within Binodini's breast. Mahendra's words denying any feeling for her had burnt their way into her. So no one cared for her! Every one felt for that silly, blushing, soft-as-butter doll!

Mahendra sat brooding. Ever since that day when he had hysterically denounced himself as a humbug in Bihari's hearing, he had felt embarrassed in his friend's presence. He felt, as it were, naked and exposed before him. That Bihari should have found out his love for Binodini when he was trying to hide it even from himself was a source of constant irritation to him. Whenever he met Bihari he felt that the latter was trying to pry into the secret of his heart. It was this

97

accumulation of annoyance which had suddenly burst out with no real provocation.

Binodini's reaction to this incident, her impulsive rushing out of the room, her entreating Bihari to stay, her offer to accompany Asha in deference to Bihari's wish, had taken Mahendra completely by surprise. He felt overwhelmed, crushed. He had worked himself into a belief that he did not care for Binodini, and yet what he had just heard had shocked him out of his complacence, robbing him of all peace. He kept on fidgeting uneasily, recalling with vain regret that Binodini had overheard his violent repudiation of her.

22

Mahendra kept on brooding. "Why need I have shouted so violently and with such vehemence that I did not care for Binodini? It is true that I am not in love with her, but that I do not care for her must have sounded very cruel. What woman would not be hurt by such words! How can I now disabuse her mind of this impression! I can't of course say that I love her but I wish I could make her understand— vaguely and non-committally—that I do care for her. It would be unfair to let her nurse the cruel and untrue idea that she means nothing to me."

He took out of his box the three letters and re-read them. There could be no doubt that Binodini loved him. Why then did she throw herself like that at Bihari? She must have done so deliberately—to warn Mahendra that if he could repudiate her so loudly, she too could retaliate. How else save indirectly could she declare what was in her mind! Having gone so far it was not impossible that she might actually grow to love Bihari. Mahendra shivered at the prospect.

His apprehension grew so fearful that he was shocked at

his own reaction. What if Binodini did overhear that he did not care for her! What did it matter? What if she did resent it! What if she turned her heart elsewhere! As a storm-tossed boat keeps on tugging at the chain that holds the anchor, so Mahendra clung desperately to Asha.

At night Mahendra took Asha in his arms and hugging her face against his breast asked, "Tell me, Chuni, how much do you love me?"

Asha wondered why the sudden question. Was he really worried by his own shameful accusation that Bihari was in love with her? Blushing all over with shame she remonstrated, "For shame! What makes you ask such a question? Do you doubt my love? Please be frank, I beg of you."

"Why then do you want to go to Kashi?" asked Mahendra trying to squeeze more sweetness out of her.

"I don't want to go to Kashi or anywhere else."

"But you did want to."

"You know why," said Asha in visible pain.

"Perhaps you felt you could be happier with your Mashima without me!"

"Not in the least," protested Asha. "I wasn't going there in search of happiness."

"I think you would have been much happier had you married someone else."

Instantaneously Asha slipped out of Mahendra's embrace and hid her face in the pillow, stiff and motionless like a log of wood. A minute later she shook with sobs. Mahendra tried to lift her up in his arms again but she obstinately clung to the pillow. Mahendra watched this reaction of his devoted wife with mingled feelings of joy, elation, pride and self-contempt.

When the submerged secret floated up to the surface it caused a general confusion in every one's mind. Binodini kept wondering why Bihari did not refute the open allegation against him. Even if the allegation was true, Binodini would have been pleased if he had bluffed and denied it.

However, it served him right. He deserved the blow Mahendra had inflicted on him. What right has a person of Bihari's calibre to fall for a goose like Asha? Binodini felt relieved that this blow-up would compel Bihari to keep away from Asha.

And yet she was haunted all the time, in the midst of her household duties, by the memories of Bihari's face, tortured with anguish, drained of all colour, pale as death. Each time she recalled the image, her heart bled with pain, all the womanly tenderness in her welling up in a surge of anguish. As a mother rocks the sick child in her arms, so Binodini rocked the unhappy image in her heart. She knew she would have no peace till she had restored liveliness to those stricken limbs, colour to that ashen face, smile to those benumbed lips.

Two or three days passed. Binodini, listless and troubled, could hold out no longer. She sat down and penned a brief note:

"Thakurpo, ever since you left us that day, looking so pale, I have prayed with all my heart for your health of body and mind. I long to see again your simple smile, to hear once more your noble voice. Please drop me a line to say how you are. Your Binod-bouthan."

She asked the *durwan* to deliver the letter at Bihari's house.

Bihari had not imagined that Mahendra could ever accuse him so vehemently and blatantly of being in love with Asha. He himself had never allowed the thought to enter his mind in so articulate a form. The first stunning effect was soon succeeded by an outburst of rage and scorn. He kept on muttering, "Baseless, unjust, filthy accusation!"

But when a thought has once become articulate it can no longer be totally suppressed. The little seed of truth in the allegation began speedily to sprout. He recalled the evening

100

when the two friends had gone to see Asha for the first time and had sat on the terrace and the lovely, bashful girl had appeared before them wrapped round with the fragrance of flowers wafted from the garden below. Knowing that she was going to be his, Bihari had looked at her with unashamed ardour. The memory of that lovely image and of his ardent gaze now haunted him, choking and oppressing him. He spent the long night lying on the roof-terrace or pacing anxiously in front of the house, brooding. The more he brooded the more articulate became the hidden secret. What had been inhibited was let loose; what had lain dormant, unknown even to him, now sprang into life at Mahendra's words overwhelming him.

He began to see the culprit in himself. What right had he to be angry with Mahendra when what the latter had said was true? In fact, the only decent thing he could do was to beg Mahendra's pardon and take his farewell. "I left Mahendra in a huff, as though he was at fault and I was the judge. It was unjust. I must now confess the wrong I did him."

He thought that Asha had left for Kashi. So one evening he walked slowly up to Mahendra's house and met Sadhucharan, a distant uncle of Rajlakshmi's, at the door. Apologising for not having been to the house for some days, he asked Sadhucharan for news of the inmates. The latter assured him that all was well.

"When did Asha-bouthan leave for Kashi?" asked Bihari.

"She didn't leave. Nor is she likely to go."

A strong impulse to rush into the house overpowered Bihari. And yet he hesitated, painfully reminded that it was no longer proper, no longer easy to mount the familiar steps leading to the inner apartments with the same simple and confident joy as before. It would be impossible now to assume the natural, friendly smile with which he used to greet and joke with every one. If only once more, for the last time, he could enter the house as before, like one of the inmates, exchange a few light words with Rajlakshmi and address the veiled Asha as Bouthan, how happy he would be!

"Why are you standing in the dark? Come inside," said Sadhucharan.

Startled out of his reverie, Bihari took a few quick steps inwards and suddenly stopped. With a hurried apology to Sadhucharan that he had an urgent piece of work to attend to, he beat a hasty retreat. That very night he left Calcutta, travelling westwards.

When the durwan took Binodini's letter, Bihari had already left. Mahendra was strolling in the little patch of garden in front of the porch and seeing the durwan return with the letter in hand, he inquired: "Whose letter is it?"

The durwan told him who had given it to him and for whom. Mahendra took the letter. His first impulse was to hand it over unopened to Binodini, without uttering a word, and watch her guilty, shamefaced reaction. That the letter carried her guilty secret he had no doubt. He recalled the previous occasion when a similar letter addressed to Bihari in her hand had come to his notice. But this time he found it difficult to resist the temptation to open the letter. After all, Binodini was living under his roof and guardianship. He was responsible for her welfare. In fact, it was his duty to ensure that she did not go astray. He was therefore morally obliged to acquaint himself with the contents of the letter.

He opened it. It was a brief note written simply and with obvious sincerity. Mahendra read the note again and again and pondered it, but failed to gauge Binodini's feelings. What and how much the words signified he could not understand. A vague fear seized him that Binodini, hurt and repulsed by him, was perhaps trying to turn her attentions elsewhere. "She is angry and has given up all hope of me altogether."

The doubt gnawed at his mind and made him restless. It

was intolerable to think that his momentary folly should cost him his hold over Binodini who had been ready of her own accord to offer herself to him. He flattered himself that Binodini's love for him was for her own good. It would save her from others. "I know my own mind, I am incapable of doing her any wrong. She can love me without any danger. She will be safe with me, since my heart is already pledged to Asha. But were she inclined elsewhere, who knows what disaster she may court!" He felt that it was his bounden duty to attract Binodini to himself, without allowing himself to be seduced.

As Mahendra went inside the house he came across Binodini in the corridor looking as though waiting anxiously for something or somebody. A jealous hatred immediately surged up within him.

"Madam, you're wasting your time," he hissed. "He won't come. Here's your letter come back."

He flung the letter at her.

"Open?" exclaimed Binodini.

Without caring to reply Mahendra walked away. Binodini imagined that Bihari had opened the letter and had returned it contemptuously. Every nerve in her body stiffened and tingled with pain and indignation. She sent for the durwan who had taken the letter but the durwan had gone away on another errand and could not be found. She shut herself up in her room. As burning drops of oil trickle down the lighted wick of an earthen lamp, so her burning heart overflowed in hot tears.

She tore up the letter in a hundred bits but found little consolation. Why was there no way of wiping out, of erasing altogether from the memory the black, shameful scrawl of those half a dozen lines? Like the enraged black bee which stings whatever comes in its way, so Binodini mad with rage prepared to wreak her vengeance on the world around her, a world which seemed bent on thwarting her, spiting her. Were all her longings, all her endeavours doomed to frustration? If all happiness was denied her, if she was condemned to a fruitless, barren existence, then there was only one way left to the fulfilment of her frustrated life—to defeat and drag into dust all those who had cheated her of her right to be happy, distorting the graceful flowering of her womanhood, robbing her of her natural, rightful due.

23

The winter was over. The spring's first breeze was in the air. After many days Asha sat on the roof-terrace in the evening, with a mat spread underneath. She held a monthly magazine in her hand and was reading very attentively, in the dwindling light of the dusk, a serialised novel. The hero of the tale who was on his way home to enjoy the Puja holidays after a year's exile had just then fallen into the hands of robbers. Asha's heart quivered in fear and excitement. At the same time the unhappy heroine of the story woke up from her sleep, crying, having been frightened by an evil dream. Asha's tears would not stop. She was an ardent admirer of Bengali novels. Whatever she read seemed to her wonderful. She would say to Binodini, "Do read this one, Eyesore dear. It's superb. I can't tell you how much I cried while reading it." Binodini would start dissecting the story, her critical judgment acting like icy water on Asha's effusive enthusiasm.

As Asha, her eyes glistening with tears, closed the magazine she decided that she must make Mahendra read the story. Just then Mahendra arrived. Asha's heart sank at the sight of his face. Making an obvious effort to be cheerful, Mahendra asked, "Which god are you meditating on, sitting alone on the roof-terrace?"

Asha forgot all about the tribulations of the hero and heroine of the story.

"Aren't you feeling well?" she inquired anxiously.

"My health is fine," replied Mahendra.

"Then you must be worried about something. Please tell me what it is."

Picking up a *pan* from Asha's casket, Mahendra replied, "I was thinking of your poor Mashima who hasn't seen you for such a long time. How happy she would be if you were suddenly to appear before her!"

Asha gazed blankly at Mahendra without saying a word. She wondered what had happened to make Mahendra suddenly revive the proposal. Seeing Asha silent Mahendra asked, "Don't you feel like going?"

A difficult question to answer. She was eager to see her aunt and yet unwilling to part with her husband.

"I shall go when your college is closed and you are able to accompany me."

"It'll be difficult for me to leave even when the college is closed. I have to work for the exam."

"In that case, it doesn't matter if I don't go."

"But why? Don't you want to go?"

"No."

"Only the other day you were anxious to go. Why this sudden change?"

Asha remained silent, her eyes fixed on the ground. Mahendra was getting impatient for a chance of unrestricted freedom to cultivate Binodini. Asha's silence irritated him. He gave way to his pent-up anger.

"Are you so suspicious of me that you must constantly keep me under watch?" he asked bitterly.

All of a sudden Mahendra found Asha's natural sweetness, gentleness and forbearance intolerable. If she wants to see her aunt, why can't she make up her mind and say, "Please send me to her anyhow," instead of this shilly-shallying—now yes, now no, now mum? What a nuisance!

Asha was shocked and scared by this sudden, bitter outburst on Mahendra's part. She could think of no answer to his mocking query. She could not understand why Mahendra was sometimes suddenly tender, sometimes suddenly cruel. The more puzzled she was the more frightened she became. Torn between love and fear she felt helpless and prostrate. How could Mahendra charge her with spying on him? Was it merely a bitter joke or was it a cruel suspicion? Should she laugh and share the joke or should she swear by her honour and deny the charge? She did not know what to do.

Seeing Asha maintain her stupefied silence the impatient Mahendra hurriedly walked away. The dusk gradually darkened into night and the fresh spring breeze of the evening grew chilly with the winter's parting breath. Asha unmindful of the fate of the magazine hero and heroine flung herself on the floor.

Late at night when Asha entered the bedroom she found that Mahendra had retired without calling her. She imagined that Mahendra was disgusted with her callousness towards her loving aunt. She got into the bed and clasping Mahendra's feet lay down with her head bent over his feet. Mahendra was deeply moved and tried to raise her into his arms. But Asha would not budge. She murmured, "If I have done any wrong please forgive me."

"You have done no wrong," said Mahendra feelingly. "It's I who am a fraud to have hurt you without any cause."

Streams of tears poured out of Asha's eyes bathing Mahendra's feet. He got up and lifting Asha seated her by his side. As soon as Asha had recovered herself she said, "Please don't imagine that I am not keen to see Mashi. It's only that I am reluctant to be parted from you. So don't be angry with me."

"There's no reason to be angry, Chuni," said Mahendra gently wiping her wet forehead. "You don't wish to leave me—could I be angry with you on that account? No, you don't have to go anywhere."

"No, I must go to Kashi."

"But why?"

"Since you have once given utterance to the suspicion that I am unwilling to go because I wish to be here to spy on you, I must go for some days at least."

"Why need you atone for a wrong which I did?"

"That I don't know. I too must have been at fault in some way, otherwise this impossible suspicion could never have been born. Why else should I have to listen to a charge which I could not have conceived even in a dream?"

"That is because you could not have conceived even in a dream how wicked I can be."

"Again! Please don't say such things. As regards Kashi, I must go there this time."

"All right, you will go," said Mahendra laughing. "But what will happen if I go astray in your absence?"

"You needn't frighten me. As if I ever nursed such a bugbear!"

"But you should. If you allow such a husband to go astray, whom will you blame?"

"At any rate, not you. So you needn't worry."

"Will you then blame yourself, if that happens?"

"Yes, yes, I will."

"Very well. In that case I shall see your uncle tomorrow and fix up about the journey."

The night was far advanced. Mahendra lay down and tried to sleep. A couple of minutes later he turned towards Asha and said suddenly, "No, Chuni, I don't think you should go."

"Why are you again stopping me?" asked Chuni anxiously. "If I don't go at least once now, your jibe will continue to prick me. So please let me go—for two or three days at least."

"All right," said Mahendra and turned over to sleep.

The day before she left Asha put her arms round Binodini and said, "Eyesore dear, please promise me one thing."

"Is there anything I would not do for you?" replied Binodini pinching Asha's cheek.

"I don't know. You seem to have changed of late—always keeping aloof from my husband."

"You know why. You heard with your own ears what Mahendra Babu said to Bihari Babu the other day. When such charges are bandied about, is it proper for me to expose myself to further suspicions? Don't you agree with me, Eyesore dear?"

Asha could not but admit to herself that Binodini was right. She herself had experienced only too recently the shame and humiliation caused by the incident. Nevertheless, she said, "So many things are bandied about, darling! If we can't put up with these little outbursts, what is our love worth? You must forget about it."

"Very well, I shall forget about it."

"I am leaving for Kashi tomorrow. Please look after my husband in my absence and see that he is not put to any discomfort. It won't do your keeping aloof from him as you've been doing of late."

Binodini remained silent. Asha caught hold of her hand and begged, "Do promise me this, Eyesore darling!"

"All right," said Binodini.

24

The moon sets on one side, the sun rises on the other. But though Asha had left there was no sign of Binodini on Mahendra's horizon. He wandered about the house ruefully, butting into his mother's room at all times on some pretext or other in the hope of seeing Binodini who successfully evaded him.

Rajlakshmi noticed that her son was moping and was worried. Poor boy, he's missing his wife! Though the thought that she herself had been made superfluous by her daughter-in-law and was of little comfort to her son hurt her, she could not bear to see him so forlorn and woebegone. She called Binodini and said, "That last attack of influenza has left me with asthma. I can no longer climb up and down stairs with impunity. Please therefore, my child, look after Mahin for me and see that his needs are well attended to. He's used to being fussed over since his childhood and can't do without it. You can see for yourself how pathetic and helpless he looks since his wife left. Fancy her leaving him like this!"

Binodini sat silent, her face slightly turned away, her fingers fiddling with the bedcover.

"What are you thinking over, Bouma?" asked Rajlakshmi. "There's nothing to think over in this matter. Let people say what they like—you are not a stranger in this house."

"Please don't press me, mother," pleaded Binodini.

"Very well, don't bother," said Rajlakshmi petulantly. "I shall myself do what I can."

She got up and made ready to climb up to Mahendra's room on the second floor. Binodini grew anxious and begged, "Please do not go up, mother. You're not well enough. I am going. Forgive me if I did wrong. I shall do whatever you say."

Rajlakshmi was completely indifferent to public gossip. Since her husband's death she had been so wrapped up in her son that she cared little for anything or anybody else. The merest suggestion that people might talk about her son and Binodini irritated her. Didn't she know her own son? Where was his equal in virtue? If anyone was so vicious as to malign her son, might the gossip's tongue rot and wither! She had an inborn contempt for people who opposed her likes and dislikes.

When Mahendra returned from college he was surprised to see his own room. As he opened the door the room smelt sweet with the perfume of sandalwood incense. The mosquito net had a frill of pink silk which hung over a spotlessly white bed cover. The old-fashioned bolster had been replaced by square-cut cushions of foreign fashion embroidered with flowered patterns in silk and woollen thread. Asha had seen Binodini working on the embroidery for many days and had several times asked her for whom they were meant. Binodini would laugh and reply, "For my funeral pyre. Death is the only bridegroom I can ever have."

Mahendra's photograph on the wall had coloured ribbons tied at the four corners of its frame and underneath it on the two sides of a small table set against the wall were two vases with flowers—like an unseen devotee's offering to Mahendra's image on the wall! The entire room wore an altogether different look. The bedstead had been shifted and the room partitioned into two halves by a couple of large clothes-horses draped over, the bedstead at the back forming the half for the night and the divan-bed on the floor for the day. The glass almirah where Asha kept her China dolls and trinkets had an inner screen of red cloth neatly crinkled against the glass so that nothing was visible from the outside. Everything in the room recalling Asha had been overlaid by a new elegance that bore evidence of a different hand.

As soon as Mahendra had stretched his tired limbs on the clean, white bedspread on the floor and rested his head against the new pillows, he was aware of a delicate perfume emanating from within. The cotton stuffing had been profusely scented and mixed with the pollen of *nagkeshar* flowers. As he closed his eyes it seemed to him that the fragrance he breathed came from the flower-like fingers that had embroidered the pillow cases.

The maid came in with a silver dish of fruits and sweets and a glass of iced pineapple sherbert. This too was something different and mutely eloquent of skilled solicitude. Everything he saw or smelt or tasted seemed a delicious revelation taking his senses by surprise and overpowering them.

As soon as he had finished relishing the delicacies, Binodini entered with a silver casket of *pans* and spices in her hand. She smiled and said, "Forgive me, Thakurpo, for having neglected you during your meals these last few days. Do not, I beg of you, complain to my Eyesore that you were not well looked after. I do my best but what to do? I have to look after the entire household."

She held out the *pan* casket before Mahendra. Even the *pan* seemed different with its special aroma of screw pine and catechu.

"It's good to be neglected occasionally," said Mahendra.

"And why, pray?" asked Binodini.

"Because one can then be repaid with interest."

"How much interest has accumulated, Mr. Creditor?"

"Since you were absent during the meal, you must stay on after it and yet owe something."

"What a swindler!" laughed Binodini. "Once in your clutches, there's no getting away."

"Whatever the ledger may say, what have I actually realised?"

"What is there to realise? And yet you hold me captive!" said Binodini as she heaved a sigh, suddenly imparting a note of gravity to the badinage.

Mahendra too became a little grave.

"Do you then look upon this house as a prison?" he asked.

Just then the bearer entered with a light and depositing it on a teapoy went away. Lowering her eyes and shielding them with her hand against the sudden intrusion of light, Binodini said, "I don't know. How can I cope with you in argument? Let me go now, I've work to do."

Mahendra suddenly caught hold of her hand.

"Since you admit you are a captive, where can you go?" he said.

"For shame!" cried Binodini. "Let me go. Why must you grab and bind one who in any case has no way left of escape?"

She wrenched free her hand and left.

Mahendra sank back on the perfumed pillow, his blood

surging up in hot waves. The spell of the hushed evening, the sweet peril of undisturbed privacy, the soft caress of the spring breeze and the imminence of Binodini's surrender made him almost beside himself with longing and with fear. Unnerved, he jumped up and hurriedly putting out the light and bolting the door and the shutters got into the bed.

The bed too felt different. Several mattresses had been put under it to make it soft and springy. Again the waft of a perfume, whether of aloe or *khuskhus* or what, it was difficult to say. Mahendra tossed about from side to side, frantically groping for a relic of the past to which he could cling for support. But none was at hand.

At nine in the evening there was a knock at the door. Binodini's voice called from outside, "Thakurpo, I've brought you dinner. Please open the door."

Mahendra jumped out of the bed and rushed to open the door. But even as he touched the bolt of the shutters he suddenly recoiled in fear and sank down on the floor.

"I've no appetite. I won't eat anything," he cried.

"Aren't you well?" inquired an anxious voice from outside. "Shall I fetch you some water? Is there anything you would like?"

"Nothing—I need nothing."

"Do not hide anything, I beg of you," implored the voice. "Even if all is well, please open the door for a while."

"No, I won't," shouted back Mahendra. "Please leave me alone."

He hurriedly got up and sank back into the bed again, resuming his fumbling in the dark for the image of the absent Asha, in the emptiness of the bed, in the tumult of his heart.

When the sleep refused to come he got up again, lighted the lamp, took up his pen and began to write a letter to Asha:

"Asha, do not leave me alone here any longer. You are my Lakshmi, my guardian angel—when you are not with me, my thoughts wander, my impulses break loose, dragging me I know not how or where. Where is the light to guide my way—the light that comes from your loving, trustful eyes! Come back soon, my angel, my pole-star, my only one! Save me, restore me to myself, make me whole again—redeem me from the sin of wronging you, from the nightmare of forgetting you, however slightly. . . ."

Thus he went on writing for the greater part of the night, apostrophising Asha in order to whip up a fervour for her in his mind. The distant church bells chimed the hour of three, the rumbling of the carriage wheels on the roads outside had almost ceased, even the dancing-girl's voice singing in the *Behag ragini* which had floated in from the upper storey of a neighbouring house was hushed and lost in the all-embracing silence of sleep. Brooding on the image of Asha, Mahendra gave vent to his excited imagination in a long letter repeating the same feeling in various ways until his tired nerves were lulled into peace and he went off to sleep the moment he lay down in the bed.

When he woke up, the morning was far advanced, the sunlight was streaming into the room. He sat up hurriedly. The night's tension had considerably relaxed. Leaving his bed his eye fell on the last night's letter resting under the weight of the ink-pot on the teapoy. He read it over and was surprised at the contents. "Good Heavens!" he exclaimed, "What have I been writing? Reads like a melodrama! Thank God it was not dispatched. What would Asha have thought of it! Half of it would have gone over her head." Recalling his inordinate reaction to the trifling episode of the night, Mahendra felt ashamed of himself. He tore the letter into bits and wrote another simple and brief one to Asha:

"How long will you delay your return? If your uncle is not likely to return soon, let me know. I shall come over to fetch you. I am sick of being alone here."

25

Asha's sudden appearance in Kashi, so soon after Mahendra's, alarmed Annapurna. She began to sound Asha by all sorts of questions.

"Well, Chuni, this Eyesore of yours you were talking of—you think there's none like her so accomplished in all the virtues?"

"Indeed, Mashi, I'm not exaggerating a bit. She's as intelligent as she is beautiful and no less accomplished."

"You will naturally see a paragon in your friend. But tell me what do others think of her in the house?"

"Mother is never tired of praising her and is beside herself the moment my Eyesore talks of leaving for her village home. No wonder. She looks after every one so well. Even if one of the servants falls ill she nurses him as only a sister, a mother would."

"What about Mahendra?"

"You know how he is, Mashi, he feels at home only with the intimate family circle. Every one else loves my Eyesore—only he has failed to pull on with her."

"How?"

"Well, with great difficulty I succeeded in bringing them together and yet he's hardly on talking terms with her. You know how shy and reserved he is. People think he's proud but that's not true, Mashi. It's just that he can't stand any one outside his restricted intimate circle."

The last words somehow made her blush hotly. Annapurna was pleased and smiling to herself said to Asha, "Indeed, it's so. When Mahin was here the other day, he did not once mention your friend."

"That's the worst of it," said Asha in a pained voice. "If he doesn't care for a person he ignores his existence altogether and behaves as if he had never set eyes on him, didn't know who he was."

"But when he loves a person," rejoined Annapurna smiling her sweet, gentle smile, "his devotion is absolute, as if he had met and known no other being, life after life. Isn't that so, Chuni?"

Asha did not reply and lowered her eyes, a smile playing on her lips.

"What news of Bihari, Chuni?" asked Annapurna. "Has he no intention of getting married ever?"

Asha suddenly became grave. She did not know what to reply. Her silence and change of colour alarmed Annapurna who inquired anxiously, "Tell me the truth, Chuni, what is the matter with Bihari? Isn't he well?"

Bihari was installed as a beloved son in the heart of this motherless woman. Her one regret was that she could not see Bihari properly settled in life before she left her home. All other desires and obligations of her little personal world had been more or less satisfied; the only painful void which kept haunting her holy seclusion was the image of Bihari unwedded, uncared for.

"Mashi, please do not ask me about Bihari Thakurpo," said Asha at last.

"Why?" asked Annapurna surprised.

"That I can't say," replied Asha and left the room.

Annapurna remained seated, lost in thought. What could have happened in that short interval to so fine a youth as Bihari that Asha should leave the room at a mere mention of his name? Irony of fate! Why was the question of his marrying Chuni ever mooted and why did Mahendra snatch her away from his hand?

After many days her eyes flowed with tears again. She said to herself, "My poor Bihari! If indeed he has been guilty of something unworthy, how much he must have suffered to be driven to it! Nothing ignoble could have come easy to him!" Her heart ached with pity as she thought of his suffering.

At dusk while Annapurna was at her devotions, a carriage stopped at the door and the coachman began to knock at the door and shout from outside. Annapurna called out from inside the prayer room, "Good Heavens! I had clean forgotten that Kunjar's mother-in-law and her two nieces were to arrive from Allahabad. This must be them. Please, Chuni, take a light to the door and open it."

Lantern in hand, Asha went to the door and opened it. She saw Bihari standing outside. Seeing Asha he exclaimed, "Hallo, Bouthan, you here! I was told you were not coming to Kashi."

The lantern fell from Asha's hand. As though scared by a ghost she ran upstairs and gasped piteously, "Mashima! Please, I beg of you, ask him to go away immediately."

Startled, Annapurna rose from her prayer-seat and asked, "Whom, Chuni? Who is it?"

"Bihari Thakurpo. He has followed me here."

She rushed into the next room and bolted the door. Bihari overheard every word of it. He wanted to run away but suddenly felt limp as though all energy had been drained out of his limbs. When Annapurna hastened down, leaving her devotions unfinished, she found Bihari seated on the ground near the door. She had not brought a lantern and could not see Bihari's face. Nor could Bihari see hers.

"Bihari!"

Alas, how different the voice sounded from the habitual affectionate tone! Its sternness carried a censure and rumbled like a thunderbolt. At whose head, Mother Annapurna, did you raise your destructive sword? * The luckless Bihari had come in this darkness to seek benediction at your holy, blessed feet!

Bihari started as though lightning had passed through his

* In Bengal the Hindus worship Kali as the Universal Mother. She carries a sword in one hand and represents the destructive aspect of the Divine Energy. Annapurna is also a name of the same Goddess in her beneficent aspect.

frame. He stood up and muttered, "Please, Kakima, no more —not a word more! I'm off."

He bowed low before Annapurna without touching her feet. As a mother offers her dead child to the dark waters of the Ganges, so Annapurna let Bihari drift away in the dark silence of the night. The carriage drove away with Bihari in it. Not once did Annapurna call him back.

That night Asha wrote to Mahendra:

"Bihari Thakurpo suddenly turned up this evening. Uncle's return to Calcutta is uncertain. Please come quickly and take me back home."

26

After the emotional tumult and vigil of the previous night Mahendra felt weak and depressed in the morning. It was the month of March and already getting warm. Instead of sitting at the table with his books as was his wont in the morning, he lay down to recline on the divan, his head resting on a pillow. The morning advanced but he lay there inert, neglecting to bathe even. The cry of the vendors could be heard from the street outside along with the ceaseless rumble of carriages on their way to office and the monotonous chant of the women-labourers working on the roof of a neighbouring house under construction and singing to keep rhythm with the beating of their mallets. The mild warmth of the southern breeze was soothing to Mahendra's overwrought nerves—such a listless, languorous morning of spring was not meant for stern resolves, heroic efforts or battles of the mind.

"What's the matter with you today, Thakurpo?" asked Binodini suddenly coming in. "Won't you have a bath? The food is ready. But why are you lying down? Aren't you well? Headache?"

She came close and touched his forehead with her hand.

"I don't feel quite well today. I won't have a bath," muttered Mahendra weakly, half closing his eyes.

"Never mind if you don't bathe, but please come and have a bite at least," pleaded Binodini.

She coaxed him into getting up and took him to the dining room where with much affectionate fussing she succeeded in making him eat. The meal over, Mahendra came back and lay down on the divan. Binodini too seated herself by his head and began gently to massage his forehead.

"Eyesore dear," said Mahendra, his eyes closed, "you haven't had your food. Please go and eat."

Binodini would not go. The curtains in the room fluttered in the warm and languid midday breeze which hummed with an idle murmur in the coconut tree adjoining the wall of the house. Mahendra's heart began to beat faster and louder and as though in tune with it Binodini's breathing became harder, causing the hair on his forehead to quiver. Neither of them uttered a word. Mahendra said to himself: "I'm floating on the ever-heaving waves of Life's endless flow. What does it matter where the bark touches the shore and, if it did matter, for how long? . . . ."

Binodini's fingers gently caressed his forehead. Gradually her head drooped, her limbs languorous with the heavy weight of her full-blooded youth. Loose strands of her hair playing in the breeze rippled on Mahendra's forehead, sending hot waves of blood coursing through his body. His breathing came so hard that he felt he would choke. Suddenly he sat up and exclaimed, "No, let me go to college." He stood up avoiding Binodini's eyes.

"Don't be upset," said Binodini. "I'll fetch your college clothes."

She laid out his clothes. Hurriedly putting them on Mahendra left for the college. But he found it impossible to concentrate on his work. He was restive and fidgety. After

118

many futile efforts to discipline his mind he returned home fairly early.

As he entered his room he found Binodini lying on the divan, face downwards, her breasts pressing on a pillow, reading a book. Her long black hair sprawled over her back. Maybe she did not hear Mahendra's footsteps. Mahendra tiptoed gently and came and stood very close to her. He heard her heave a deep sigh.

"Benign lady," he called softly, "do not waste your pity on imaginary characters. What are you reading?"

Binodini started and hurriedly sat up, hiding the book in the folds of her sari. Mahendra tried to wrest it from her. After much scuffling and jostling Mahendra succeeded in snatching the book from the overpowered Binodini. He read the title *Visha Vriksha.** Breathing heavily and fuming, Binodini remained silent, her face turned away.

Blood was surging up in Mahendra's breast. With a great effort he pulled himself together and said laughing, "How you fooled me! I thought it was something mysterious—a secret. Fancy, after all this scuffle what comes out is only *Visha Vriksha.*"

"What secret did you imagine I was hiding?"

"Well—say, for example, a letter from Bihari," blurted out Mahendra.

Suddenly lightning flashed out of Binodini's eyes. It seemed the god of love who was fiddling with his arrow all this while was burnt to cinders once again.† Like a flame suddenly lighted, Binodini jumped up from her seat. Mahendra caught her hand and begged, "Please forgive me, forgive a jest."

"A jest!" hissed Binodini wrenching her hand free. "At

---

* The well-known novel by Bankim Chatterji. *Lit.*, "The Poison Tree." The book has been already referred to in previous pages.
† Reference to the well-known Hindu legend of Kama, the god of love, being burnt to cinders for having dared to aim his dart at Shiva.

whose expense? Were you worthy of his friendship, I could forgive your jest. But you are too mean—you are incapable of friendship and yet you have the cheek to gibe!"

She was about to sweep out of the room when Mahendra caught hold of her feet clasping them with both his hands. Suddenly a shadow fell across. Mahendra let go his hands and looked up. Bihari was standing.

"I apologise for the untimely intrusion," said Bihari calmly, his icy gaze piercing both of them, "but I won't stay long. I came to say that I had been to Kashi, not knowing that Bouthan was there. I had no chance of begging her pardon for that unwitting impertinence, so I came to offer my apology to you. If I have been guilty of a wrong, knowingly or unknowingly, I beg of you to see that she is not made to suffer for it."

Having been caught unawares in a moment of weakness Mahendra was raging with fury. He was incapable of a generous impulse at the moment. He smiled wryly and sneered, "The guilty conscience, eh? I did not invite you to confess or to deny—why then this farce of forgiveness and playing the saint?"

Bihari stood rooted to the ground like a wooden puppet. His lips trembled as though he was struggling hard to say something. Binodini intervened.

"Don't say a word, Bihari Thakurpo," she cried. "What this person has said has only fouled his own tongue. It has not stained you in any way."

Whether he heard Binodini's words or not is doubtful. Like a person walking in his sleep, Bihari turned his back and retraced his steps. Binodini followed him pleading anxiously, "Bihari Thakurpo, have you nothing to say to me? If it's scorn you feel, then fling scorn in my face!"

But Bihari made no reply and walked ahead. Then Binodini rushed in front and caught hold of his right hand in both her hands, but he flung her violently aside in a gesture of supreme contempt and walked away, little noticing that his blow had felled Binodini to the ground.

Hearing the sound of a fall Mahendra rushed up to Binodini and saw that her left elbow was bleeding. "A nasty cut," he commented and immediately tore a strip from his fine muslin tunic and was about to bandage the wound when Binodini snatched her arm away exclaiming, "No, please don't touch it, let it bleed."

"Let me apply a tincture and bandage it. It'll relieve the pain and heal the wound rapidly."

"I do not want the pain to be relieved," said Binodini moving away from Mahendra. "Let it remain as mine."

"I am sorry I forgot myself and was guilty of an impertinence before others," apologised Mahendra. "Can you forgive me?"

"Forgive you for what? You did well. You think I'm afraid of people? I don't care at all. Why should I run after those who know only how to hurt and fling aside? And they who clasp my feet and hold me to themselves—do they mean nothing to me?"

Mahendra was thrilled. He asked tremulously, "Then you won't spurn my love, Binodini?"

"I'll wear it as a crown. I haven't had so much love in life that I can afford to reject what is offered!"

Mahendra took both her hands in his and said, "Then come into my room. We have hurt each other today and until we wipe out every trace of that wound, I shall have no peace."

"No, not today. Let me keep to myself today. If I have caused you any pain, please forgive me."

"You too must forgive me, or else I shall have no sleep at night."

"I forgive you."

Mahendra was excited and wanted then and there to snatch from Binodini a token of her forgiveness and love, but a look at Binodini's face made him withhold himself. Binodini walked down the steps; Mahendra slowly went up to the terrace and began to pace up and down. He felt an exhilaration, a thrill of liberation at the thought that Bihari had at last suddenly discovered his secret. The strain and self-debasement that came of continual hiding and subterfuge were considerably lightened and Mahendra said to himself, "I no longer wish to pose as a good man—I am in love—that is no mere pose. It is true." The pride of love so intoxicated him that he began almost to compliment himself on having ceased to be good. He felt he could challenge the whole world, spread out before him under the silent, twilight sky, in the supreme assurance, "Let them malign me if they will—I am in love. I love." The image of Binodini filled his mind, blotting out the sky, the world and all obligations. It was as though Bihari had suddenly upset and broken the closed ink-pot of Mahendra's subconscious, letting the black of Binodini's eyes and hair overflow, wiping out in one overspreading smudge all the whiteness and all the writing of the past.

27

As soon as Mahendra woke from sleep the next morning, his heart was flooded with a delicious exhilaration. The early morning sun had, as it were, touched all his thoughts and anticipations with its golden hue. How beautiful seemed the earth, how enchanting the sky! Like the pollen of flowers blown by the wind his mind seemed to float lightly in the air.

A Vaishnav * mendicant was singing to the beat of drum and cymbals outside the main door down below. The durwan was about to drive him away when Mahendra forbade him

* A religious sect.

and flung a rupee to the mendicant. The bearer carelessly dropped the kerosene lamp and it broke into bits. Frozen with fear he looked up helplessly at Mahendra who merely remarked gently, "Please mop up the broken bits and see that no one steps on the glass." No damage, no wrong, seemed a wrong any more.

Love, hidden all these days behind a screen, had suddenly flung the barrier aside and appeared before him. The curtain had lifted revealing the world in an altogether new light. The earth's pettiness and squabbles had vanished and everything seemed wonderful, the trees, the birds, the crowd on the road, the din of the market-place. Where was this all-pervading loveliness hidden before?

It seemed to Mahendra that today his meeting with Binodini would not be the usual, daily routine. It would be something different, needing poetry for conversation and music for expression. Today would be a page from the Arabian Nights, filled with beauty and glory, released from the bondage of inhibition and convention—real and yet dream-like, unbound by the commandments of society and the hard realities of the world.

Excited and restless he wandered about the house and did not go to college, not knowing when the wonderful moment would happen, which no almanac could foretell. Now and again Binodini's voice would reach him from the kitchen or the pantry. He resented her association with the mundane and matter-of-fact world, having in his imagination lifted her far above such vulgar concerns. The time would not pass. The midday meal was over and the household was hushed in the stillness of the afternoon. But there was no sign of Binodini. His nerves tingled in an agony of suspense, torn between hope and despair, joy and pain.

His eye fell on yesterday's book still lying on the divan. The memory of the delicious scuffle with Binodini over the possession of the book caused a thrill to pass through his frame. Seizing the pillow on which Binodini had pressed her weight he laid his head on it and began to turn over the leaves of *Visha Vriksha*. Gradually he got absorbed in the story and did not notice the passage of time until it struck five.

Binodini appeared with an enamelled brass tray carrying dishes of fruit and sweets and a cut melon, sugared and iced and perfumed. Placing the tray in front of Mahendra she said, "What's the matter with you, Thakurpo? It's five and you have neither washed nor changed!"

Mahendra was stupefied. How could Binodini not know what the matter was with him? Was such a question possible? Did she not understand that today was different from all other days? He was suddenly scared lest his anticipations turn to dust by a rebuff and therefore refrained from advancing any claims on the basis of yesterday's episode.

He sat down to eat. Binodini went and fetched from the terrace the woolen garments spread out to dry in the sun and began dexterously to fold and deposit them in the wardrobe.

"Wait a minute," said Mahendra. "Let me finish eating, then I'll help you."

"Help me? For God's sake do what you like, but don't try to help me," said Binodini in mock entreaty.

"Indeed! You think I'm no good, don't you? Well let's see."

He began to make clumsy attempts at folding the garments. Binodini snatched them from his hands, adding cuttingly, "Please, Sir, don't add to my work."

"Very well then, let me at least watch you and learn."

He seated himself on the floor beside Binodini who went on folding and arranging the clothes, now and again playfully dusting them against his back.

Thus began the long-looked-for moment. It was altogether different from the way Mahendra had imagined it would be. It lacked the dignity of a romance worthy of being poetised in verse, or sung in ballad or narrated in a novel. And yet Mahendra was not disappointed. In fact, he felt relieved. He

124

had been secretly worried as to how to give shape to his imagined dream, what the prelude should be, what to say, how much to express and how, and above all how to save it from the anticlimax of the commonplace. This simple and easy way of playful intimacy amid the dusting and folding of clothes came to him as a godsend, rescuing him from the ordeal of an imaginary and impossible ideal.

Just then Rajlakshmi entered. Looking at Mahendra she asked, "What are you doing here, Mahin, while Bouma is arranging the clothes?"

"Look at him, Pishima," complained Binodini, "he's merely adding to my labour!"

"Indeed!" rejoined Mahendra. "I was in fact helping her, mother."

"Heavens!" exclaimed Rajlakshmi. "You helping her!" Then turning to Binodini she added, "You know, Bouma, he has been so pampered since childhood that he is incapable of doing anything for himself."

She looked tenderly at her beloved helpless son. Her main topic of conversation with Binodini was always how to pamper and surround with every comfort her overgrown baby incapable of looking after himself. She had noted with great relief and satisfaction that Binodini was now looking after him for her. That Mahendra had at least learnt to appreciate Binodini's worth and was anxious that she should stay on made her very happy. She said to Binodini—deliberately for Mahendra's benefit, "Now that you have aired and put away Mahin's warm clothes, I should like you, dear, to embroider his name on the kerchiefs tomorrow. What a shame that instead of looking after you, I should make you slave like this!"

"If you talk like that, Pishima," said Binodini, "I shall imagine that you look upon me as an outsider."

"No, my dear, you are nearer to me than my very own," said Rajlakshmi affectionately.

After the clothes had been put away Rajlakshmi asked,

"Shall we now put the syrup on the fire * or have you something else to attend to?"

"No, Pishima, there's nothing else to do. Let's go and make the sweets."

"But, mother," intervened Mahendra, "only a minute ago you regretted that you were making her slave, why then are you dragging her back to work?"

"This dear angel," replied his mother tapping Binodini affectionately under the chin, "loves to work."

"I was free this evening," continued Mahendra, "and thought I would read out a book to the Eyesore."

"We can both listen to the reading in the evening, Pishima," suggested Binodini.

Rajlakshmi thought, "Poor Mahin, he is feeling lonely and lost. We must all help to keep him entertained." So she said aloud, "Excellent. As soon as we have prepared Mahin's dinner, we shall come up and listen to the book. What say you, Mahin?"

Binodini threw a quick look at Mahendra. He replied, "Very well." But it was obvious that he had lost his enthusiasm for the proposal. Binodini went down with Rajlakshmi.

Mahendra was piqued and said to himself, "Let me also go out and return late." He changed his clothes but could carry his resolve out no further. For a long time he paced up and down the terrace, looking anxiously at the stairs. Finally he went and sat inside the room sulking. "I shan't touch the sweets tonight. I shall make mother understand that keeping the syrup so long over the fire ruins the sweets."

At dinner † Binodini brought Rajlakshmi up along with her. For fear of asthma the latter hardly ever climbed the stairs nowadays but today she did so at Binodini's special request. Mahendra sat down to eat, looking very grave.

* For making sweets.
† In a traditional Hindu household the women eat separately and later, after they have attended on the men at meals.

"What's the matter, Thakurpo?" protested Binodini. "You're hardly eating anything."

"Aren't you well?" asked the mother anxiously.

"I made these sweets with great care," went on Binodini. "You must try some at least. But—maybe, they're not well made! In that case please don't take them. No, no, you mustn't touch them. It's no good swallowing them under duress."

"How embarrassing!" said Mahendra laughing. "It's precisely the sweets that are most tempting. I'm enjoying them thoroughly. Why must you prevent me from eating them?"

He finished the plate, leaving not a speck behind.

After the meal the three of them came and sat in Mahendra's room. Mahendra refrained from recalling his original proposal, but Rajlakshmi said, "You were talking of some book. Why not begin?"

"I don't think you'd care to listen to it," replied Mahendra. "You see, there are no gods and goddesses in it."

"What a thing to say!" thought Rajlakshmi. She had come fully resolved to enjoy whatever Mahendra read. Were he to read out Turkish she would enjoy it. Poor boy feeling lonesome—the wife away in Kashi—whatever pleased him must please the mother.

"There's that anthology of moral precepts in Pishima's room," suggested Binodini. "Why not read that out this evening? It'll please Pishima and the evening will pass pleasantly."

Mahendra shot a piteous look at Binodini. Just then the maid came and announced that a lady had come and was waiting downstairs in Rajlakshmi's room. Kayet Thakrun * was an intimate friend of Rajlakshmi's. It was not easy for the latter to miss the luxury of a chat with her in the evening. Nevertheless she said to the maid, "Please apologise to

---

* *Kayet* is the proper name, *Thakrun* an honorific suffix like the obsolete *Mistress* in English.

Kayet Thakrun that I am busy in Mahin's room and request her to come tomorrow positively."

"But why, mother, why don't you go down to her?" suggested Mahendra hurriedly.

"Don't bother to get up, Pishima," said Binodini. "I'll go and sit with Kayet Thakrun."

Unable to resist the chance of a spicy, feminine gossip, Rajlakshmi said, "You stay here, dear. Let me go down and see if I can get rid of Kayet Thakrun. Please begin the reading and do not wait for me."

As soon as Rajlakshmi had left the room Mahendra burst out. "Why do you deliberately torture me?"

"What a thing to say!" replied Binodini affecting to be surprised. "I torture you? How? Maybe I should not inflict my presence on you. Let me go."

She tried to get up, looking dejected. Mahendra caught her by the hand exclaiming, "That's precisely how you torment me!"

"I am sorry I didn't realise I was such a pest. How strong you must be to have suffered me so long—without any visible signs of pain or ravage!"

"How can you know from the outside?" sighed Mahendra as he pulled her hand and rested it against his heart.

Binodini uttered a cry. Mahendra released her hand and asked anxiously, "Did I hurt you?"

He noticed that yesterday's wound had begun to bleed again.

"I am sorry, I forgot about the injury," apologised Mahendra looking crestfallen. "I must apply something and bandage it up today. I insist."

"It's nothing," said Binodini. "Please don't bother. I won't have anything done to it."

"Why not?"

"Where's the question of why not? I won't let you doctor me. Let it remain as it is."

Mahendra became grave. It was tantalizingly difficult to understand a woman's mind.

Binodini rose to go. Chafing under hurt pride Mahendra made no attempt to detain her. He merely inquired, "Where are you off to?"

"There's plenty to do," answered Binodini as she slowly left the room.

Mahendra remained seated for a minute. Then he jumped up and ran after Binodini to fetch her back. But something held him back as he reached the head of the stairs. He turned back and began to pace up and down the terrace.

Binodini was constantly luring him on and yet would not let him come near her even for a moment. He had already lost one boast—that he was invulnerable. Must he now lose face altogether and confess that he was incapable of winning another heart, however much he tried? To be conquered without making a conquest in return—this defeat on both the fronts was very galling to Mahendra's self-esteem. His pride both as a moralist and as a lover lay in the dust. Having lost his dignity he got nothing in return. Like a beggar he was forced to keep vigil outside a locked door, empty-handed in the dark.

Every year in April Bihari received a consignment of mustard-flower honey from his estate. He used to send it over to Rajlakshmi. This year too the honey was received. Binodini took the jar to Rajlakshmi and said, "Pishima, Bihari Thakurpo has sent honey."

Rajlakshmi directed that the jar should be stored in the pantry. Binodini did so and came and sat by Rajlakshmi.

"Bihari Thakurpo never neglects to remember you. The poor boy is motherless and dotes on you as a mother."

Rajlakshmi had always looked upon Bihari as Mahendra's shadow. She took him for granted as a free, unpaid, ever-willing, ever-handy adjunct to her household. But when Binodini referred to her as mother to the motherless Bihari, Rajlakshmi's maternal heart was suddenly touched. "Indeed, it is true, he does look upon me as mother," she thought and recalled how in sickness, in times of trouble and difficulty Bihari had always served and helped her with unstinted devotion without waiting to be asked. So naturally was the devotion offered and so easily accepted that she was almost unaware of her need to be grateful, as she was unconscious of her need to breathe. She had hardly ever bothered to inquire after him and recalled how she used to resent Annapurna's doing so, thinking, "She professes her solicitude for Bihari so as to keep him under her thumb."

She sighed and remarked, "Yes, Bihari is like my own son." It occurred to her that in fact Bihari had done much more for her than her own son ever did, without having received anything from her in return. His devotion was unselfish and steadfast. She heaved another long sigh.

"Bihari Thakurpo loves your cooking very much," said Binodini.

"No other fish curry he relishes so much," said Rajlakshmi with pride in her voice.

Suddenly it occurred to her that she had not seen Bihari for several days. She asked, "How is it, Bou, that I don't see Bihari these days?"

"I too was wondering, Pishima," replied Binodini. "But the way your son has been obsessed with his bride since the wedding, is it any wonder that his friends hardly find it worth while to call?"

The argument went home immediately. It was indeed true that Mahendra's infatuation with his wife had alienated all his well-wishers. Bihari had a legitimate grievance. Why should he call? Having thus enrolled Bihari on her side in her own grievance against Mahendra's shameless behaviour, her sympathy with Bihari increased. She began to relate to Binodini how much Bihari had done for Mahendra, how much he had suffered on his account, since their early boyhood. Speaking on Bihari's behalf she gave vent to her own hidden grievance against her son. What would become of this world and its obligations if men neglected their life-long loyalties for the sake of a new-found wife!

"Tomorrow is Sunday," said Binodini. "If you invite Bihari Thakurpo to lunch, he'll be happy."

"An excellent suggestion. Let me ask Mahin to send him an invitation."

"No, Pishima, you must invite him yourself."

"Do I know how to read and write like you people?" asked Rajlakshmi.

"It doesn't matter. I'll write the letter for you," offered Binodini. She wrote the letter and sent it.

Sunday was a day to look forward to. Since the night before, Mahendra's imagination was worked up and inflamed, even though nothing had so far happened in conformity with its anticipations. Nevertheless, the day dawned sweet as honey. The gathering din of the awakened city sounded like music to his ears.

But what was this hullabaloo going on in the house? Was mother observing a ceremonial ritual? Today she was herself supervising all household operations instead of resting and leaving it to Binodini as usual. It was getting on to be ten in the morning and Mahendra had not yet had a glimpse of Binodini despite all his attempts. He tried to read a book but found it impossible to concentrate his mind on it. He took up a newspaper but could not get beyond the advertisement column. For fifteen minutes his eyes were glued to it while his mind wandered far away; finally unable to control himself any longer he went downstairs. He found his mother seated in the veranda outside her room, cooking on a portable oven. Binodini, the loose end of her sari girdled round her waist, was assisting her.

"What's the matter today?" asked Mahendra. "Why all this hubbub?"

"Hasn't Bou told you?" asked Rajlakshmi. "I've asked Bihari to lunch."

Bihari to lunch! A flame of wrath shot through Mahendra. "But I shan't be here, mother," he said.

"Why?"

"I have an engagement outside."

"You can leave after lunch. The food won't be delayed."

"I am invited to lunch outside."

Binodini threw a quick look at him. Then turning to Rajlakshmi she said, "Let him go, Pishima, if he is invited out. It won't matter if Bihari Thakurpo eats alone."

But the mother could not reconcile herself to the prospect of her son not sharing the food cooked by her own hands. The more she pressed Mahendra the more adamant became his refusal. "It's an important invitation which cannot be ignored. It would have been better if I had been consulted before inviting Bihari." And so he went on.

Mahendra was angry. He knew he could punish his mother best by not eating her food. Rajlakshmi lost all her enthusiasm for cooking and felt like throwing everything away. Binodini tried to console her. "Please don't be upset, Pishima. Thakurpo is bluffing. He won't go out today."

Rajlakshmi shook her head and said, "No, child, you don't know Mahin well enough. He's obstinate. Once he has made up his mind, nothing can change it."

When the time came it was discovered that Binodini knew Mahendra better than his mother. Mahendra had understood that it was Binodini who was responsible for the invitation to Bihari. Hence the intense jealousy and anger. And hence also the reluctance to absent himself from the scene. He must be there to watch what Bihari said and did, what Binodini said and did. It would be painful to witness the scene, but witness he must.

After many days Bihari entered Mahendra's house today. A momentary hesitation held him back before he passed the

132

door of a house which since childhood had been a second home to him, where as a child he had indulged in so many pranks. Controlling the painful spasm of memory, he forced a smile on his lips and went in where Rajlakshmi was sitting, freshly bathed. He bent low and touched her feet—a formality which he did not observe when he was a frequent visitor to the house. Today he behaved as though he had returned from a distant exile. Rajlakshmi affectionately placed her hand on his head.

Today she was particularly cordial and full of tender solicitude. She asked, "How is it, Bihari, that we haven't seen you for several days? Every day I would say, today Bihari will turn up, but no, there was no sight of you."

Bihari laughed and replied, "If I had turned up daily, you would hardly have thought of me, mother. But where is Mahinda?"

Rajlakshmi's face was clouded as she replied, "Mahin's been invited out today. He couldn't stay on."

Bihari was cut to the quick. Was this the end of a lifelong friendship? Heaving a deep sigh he made an effort to brush aside all painful thoughts and asked, forcing a lively tone, "What dishes have you cooked today, let's hear?" He began to talk of his favourite dishes as cooked by her hand. Whenever he happened to eat at Rajlakshmi's, he made it a point to seem greedy and affected an excessive appetite for her cooking—a trick to please and stimulate a maternal solicitude. Rajlakshmi laughed with pleasure as Bihari made inquiries about her dishes and assured her greedy guest that he had nothing to fear.

Just then Mahendra strolled in and asked in a formal, dry tone, "How are you, Bihari?"

"I thought you had gone out?" exclaimed his mother.

"I managed to put off the invitation," replied Mahendra trying to hide his embarrassment.

When Binodini appeared, fresh from her bath, Bihari at first could not say anything to her. The memory of the last scene was still sore.

"Well, Thakurpo," said Binodini coming nearer, "you don't seem to know me!"

"Can every one be known?" replied Bihari.

"If you have the sense, yes," murmured Binodini. Then she announced in a louder voice, "Pishima, the food is served."

Mahendra and Bihari sat down to lunch. Rajlakshmi watched them eat while Binodini served them.

Mahendra had little appetite for food and kept on watching Binodini serve. He had a suspicion that Binodini was deriving a special delight from serving Bihari. If the most palatable tid-bits were poured into Bihari's plate, Mahendra was in no mood to appreciate that that was as it should be, since he himself was the host and Bihari the guest. In any case it was not something he could protest against openly. In consequence he burnt all the more inwardly. When Binodini was about to serve Bihari a special dish of out-of-season mango-fish secured with great difficulty, Bihari exclaimed, "Please, not me—give it to Mahinda who is particularly fond of it." But Mahendra angrily waved it aside, saying with acerbity, "No, I don't want it." Binodini quietly and without any more ado poured the fish curry into Bihari's plate.

As soon as the meal was over and the two friends had come out of the room, Binodini hurried out after Bihari and said, "Bihari Thakurpo, please don't go as yet. Come and sit down upstairs."

"Won't you have your food?"

"No, it's Ekadashi *—I'm on fast today."

A flicker of a cold and mocking smile played on Bihari's lips, as though to say, so all the trappings of virtue are there! Ignoring the sneer—as she had put up with the wound on her elbow—she repeated her request very gently and humbly, "Please come and sit down for a while. I beg of you."

Mahendra flared up savagely and barked, "How ridiculous!

* The eleventh day of the moon is observed as a fast day by the orthodox Hindus.

Why must you pester him to stay when he may have work to do, when he probably doesn't wish to stay? I don't understand the meaning of this fussing and cajoling."

Binodini laughed aloud. "Look at him Bihari Thakurpo, listen to what your Mahinda says! Fussing and cajoling mean just fussing and cajoling, as any dictionary will tell you." Then turning to Mahendra she added, "Say what you will, Thakurpo, no one else has had the meaning of fussing and cajoling so massaged into his skin since babyhood as you."

Bihari turned to Mahendra and said, "Mahinda, I've something to say to you. Please come over here."

Bihari drew Mahendra aside without taking any notice of Binodini and without a word of leave-taking. Binodini stood on the veranda holding on to the railing and gazing vacantly into the emptiness of the outlying courtyard.

Coming outside Bihari said, "I should like to know, Mahinda, if this is the end of our friendship."

Mahendra was fuming. The last jeer of Binodini was whirling round and scorching the inside of his brain like a lightning current. He burst out, "Reconciliation may suit your strategy but I am not dying for it. I want no intruders in my domestic life. The privacy of my home must remain private."

Bihari left without a word. Consumed by jealousy Mahendra swore that he would not see Binodini. He spent the day prowling about the house furtively, going up and down, longing for a sight of Binodini.

28

Asha asked her aunt, "Auntie, do you often think of Uncle?"

"I became a widow at the age of eleven," replied Annapurna. "I have only a shadowy memory of my husband left with me."

"Of whom then do you think?" asked Asha again.

"Of Him in whom my husband is now merged."

"Does it bring you any happiness?"

Annapurna affectionately patted Asha's head and replied, "How can I explain to you, my child, what only my mind feels and He knows?"

Asha wondered if he of whom I think day and night knows what I feel. I am not literate enough to write long letters. Is that any reason why he doesn't write to me any more?

Asha had received no letter from Mahendra for several days and kept on wishing, if only my Eyesore were with me! How well she would put on paper what I feel and long to express but cannot!

She was reluctant to write herself, knowing that her miserable, ill-written scribble would not please her husband. The more carefully she tried to write, the worse became the scribble. The more she tried to express her feelings, the more confused became the expression. Why were husbands not like the gods who, invisible themselves, see, hear and know everything? Why couldn't she merely write 'Beloved Lord' and let him understand the rest from the blank sheet? God has planted so much love in my heart—why couldn't He provide me with just a little power of expression?

It was evening. Asha had just returned home from her evening worship at the temple and was sitting by her aunt's feet, gently rubbing them. After a spell of silence she suddenly said, "Mashi, you have often said that a woman's religion consists in the devoted service of her husband. But what is to become of the woman who is foolish and lacks the necessary understanding of her husband's needs—how is she to serve?"

Annapurna looked at Asha and said nothing for a moment. Then heaving a half-stifled sigh she replied, "I too am a foolish woman, my child, and yet I continue in my devotions to the Lord."

"He knows your heart and is pleased. But suppose a husband turns away from the devotion of a foolish wife?"

"All are not given the power to make every one happy, my child. But if a woman does her best to love and serve her husband and fulfils her other obligations, then even if the husband spurns her devotion, the Lord Himself takes it unto Him."

Asha did not reply and remained silent. She tried hard to derive consolation from what her aunt had said but failed to convince herself that even God could fulfil the heart of a woman spurned by her husband. She continued her gentle massage of the aunt's feet, her head hanging low, her eyes on the ground. Annapurna then took her by the hand and drawing her to herself kissed her forehead. Swallowing hard to release her voice choked with emotion, she said, "Chuni darling, you cannot learn by precept the wisdom that comes from a living experience of sorrow. Your aunt too at your age had once cherished a naïve belief in the law of give-and-take. Like you I had felt that my love and devotion must necessarily make the other one happy. Why should not my worship bear fruit? Why should I not earn at least the credit for wishing and striving well? But a rebuff awaited me at every step and finally I came to the desperate conclusion that my whole life had been a waste and a futility. That very day I gave up the world and came over here. But now I realise that nothing I had done was in vain. Oh my child, our real and ultimate commerce is not with each other but with Him who is the supreme giver and the supreme taker. He has accepted everything I had to offer. If I had only known it then, if I had known that my real bargain was with Him, that in living and loving I was carrying out my deal with Him, that I was living His life and loving His world, how much pain I would have spared myself!"

Asha pondered a great deal as she lay in bed at night but

could not understand, could not grasp anything. She had unbounded regard for her saintly aunt and could not altogether ignore what she had said, and so she in a way clung to the words without fully knowing what they meant. She sat up in bed and in the hushed darkness of the night bowed low before Him who reigned supreme in her aunt's heart, murmuring, "I am a child and do not know who or what you are. I know only my husband. Please do not be annoyed with me on that account. Please, O Lord, tell my husband to accept the love I give him. If he spurns it, I shall not live any more. I am not saintly like my aunt and will not find comfort and refuge in you." She bowed low again and again.

On the evening before the day she was to return to Calcutta with her uncle, Annapurna took Asha in her lap and said, "Chuni, my little mother, I have no power to shield you from life's pain and rebuffs and misfortunes. I have only one piece of advice to give you—wherever you are, whatever happens, hold on to your faith, be steadfast in your devotion."

Bowing low and touching her aunt's feet, Asha murmured, "Bless me, Mashima, that it may be so."

29

When Asha returned home Binodini was full of reproaches. "Could you not have written me a letter even once during all this long absence?"

"What about you, darling? Why didn't you write?"

"Why should I write first? It was for you . . . ."

Asha flung her arms round Binodini's neck and made apologies. "You know, dear Eyesore, how ill-equipped I am to write. I feel particularly shy to write to one so clever and learned as you."

In no time the two friends were as affectionate and intimate as before.

"Your constant company," said Binodini, "has so spoiled your husband that he simply can't do without some one fussing over him."

"That is why I put you in charge. Who knows better than you how to entertain!"

"It was easy enough during the day—I would pack him off to college and feel easy. But in the evening it was difficult to evade him. I must sit and chat with him or read out a book to him—no end to his claims."

"Serve you right! You must pay for being so charming."

"Take care, my dear. Sometimes he behaves so ridiculously that I wonder if I am really not an enchantress."

"Indeed you are. Who is one if not you? I wish I had a little of your magic."

"Why, whom would you like to bewitch? Hold on fast to what you have and don't you try to seduce another. It's not worth it."

Asha pouted and pushed Binodini away, chiding, "Don't be absurd, darling."

At their first meeting since her return from Kashi Mahendra's first words to Asha were: "You seem to have kept very well in Kashi. You look pretty plump—almost chubby."

Asha flushed red with embarrassment. Her body had no business to look so fit. Everything was wrong with the foolish Asha. When her mind was on the rack, her wretched body flourished. She lacked the power to give expression to her feelings and on top of it her body gave evidence against her.

She asked softly, "How have you kept?"

Once his answer would have been half playful, half sincere: "I was pining for you." Today the same words were choked before they could be uttered. He replied, "So, so."

Asha looked at him and noticed that he had grown thinner, his skin was pale and an unnatural brightness shone in his eyes, as though a deep-seated hunger were consuming him with its flame. Asha's heart was wrung with remorse. Why did she leave the husband behind and go to Kashi when he was not well? He getting thinner and she fatter— the indecent contrast filled her mind with shame. She loathed her own health for it.

Not knowing what else to say Mahendra remained silent for a while. Then he asked, "I hope Kakima was well?" Having been assured by Asha on that point, he was at a loss for a further topic of conversation. He did not know what to do and to hide his embarrassment took up an old newspaper and pretended to be absorbed in it. Asha bent her head and kept gazing at the floor, wondering, "Why has he nothing to say to me after such a long absence? Why can't he even look at me? Is he angry with me because I didn't write for a few days, because I overstayed to please Mashima?" She wished she knew what exactly her sin was so that she could make amends. Afflicted with grief, remorse and fear, she looked around for her own lapses.

When Mahendra returned from college and sat down to partake of the afternoon refreshments, Rajlakshmi was there and Asha too stood leaning against the door, a veil drawn over her face. But no one else was there.

"Is anything wrong with you today, Mahin?" asked Rajlakshmi anxiously.

"No, no, why should there be?" replied Mahendra annoyed.

"Then why aren't you eating well?"

"I am eating a lot. How much more can one eat?" Mahendra's voice was vexed and sharp.

Later in the day—it was a summer evening—Mahendra went up to the roof-terrace and strolled up and down wrapped in a muslin shawl. He was hoping against hope that Binodini would turn up for the usual reading together. Only a couple of chapters remained of *Ananda Math*. * He found it hard to believe that Binodini would be so cruel as to deprive

* The well-known novel by Bankim Chatterji.

140

him of the joy of listening to them. But the evening merged into night, the usual reading hour was long past and there was no sign of Binodini. Weary with the weight of disappointment Mahendra retired to his bed.

Decked in fine clothes and looking bashful, Asha slowly entered the bedroom—to find that Mahendra was already in bed. She hesitated, not knowing what to do, and was overcome with shyness. The intervening separation made it difficult for her to resume where she last took off. She needed to be courted again and waited as it were for a fresh invitation. She stood for a long time near the door but there was no response from Mahendra. Slowly and softly she advanced step by step, frightened and embarrassed by the tinkling of her ornaments. With bated breath and a heart beating fast she approached the mosquito net and saw that Mahendra was asleep. Her lovely dress and ornaments then seemed to her a mockery and she felt as if every limb was wrapped round with derision. She wanted to run from the room and hide herself somewhere.

She controlled the wild impulse and gently and very cautiously got into the bed. Despite her care there was enough sound and motion in the bed to have wakened up Mahendra had he been really asleep. But he was not and therefore remained motionless with eyes closed. He lay on his side, his face turned the other way, his back towards Asha. Though he could not see her face he could understand that she was weeping silently. His own callousness weighed on him like a millstone grinding his heart in agony. But what was he to do? He didn't know what to say to her, how to pet her. He was angry with himself but however much he tortured himself, he remained inert, unable to find a way out. He was afraid of the morning when he would no longer be able to feign sleep and would have to face Asha.

Asha herself saved him. Very early, before daybreak, she crept out of the bed, still decked in her finery, and left the room steeped in her humiliation.

30

Why this change? What have I done? Asha brooded, unable to understand. The real source of mischief escaped her altogether. She had not the faintest suspicion that Mahendra could be in love with Binodini. Inexperienced in the ways of the world, she was incapable of imagining that her husband could be different from the image she had formed of him after marriage.

Mahendra left for college earlier than usual that day. It had been a ritual with Asha to stand at the window and watch him leave and catch his parting glance as he looked up from the carriage. Today also she came and stood by the window as soon as she heard the carriage arrive. Mahendra too looked up from force of habit. He saw Asha standing by the window, unwashed, in shabby clothes, her hair undone, her face drawn and pale. Immediately he lowered his gaze and pretended to look at a book lying in his lap. The carriage drove away without their eyes meeting in a last lingering look, without the usual smile so pregnant with meaning.

Asha sank down on the floor. All savour had gone from her life and world. It was 10-30 in the morning; outside on the roads the din of the awakened city had risen to its full crescendo. An endless procession of carriages rumbled their way to the offices in the city and one tram followed closely on another. In the din, bustle and excitement of the workaday world, Asha nursing her bewildered and wounded heart seemed strangely out of place.

Suddenly it flashed across her mind that Mahendra had been upset by Bihari's visit to Kashi. That was the only plausible reason she could think of, for nothing else had happened in the interval. On the other hand such a cause was hardly reasonable. How was it her fault if Bihari went to

142

Kashi?—unless, unless—her heart nearly stopped as the terrible suspicion dawned on her—Mahendra suspected that she and Bihari had secretly arranged a tryst in Kashi. What a base suspicion! How shameful! It was bad enough her name having been associated with him, but that Mahendra should smell an affair, it was too shameful—she couldn't survive it. But even if there had been a cause for suspicion, even if she were at fault, why didn't he say so? Why didn't he chastise her? Instead of openly charging her he was merely evading her as though he was secretly ashamed of his own suspicion. In fact he went about with a guilty face. An angry judge doesn't go about with a hang-dog expression!

The glimpse of Asha's pitiful, woe-begone face which Mahendra had caught from his carriage haunted him the whole day. Whether he was listening to a lecture in the college or sitting with his student companions, he could not get rid of the image of the window and of Asha standing behind it, unbathed, her hair in disorder, her clothes shabby, her face like a mask of anguish.

The classes over, Mahendra wandered around the Goldighi Square until sunset, unable to decide how he should behave towards Asha—with benevolent hypocrisy or callous brutality! The question of his giving up Binodini did not once arise in his mind. He was lacerated in the struggle between the conflicting claims of pity and love.

Finally he sought refuge in the consolation that very few wives could boast of enjoying as much love of their husbands as Asha was still privileged to receive. Why should she not then be content with that much love and solicitude? His heart was big enough to accommodate both Binodini and Asha: his love for Binodini was so platonic that it could not possibly come in the way of his marital obligations.

Thus he succeeded in lifting from his mind the oppressive weight of his guilt. Without giving up either, he would have both Binodini and Asha eternally revolving round him like two luminous planetary satellites. The thought made his heart swell with joy and pride. Tonight, he resolved, he would retire to bed early and taking Asha in his arms would smother her with tenderness and affection and wipe out all her misgiving and sorrow with sweet words. Intoxicated by the prospect he hurried home.

Asha was not present at the meal, but surely she would come to bed as usual! He lay down in bed in that hope. But what haunted the solitude of the room and the emptiness of the bed was not the memory of the romantic hours filled with the ever-renewed ardour of passion which he had spent with Asha in the early days of their married life, but something utterly different. As when the sun rises the light of the moon fades, so the memory of Asha waned in the waxing light of a more powerful luminary. The gentle image of the timid, shy girl-wife was blurred over and lost in the dazzling light of a full-blown beautiful woman. He recalled the playful scuffle with Binodini over the book, *Visha Vriksha*; Binodini reading out to him *Kapalakundala* * till the evening passed into night and the household save those two was hushed into sleep, Mahendra listening and Binodini reading aloud in the solitude and silence of the night, her voice softer and softer until charged with emotion it was barely audible and she recovered herself with a supreme effort and threw the book away. "Let me see you to the stairs," Mahendra would say. Recalling the scene over and again Mahendra shivered in an ecstasy of delight.

The night was far advanced. Now and again a mild fear crept on him that perhaps Asha would turn up, but Asha did not come. Mahendra said to himself, "I was ready to do my part, but if Asha is so unreasonable and peevish as not to turn up, what more can I do?" Freed from his moral obligation he gave himself up at dead of night to thoughts of Binodini without inhibition or scruple.

When the clock struck one, Mahendra could no longer

* Another novel by Bankim Chatterji.

stay in bed. Pulling up the mosquito net he came out of bed and went up to the roof-terrace. The summer moonlight was enchanting. The vast, overspreading silence of the city in sleep was almost tangible, like the still waters of a calm sea. A gentle breeze was blowing over the innumerable roofs of the city lulling it into a deeper sleep.

Mahendra could no longer bear the suppressed longing of many days. He had not had a glimpse of Binodini since Asha's return from Kashi. The tense solitude of the moon-drunk night held Mahendra under a spell and drove him irresistibly towards Binodini. He went down the stairs and stood in the veranda facing Binodini's room. The door was open. Mahendra went into the room and found that the bed had not been slept in. Hearing footsteps in her room Binodini asked from the open veranda to the south of the room, "Who's there?"

"It's I, Binod," replied the frightened Mahendra in a subdued voice. He went up to the veranda and found Rajlakshmi and Binodini lying on a mat on the cool floor. Rajlakshmi asked, "How are you here at this time of the night, Mahin?" From beneath her deep dark eyebrows Binodini's eyes shot flames of wrath at him. Mahendra made no reply and beat a hasty retreat.

31

The next morning was cloudy. After several days of blistering heat the simmering sky was overcast with gathering masses of dark, soothing clouds. Mahendra had left early for college. His discarded clothes were lying on the floor. Asha had taken out the soiled garments for the laundry and was counting them and searching pockets before handing them over to the dhobi. Mahendra had warned her of his absent-mindedness and requested her to turn out and empty each pocket before letting the garment go to the dhobi. In one pocket she found a letter.

Had the letter then and there assumed the shape of a poisonous snake and bitten her finger, it would have been better. The deadly poison takes no more than five minutes to complete its fatal work after entering the body. But the poison in the mind is far worse—it brings the agony of death but not death.

The letter was open and written in Binodini's hand. As soon as Asha recognised the hand she went ashen pale. Hurrying inside the adjoining room she read the letter:

"Not content with your shameful behaviour last night you have sent me surreptitiously a letter this morning through Khemi. * For shame! What must she have imagined! Are you bent upon disgracing me before the whole world?

"What do you want of me? Love? You have received nothing but love since your childhood and yet there is no end to your greed, to your cupidity. Why this congenital covetousness, this begging itch?

"I have no right to love or be loved in this world. That is why I play at love to lighten my sorrow. When you were free you also joined in the idle game. But playtime does not last for ever. Now that you have been called back to duty at home, why this sneaking into the playroom? Shake off its dust and go back home. Having no home, I shall carry on the game in my mind without calling you to join it.

"You write that you love me. Make-believe is permissible in play, but if you mean the words in earnest, I do not believe it. At one time you thought you were in love with Asha. It was false. Now you imagine you are in love with me. That too is false. You love only yourself.

"A burning thirst for love has parched my mind and I know it too well. I implore you again and again, please give

* A maid's name.

146

me up, do not pester me, do not put me to shame with your shamelessness. I have no desire to play the game any longer. Much as you may call me, you will get no response whatsoever. You have called me 'heartless' in your letter. It may be true but my pity too is no less real. Today out of pity for you I renounce you. If you inflict on me a reply to this letter I shall know that my only safety against you is in flight."

No sooner had Asha read the letter than the ground seemed to give way under her feet, her muscles and nerves were as though no longer under control, she felt as though there was not enough air left to breathe, as though the sun had withdrawn all the light from her eyes. She groped for support on the wall, on the almirah, on the back of the chair before she gradually fell down in a faint. When soon after she came to herself she tried to re-read the letter but was too distracted to understand what she read. She felt the black letters dancing before her eyes. What had happened? How did it happen? Did it mean the end of everything? What should she do, whom should she call, where should she escape? She could not understand, could not think. Like a drowning person waving his arms and clutching at air, she tried frantically to cling with all her might to some support, any support—until out of the depth of her anguished heart came the cry, "Mashima!"

As soon as she had uttered the beloved name, the frozen flood of tears was released. She sat down on the floor and burst into repeated fits of weeping. When the fits subsided she asked herself, "What shall I do with the letter?" If the husband knew that the letter had fallen into her hand, how ashamed and humiliated he would feel! She must spare him that humiliation. She decided to replace the letter in the pocket of the tunic and hang the tunic in the wardrobe instead of giving it for wash.

She went back to the bedroom, letter in hand, and found that the dhobi had fallen asleep, his head resting on the pile of clothes. She recovered the tunic and was about to replace the letter in the pocket when she heard, "Eyesore dear!" She hurriedly threw both the tunic and the letter on the bed and sat over them. Binodini entered the room complaining. "The dhobi has been mixing up our clothes with others'. Let me take away the unmarked clothes and put a mark on them."

Asha could not look Binodini in the face. Afraid of revealing the expression on her face she turned towards the window and gazed upwards at the sky, her lips trembling, the tears overflowing her eyes. Binodini stood still and looked at Asha. "I see," she said to herself. "She has learnt of the last night's incident and is angry with me. Why with me—as though I was the culprit?" Without forcing any conversation on Asha, Binodini picked up a few clothes and hurriedly left the room.

The shame for her days of artless friendship for Binodini weighed on Asha's mind even in the midst of her bitter sorrow. She felt like re-reading the letter to see what relation there could be between its cruel contents and the ideal she had formed of her friend's character. As she opened the letter Mahendra suddenly burst into the room. Something must have happened to make him suddenly leave the college in the midst of a lecture and hurry back home.

Asha hid the letter in her sari. Seeing Asha in the room Mahendra stood still for a while in confusion and then looked around the room anxiously. Asha understood what he was looking for but did not know how to flee the room unnoticed and leave the letter in the right place for Mahendra to pick up.

At last Mahendra began picking up and searching each garment one by one. Asha could not bear to watch any longer the frantic and futile search and threw the tunic and the letter on the ground. To keep herself steady she held on to the bedpost with her right hand, hiding her face in the arm. Mahendra pounced on the letter with the speed of lightning and then stood still for a second looking at Asha. She heard his steps hurrying down the stairs. The dhobi pleaded, "Ma-thakrun, how much longer shall I wait for the clothes? It's getting late and my quarters are some way off."

32

Rajlakshmi did not send for or speak to Binodini in the morning. Binodini went into the pantry as usual but Rajlakshmi took no notice of her. Binodini understood what the matter was; nevertheless, she asked Rajlakshmi, "Aren't you feeling well, Pishima? No wonder. Shocking, the way Thakurpo behaved last night! Rushed in like a mad person! I couldn't sleep after that."

Rajlakshmi remained silent and sullen, without making any response whatsoever.

Binodini continued: "May be he had a slight argument with the Eyesore and came running to lodge a complaint or to seek advice—too impatient to wait for the night to end. You needn't be annoyed with me, Pishima. Whatever your son's other virtues, patience is not one of them. That you must concede. He's always falling foul of me on that account."

"You are wasting your words, Bou," said Rajlakshmi coldly. "I'm in no mood for argument today."

"Nor am I, Pishima. I was merely making up false excuses to cover up your son's shame to spare you pain. But the way he has broken loose, it's difficult to cover it up any longer."

"I am well aware of my son's virtues and lapses. What I did not know was that you were such a seductress."

Swallowing a retort that came to her lips Binodini replied, "You are right, Pishima. No one knows any one else. Most of us hardly know our own minds. Didn't you ever, out of spite

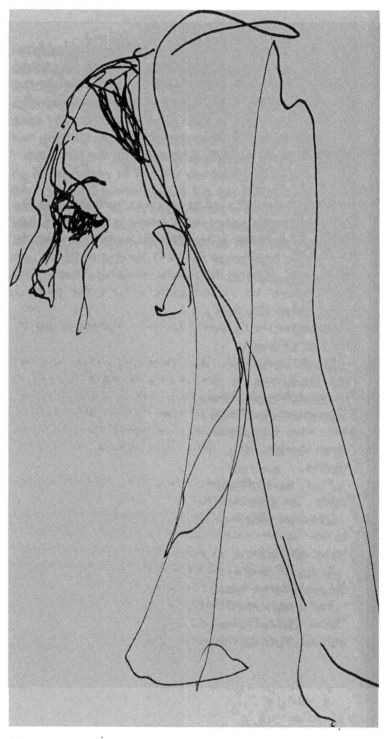

against your daughter-in-law, wish this seductress to divert your son's mind? Look within yourself and see if it is not so!"

Rajlakshmi flared up like a hot flame.

"Cursed creature, how dare you charge a mother with such infamy against her son! May your tongue rot!"

"Pishima," replied Binodini calmly and with composure, "we are an artful, decoying sex. What cunning there was in me, you understood better than I did. I too saw through your cunning better than you did yourself. But the cunning was there—or else all this would not have happened. Half knowing, half unconscious I laid a snare; you too laid one, half witting, half unwitting. Such is the way of our sex. We are a race of seductresses."

Choking with anger Rajlakshmi swept out of the room. Binodini remained standing where she was for some time, her eyes flashing fire.

The morning's household duties over, Rajlakshmi sent for Mahendra: he understood that it was about the last night's incident. He had just received Binodini's letter and was like one demented. Binodini's rebuff had let loose the tidal wave of his desire which was now sweeping him along irresistibly towards her. He was therefore in no mood for argument with his mother. He knew that she would upbraid him about Binodini and was afraid that her diatribe would provoke him into blurting out the truth and result in a bitter domestic feud. It was therefore best to escape from the house for a while and review the situation calmly. Leaving a message for his mother with the servant that his presence was urgently required at college and that he would see her on his return, he hurriedly dressed and fled from the house like a runaway child, without waiting to eat, and having in his hurry left behind the fatal letter which he had read and re-read the whole morning, carrying it about in the pocket of his tunic.

After a heavy downpour the sky was still heavy with clouds. Binodini, sore in mind, was in a state of extreme irritation and, as was her wont in such moods, was working furiously to distract her thoughts. Collecting all the household garments in a heap, she sat down to mark each one of them. When she went to collect the clothes from Asha and saw her mood, her irritation was further inflamed. If she was to be branded as a sinner, then why should she merely suffer the shame and ignominy of it and not taste the pleasure of sinning!

Again the patter of rain outside. Binodini sat on the floor of her room, a stupa of clothes in front of her. As the maid Khemi handed each garment to her, Binodini inscribed a letter on it with the marking ink. Suddenly Mahendra rushed into the room without knocking on the door. The maid threw the clothes down in confusion and covering her head fled. Binodini put down the garment she was holding in her lap and leapt up like a flash of lightning.

"Get out of my room," she hissed.

"Why, what have I done?"

"What have I done?" mimicked Binodini. "Chicken-hearted coward! As if you have the guts to do anything? Neither the guts to love nor the guts to do your duty! Why must you merely drag me down into disgrace?"

"Are you suggesting that I don't love you?"

"That's precisely what I am saying. This prowling like a thief, blowing hot and cold, now this side, now that—I loathe this cowardly mentality of a sneak. It sickens me. Get out of here!"

Mahendra was stupefied.

"You despise me, Binod?"

"Yes, I do."

"I can still make amends, Binod. If I cease wobbling, if I make up my mind to give up everything and go away, will you come with me?"

He grabbed both hands of Binodini and drew her into his arms with all his force.

"Let go. You're hurting me," cried Binodini.

152

"Let it hurt. Tell me, will you come with me?"

"No, I won't. Never!"

"Why not? You have trapped me into this hell, you can't throw me away. You must come."

He clasped her violently to his heart and holding her tight, continued: "Not all your contempt will turn me away. I shall take you away with me and will make you care for me."

With a violent effort Binodini wrenched herself free.

"You've set the house on fire," went on Mahendra. "You can neither put out the fire nor flee yourself."

His voice rose as he spoke until he almost shrieked, "Why did you make a sport of me, Binod? You can't now get away by calling it a mere game. Now there is only one death for us both."

Rajlakshmi rushed into the room and said, "What are you doing, Mahin?"

For a moment Mahendra's frenzied eyes rested on his mother. Then he turned them again on Binodini and pleaded, "I'm giving up everything and going away. Say you will come with me."

Binodini looked at the wrathful face of Rajlakshmi. Then she came forward and calmly held Mahendra's hand and said, "I'll come."

"Give me one day only," said Mahendra. "I am going now. From tomorrow there will be only you and me."

Mahendra went away. Just then the dhobi came and pleaded, "Ma-thakrun, I can't delay any more. If you have no time today, I shall come tomorrow to take away the clothes."

Khemi came and reported that the coachman was asking for the horse's feed. Binodini used to measure and dole out seven day's ration and send it to the stable and standing by the window used to watch the horse eat.

One of the servants, Gopal, came and complained, "Bou-thakrun, Jhadu bearer has had a scene with Dadamashai (Sadhucharan) and says that as soon as his kerosene account is paid off, he will take his salary from the steward and walk off."

Thus the daily household routine went on as usual.

33

Bihari gave up the Medical College just before the final Examination. To those who were surprised his reply was, "Let me first mind my own health before I look after others'."

Bihari was by nature restless and active. He must always be at something, though he lacked the natural incentive of ambition or the need to earn a living. After graduating from the Arts College he had joined the Shibpur College of Engineering. Having learnt as much engineering as was necessary to satisfy his curiosity about the science and to equip him with a certain amount of skill with his hands, he joined the Medical College. Mahendra had joined the college a year earlier. Their friendship was a byword among their college mates who used to refer to them teasingly as the Siamese Twins. They were now in the same class, Mahendra having failed in the first examination. The sudden break in friendship was a puzzle to their classmates who could not understand why Bihari studiously avoided even a chance encounter with Mahendra. Every one expected Bihari to pass the examination with flying colours but Bihari did not even sit for it.

Next to Bihari's house was a one-room tenement occupied by a poor Brahmin by name Rajendra Chakravarty who worked as a compositor in a press on a salary of twelve rupees a month. Bihari offered to adopt his son and to teach him reading and writing. The Brahmin was overjoyed and handed over his eight-year Basanta to Bihari's tutelage.

Bihari began to educate the boy in his own fashion. "I won't let him touch a written text till he is ten years old," he said. "Till then everything must be oral." He played with him, took him to the park, to the Zoological and Botanical Gardens and the Museum and spent practically the whole day with him. He gave him conversational lessons in English, told him stories from History and tried to discover and develop by various tests and experiments the natural aptitudes of the child and was so absorbed in the task that he had little leisure for anything else.

One evening it was difficult to go out. The rain which had stopped for a while at midday had been pouring since the afternoon. In the large living room on the first floor of his house Bihari, seated by the lamp, was engaged in his latest hobby with Basanta.

"Tell me, Basanta, how many beams are there in this room? No, you can't count them. Just say it straight away."

"Twenty."

"Wrong! Eighteen."

Bihari got up and suddenly opening a shutter asked, "How many panels are there in this shutter?"

He closed the shutter.

"Six," replied Basanta.

"Good. Now tell me, what's the length of this bench? And hold this book and guess its weight."

While Bihari was thus engaged in lessons in sense-training, the servant came and announced, "Sir, a lady . . . ." Before he could complete the sentence Binodini entered the room.

"What's this, Bouthan?" exclaimed Bihari in surprise.

"Have you a female relative in the house?" asked Binodini.

"No female—either related or unrelated. My only aunt is in our village home."

"Then please take me to her."

"What am I to say to her?"

"Introduce me as a maid-servant. I shall do the household work."

"She'll be not a little taken aback. She hasn't informed me

of her need of a maid. But first tell me why you want this. Basanta, please go to bed."

Basanta left. Binodini said, "You'll hardly understand the real trouble from a mere narration of what has happened."

"Never mind if I fail to understand or if I misunderstand. No great harm."

"Very well. You're free to misunderstand. Here it is. Mahendra is in love with me."

"It's no news. Nor is it news such as I would like to hear repeated."

"Nor am I anxious to repeat it. I have come to you for protection."

"Why? Aren't you glad? Since when have you changed? Who is responsible for leading Mahendra up the garden path?"

"I. I won't hide it from you. I am responsible for what has happened. But whether I am wicked or otherwise, please for once try to understand me. With my own burning heart I have set Mahendra's house on fire. Once I thought I cared for him, but it's not so."

"Does one set another's house on fire out of love?"

"That's only a maxim from books. I have no mind for such hackneyed wisdom. Please Thakurpo, lay these maxims aside and for once look into my heart. Listen to me, let me tell you all I am, good and bad together."

"It's not for nothing that I cling to bookish maxims, Bouthan. Let the Omniscient take care of the heart and its mysterious workings. We mortals are likely to err if we don't hold fast to what the books tell us."

"Listen to me, Thakurpo. Let me confess without shame that you could have turned me back. It's true that Mahendra is in love with me, but he is dense and blind and incapable of understanding me. Once I believed that you had understood me, that you had some regard for me—please don't suppress the truth."

"It's true that I did have a high regard for you."

"Nor were you mistaken, Thakurpo. But if you did understand, if you did care, why did you stop at that? What held you back from loving me? I have today cast off shame and come to you, and unashamedly I put it to you, why did you not love me? My ill luck—that you too should have fallen for Asha! No, you can't be angry with me! Please sit down, Thakurpo. I want to speak frankly, without any reservations. I knew of your love for Asha even before you became aware of it yourself. But what baffles me is, what is it you people see in Asha? What is there positive about her, be it good, or bad? Has God given you men only eyes but no insight? How soon and how easily you men are fooled! Stupid! Blind!"

Bihari stood up and said, "I am ready to listen to whatever you say to me today. I have only one request—please don't discuss what need not be discussed."

"I know where it hurts, Thakurpo. But please bear with me and try to understand what agony I must have gone through to have cast off all shame, all fear and come running to you tonight—to one who once did have regard for me, who, had he only loved me, would have saved me and turned my frustration into fulfilment. It's the truth I am telling you, had you not been in love with Asha, her life wouldn't have been ruined today."

"Why, what's happened to Asha?" asked Bihari suddenly losing colour. "What have you done to her?"

"Mahendra is preparing to forsake his home and to take me away with him."

"That can't be," suddenly roared Bihari. "Under no circumstances!"

"Under no circumstances?" repeated Binodini. "Who can hold back Mahendra today?"

"You can!"

Binodini remained silent for a while. Then resting her eyes on Bihari she said, "For whose sake should I do it? For your Asha's sake? Is there no such thing as my own happiness or sorrow? To renounce all my rights in this life for the sake of your Asha, for the good of Mahendra's family—I am not such a saint as that. I am not so deeply versed in the scriptural ethics. I must have something in return for what I give up."

Bihari's face hardened until his expression became severe. He said, "You have tried to tell me many plain truths. Let me also be frank. The mischief you have done today and the words you are uttering now are largely derived—in fact, stolen—from the novels you have read. Mostly melodramatic, theatrical!"

"Melodramatic? Theatrical?"

"Yes, melodramatic, theatrical. And not of a high order either. You think that what you are saying is your own, but it is not so. It's an echo of the printing press. Had you been an utter simpleton, a silly, brainless girl, even then you wouldn't have been denied some love in this world—but the heroine of a play is attractive only on the stage, no one wants her at home."

Binodini's passionate and proud air suddenly subsided like a hooded snake under the spell of a charmer. She sat still for a long while, her head bent low. Then without raising her head she asked gently, "What do you wish me to do?"

"Nothing dramatic or sensational. Do what a normal woman's good sense would impel you to do. Go back to your village."

"How do I go?"

"I shall take you to the railway station and put you in a ladies' compartment."

"Then may I spend the night here?"

"No. I don't trust myself so much."

Binodini suddenly dropped on the floor and clasping Bihari's feet with her arms pressed them hard to her breast.

"So you do own a little weakness, Thakurpo," she murmured. "Please keep it. Don't freeze into purity like a stone god. Be human and just a little bad by loving the bad."

She kissed his feet again and again. This sudden impetuous and unexpected behaviour took Bihari completely by surprise and for a moment paralysed his will. The tension in his body and mind seemed suddenly to relax, as though all the knots were loosened. Binodini felt the silent tremor of his limbs and letting go his feet raised herself on her knees in front of Bihari's chair, clasping his neck in both her arms.

"Dearest," she murmured, "I know you can't be mine for ever, but let me have your love just for once, even though for a moment. I shall then disappear in the wilderness of my village and will ask nothing any more of any one. Give me something, just a little, to cherish as a memory till my death."

She closed her eyes and raised her lips near to his. For a moment the two remained motionless in the hushed stillness of the room. Then Bihari heaved a deep sigh and gently removing Binodini's arms from his neck got up and went and sat in another chair. He made an effort to recover his choked voice and said, "There is a passenger train at one in the morning."

Binodini remained silent for a while. Then she murmured faintly, "I'll go by that train."

At this moment Basanta suddenly re-entered the room, bare-footed and without an upper garment, his fair and young body shining with health. He came and stood by Bihari's chair, looking gravely at Binodini.

"Why aren't you in bed?" asked Bihari.

Without replying Basanta kept on staring at Binodini. She stretched her arms towards him. After a momentary hesitation Basanta slowly walked into them. Binodini hugged the child to her heart and began to weep.

34

What is unthinkable does happen and what seems unbearable comes to be borne—otherwise Mahendra's household would hardly have survived that night and that day. Having asked Binodini to get ready, Mahendra posted a letter to her that very night. The letter was delivered at the house the following morning.

Asha was still in bed. When the bearer brought the letter to her, the blood rushed into her heart with a violent thrust. A turmoil of mixed hope and fear whirled within it. Hurriedly raising herself in bed she looked at the envelope and saw Binodini's name written in Mahendra's hand. She sank back on the pillow and returned the envelope to the bearer without a word.

"To whom am I to give it?" asked the bearer.

"I don't know."

It was eight in the evening when Mahendra came rushing up like a storm and paused outside Binodini's room. He found the room in darkness. Taking a match-box from his pocket he lighted a match and saw that neither Binodini nor her things were in the room. He crossed over to the veranda on the south. It was deserted. He called out, "Binod!" There was no response.

"What a fool I was! What an utter fool!" he chafed. "I should have taken her along with me then and there. No doubt, mother gave her such hell that it was impossible for her to stay in the house."

No sooner did the suspicion strike his mind than he was convinced that it must have been so. Bursting with impatience he rushed to his mother's room. That room too was in darkness, though he could see dimly that Rajlakshmi was lying in bed. He barked out angrily, "Mother, what have you people been saying to Binodini?"

"Nothing," replied Rajlakshmi.

"Then where is she?"

"How do I know?"

"You don't know!" said Mahendra sceptically. "Very well, I'm going to look for her. I shall find her wherever she is."

He turned on his heels. Rajlakshmi hurried out of bed and trailing behind him kept on crying, "Mahin, please don't go away. Come back. Listen to me!"

But Mahendra had rushed out of the house. A moment later he came back to the gate and asked the durwan, "Where's Bahu-thakurani gone?"

"We don't know, Sir. She didn't say anything."

"Don't you know?" asked Mahendra in a stern, contemptuous voice.

"No, Sir," replied the durwan with folded palms.

Mahendra muttered to himself, "Mother has coached them." To the durwan he said curtly, "Very well, let it be."

In the deepening gloom of the dusk relieved by the city's gas lights, the vendors on the road were hawking ice and fish. Mahendra walked on and was soon lost in the noisy crowd.

35

Bihari was not in the habit of brooding on himself at night. In fact he did not at any time consider himself a fit subject for meditation and regarding the world around him as more important than himself was happy with his books, his work, his friends and his surroundings. But a day came when the terrific impact of a shock suddenly blighted the world around him, leaving him stranded on the lonely peak of his own suffering. Since then he developed a fear of being alone with himself and tried to drown himself in work so as to give no opportunity to his self to obtrude itself.

But today he found it impossible to ignore the prisoner within. He had accompanied Binodini to her village home the previous day and since then his heart writhed in pain in its deep cavern, constantly tugging at him and keeping him aware of itself in the midst of work or in the company of others. He felt depressed, dejected and overcome with weariness.

It was nine in the evening. The south breeze from the sea which makes the end of the day in summer so pleasant was blowing frenziedly on the roof-terrace opening on Bihari's bedroom. It was a moonless night and Bihari was sitting in the darkness, reclining in an easy chair. He was in no mood to teach Basanta and had dismissed the pupil early in the evening. His heart, like a child forsaken by its mother, was stretching its arms and groping in the darkness for some comfort, some companionship, some sweet savour of his usual, carefree, extroverted existence. The banks of his well-regulated, disciplined personality seemed to have given way, letting loose the turbid waters of the subconscious so long held in check, which now swept him along towards images and thoughts he had vowed never to invoke.

The long story, from beginning to end, of his friendship with Mahendra, inscribed in many colours on the rolled-up scroll of his memory, like a map charted with land and water, rivers and mountains, was unrolled before his mind. He recalled one by one the shocks which had upset the equilibrium of the little world which was his life—in its collisions with other wayward planets. Whence came the first shock? He could see etched on the darkness in front of him the bashful, girlish face of Asha radiant with the soft gold of the sunset and could hear the blowing of the conches heralding the hour of the wedding. This benign planet emerging from an unknown horizon of fate had come and stood between

162

the two friends, causing a slight rift between them and an obscure pain which he dared not express, which he dared not even admit consciously in his mind. And yet this pain glowed with the light and sweetness of a rare affection which was a fulfilment in itself.

In the wake of the benign planet came the Saturn scattering to the winds the devotion of friends, the bond of wedded love, the peace and sanctity of the family. Bihari strove with all the scorn which righteousness can muster to drive away the image of Binodini from his mind. But strangely enough his scorn melted even as he felt it, without marring the image of the enchanting and baffling beauty which remained steadily luminous on the breast of darkness, its dark, mysterious gaze riveted on him. The panting, turbulent south breeze of summer was like the excited breath of that image caressing Bihari's limbs. Gradually the dazzle of that unflinching, fiery gaze began to dim and the sharp, piercing eyes burning with thirst seemed to soften and melt in an overflow of tears, turning the look into one of profound tenderness. The image drew near and sinking on the floor clasped Bihari's knees against its breasts in a tempestuous embrace. Then it seemed to grow like an enchanting fairy creeper enveloping Bihari with its soft tendrils and raising its lovely face like a full-blown flower breathing the perfume of desire into Bihari's lips. Bihari closed his eyes trying to banish the image from the screen of his mind but his will seemed powerless to raise its hand against it. A feverish, abortive kiss trembled on the edge of his lips in an agony of unfulfilment. A thrill of ecstasy held him under its spell.

Unable to bear the darkness and the solitude any longer he hurried inside the lighted bedroom. His eyes fell on a teapoy in one corner of the room on which lay a photograph wrapped in silk. Unwrapping the photograph Bihari sat down in the centre of the room, directly under the light, and placing the photograph in his lap began to gaze at it.

It was a picture of Mahendra and Asha taken together

soon after the wedding. On the back of it was inscribed 'Mahinda' in Mahendra's hand and 'Asha' in her hand. The picture had preserved intact the sweet rapture of their newly wedded love. Mahendra was seated in a chair, his face radiant with the joy of newly discovered love. By his side stood Asha. The photographer had succeeded in removing her veil but not the bashfulness from her face. Poor Asha was now stranded and was eating her heart out while Mahendra had drifted far away; the unthinking picture by preserving intact the ecstasy of love on his face had merely turned it into a testament of fate's mockery.

Keeping the picture in his lap Bihari tried to invoke the aid of Asha as a talisman to drive away the image of Binodini, but Binodini's soft arms pulsating with the ardour of full-blooded love continued to cling round his limbs. Bihari tried to despise her by repeating in his mind, "How could you break up such a lovely and loving home?" but Binodini's feverish lips raised so invitingly close to his in a passionate supplication seemed to murmur, "I love you. In the whole wide world you alone are mine."

What sort of a reply was this? Could "I love you" be a sufficient answer to drown the pitiful wail of a broken home? The evil charmer! And yet even as he muttered the words with what he hoped was utter contempt he had a suspicion that there was a quiver of tenderness in the notes. How could he truly and whole-heartedly reject the gift of measureless love freely offered, at a time when he himself had just been rejected and cast on the wayside as a beggar, disinherited of his right to a lifelong friendship and devotion! Such a gift had never come his way before. The only return he had ever had for his self-effacing devotion had been a few miserable crumbs from the storehouse of love. And now when the Lady of Love had herself sent her choicest dishes of love prepared solely for him and offered on a plate of gold, how should the poor, hungry wretch deny himself such feast!

Absorbed in this reverie, with the picture still in his lap, he was startled by a sound. Looking up he saw Mahendra in the room. As he rose up from his seat in sudden confusion the picture slipped down from his lap on to the carpet, unnoticed by him.

"Where's Binodini?" asked Mahendra unceremoniously.

Advancing to greet Mahendra, Bihari took his hand in his and said affectionately, "Mahinda dear, please sit down for a while and we shall talk over everything."

"I have no time to sit and argue. Tell me, where is Binodini?"

"Your question cannot be answered as simply as that. You must sit down for a while and listen with patience."

"Are you going to preach? I have read enough sermons in childhood."

"No. I have neither the right nor the power to preach."

"You'll revile me then? I know I am a villain and a humbug and every name you can call me. But what I want to know is, do you know where Binodini is?"

"Yes, I do."

"Will you tell me?"

"No."

"You must. You have stolen her and kept her hidden. She is mine. You must return her to me."

Bihari remained silent for a minute. Then he said coldly, "She is not yours. Nor did I steal her. She came to me of her own will."

Mahendra flared up. "You're lying!" he shouted. He rushed to the closed door leading to the next room and began to pound violently on it, shouting, "Binod! Binod!"

A sound of sobbing reached him from inside the room. He shouted, "Don't be afraid, Binod. It's I Mahendra come to rescue you. No one dare lock you up as a prisoner."

Putting his whole weight against the door he threw it open and rushed into the room steeped in darkness. He could see a shadowy form in the bed crouching in fear and clinging to a pillow with a stifled cry. Bihari rushed into the room and lifted up Basanta in his arms, murmuring consolingly, "Don't be frightened, Basanta. There's nothing to fear."

Mahendra rushed out and went about the house looking into every room. When he returned, the room had been lighted and Basanta was back in bed though still giving out an occasional sob of fear, while Bihari sat by his side gently caressing him to sleep.

"Where have you put Binodini?" asked Mahendra impatiently.

"Please don't shout, Mahinda," remonstrated Bihari. "You have already scared this little boy; you may make him ill. As for Binodini you have no business to know where she is."

"High-souled saint, don't spout holy ideals at me," mocked Mahendra. "What were you doing in the night with my wife's portrait in your lap? Meditating on what divinity? Mumbling which sacred verses? Hypocrite!"

He flung the framed photograph on the floor and stamped on it with his shoes, trampling the glass into bits. Then lifting up the print he tore it into pieces, flinging them on Bihari. Frightened by this violent frenzy Basanta broke into a renewed fit of sobbing. Choking with silent rage Bihari pointed to the door and ordered, "Get out!"

Mahendra swept out of the house like a tempest.

36

Watching the landscape from the window of the deserted ladies' compartment as the train swept past cultivated fields and villages with their shady groves, Binodini felt a nostalgia for the peace and calm of the country life. Her imagination built for her a sheltered nest set in sylvan surroundings where in the company of her favourite books she would succeed in healing the bitter pain and burning of the wounds inflicted on her heart by her sojourn in the city. Gazing at the unending stretch of empty, greying summer fields tinged with the mellow light of the sunset, she felt she needed nothing, she merely wanted to close her eyes and sink all her memories in a similar golden light of peace, to rescue her little boat from the stormy and turbulent waves of life and paddle it silently to the bank and tie it under the still branches of a banyan tree brooding in the silence of the day's end. No, she wanted nothing else. Now and again the fragrance of mango blossom was wafted into the compartment, fanning her longing for the peace of her village home. "Just as well," she murmured to herself. "It is better so. I am sick of myself and long only to forget myself in a deep slumber. I'll be a village girl once more and live in peace and find comfort in my duties at home and in the village."

Having lulled her troubled heart with hopes of peace, Binodini entered her cottage. But alas, where was the peace! There was only loneliness and poverty. Everything in the cottage was shabby and tattered, dirty and decrepit. The damp and foul odour of the closed room almost choked her. What little furniture was there had crumbled to pieces under the combined onslaught of white ants, rats and the dust. It was dusk when Binodini entered the cottage, and the room was wrapped in complete darkness. Somehow she managed to light an earthen lamp which immediately filled the air with the rancid smoke of mustard oil. Its dull, morose light only added to the squalor of the room. What she had not minded previously now seemed to her unbearable. Her rebellious spirit revolted at the sight and burst into a violent protest: "Not for a minute can I survive here." A couple of her old books and magazines covered with dust lay in a niche in the wall. She had not the heart to touch them. Outside the wind had stopped and the only sounds in the mango grove were the ceaseless chirping of the crickets and the droning of the mosquitoes.

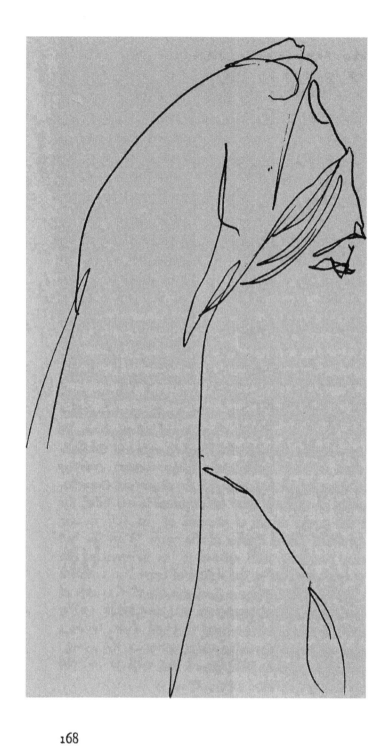

An aged female relative on the husband's side who used to stay with and look after Binodini had gone to visit her daughter who lived with her husband some distance away. Binodini went to call on the neighbors who gaped at her with mouths open. "Fancy! Who would have thought it! Look at her, how fair and smart, just like a memsaheb!" They looked at each other and exchanged meaningful glances, as though the evidence fully confirmed the rumours.

At every step Binodini realised more and more how far away she had drifted from the village life. She was virtually an exile in her own cottage, unable to relax in peace anywhere.

The ancient postman was known to her since childhood. The next morning on her way to the village tank for her bath she saw him walking on the road with the post bag on his shoulder. Unable to restrain her eagerness she threw down the bath towel and ran up to the postman inquiring, "Panchuda, is there a letter for me?"

"No," replied the old man.

"There may be one," said Binodini anxiously. "Please let me see."

She took the half a dozen letters in her hand and looked at the addresses carefully. None was for her. Dejected and in low spirits, when she reached the bathing steps of the tank, the neighbour-girls winked and smiled mischievously.

"Good Lord, Bindi!" exclaimed one of them, "why this anxiety for a letter?"

"Well, well," said a more impudent one, "how many of us are so lucky as to get a letter by post? Our husbands, brothers, brothers-in-law also work in towns but does the postman ever take pity on us?"

And so the taunts became more obvious and the glances more mocking. Binodini had begged Bihari to write to her at least twice a week, if not every day. There was little likelihood of a letter arriving that morning but so keen was her longing for the letter that she clung even to the remotest possibility. It seemed to her as though an age had passed since she left Calcutta.

Scandalous rumours about her and Mahendra had preceded her arrival in the village. How widespread and malicious they were was soon brought home to her by the grace of friends and foes. Where was the peace? She tried to keep away from the neighbours which only angered them the more. They resented being denied the luxury of mocking and railing at a fallen sister.

It is useless to try to hide oneself in a small village, impossible to find a dark nook where one can heal one's wounds in solitude. Prying eyes peep out of everywhere to spy on the sore spots. Writhing like a live fish in a basket, the more Binodini struggled the more she hurt herself. Even the right to relish the full savour of pain was denied to her here.

On the second day, after the hour of postal delivery was past, she shut herself in the room and wrote:

"Do not be afraid, Thakurpo, I am not going to inflict a love letter on you. You are my tribune and I bow down to you. You have chastised me severely for the sin I committed and I am carrying out your sentence against me. My only regret is that you cannot see for yourself how stern is the sentence. Could you see it you would be moved to pity. Of that chance too I am deprived. However, I shall bear it all, thinking of you, bowing down to you. But tell me, my lord, is not a prisoner entitled to his rations at least?—not delicacies but the barest minimum to keep him alive! A two-line letter from you is all the food I ask for. If I am denied it, my sentence will be, not exile but death. Please do not, O judge, put me to too cruel a test. There was no end of pride in my sinful heart. I could not imagine even in a dream that one day I would have to humble myself so abjectly before any one. You have won and I won't rebel. But please have pity on me and help me to survive. Give me just a little food to enable me to stand the rigour of this exile in the wilderness. Nothing then can stand in the way of my carrying out your sentence loyally. This is the only little indication I am conveying to you of my suffering. What else is in my mind I have vowed not to inflict on you, even though my heart is bursting to vent itself. But I shall keep my vow. Yours Binod Bouthan."

She posted the letter. The neighbours were scandalised. The shameless wench! Shutting herself up in her cottage and writing letters and accosting the postman! Does a few days' stay in Calcutta kill all shame and sense of right and wrong?

There was no letter the next day either. Binodini spent the day in a state of stupefaction, her face set hard. Lacerated by the scourge of insult and derision from every side, from within and without, the destructive forces lying dormant in the dark depths of her subconscious were whipped up into a demoniac fury, savage and cruel. Terrified, Binodini shut herself up in the room.

She had nothing of Bihari with her, no concete souvenir, no photograph, not even a scribbled note. She groped in the emptiness around her for some symbol, some keepsake which she could clasp against her heart, whose warmth might force tears into her eyes, something which would help to thaw the frozen bitterness of the heart and put out with the flood of tears the rising flame of rebellion within her, so that she could carry out with love and devotion the stern discipline which Bihari had imposed on her. But like the cloudless midday sky her heart continued to burn unabated, with not a trace of a tear in the eyes.

She had heard that the power of single-minded meditation was such that any one invoked through it could not but come. So she closed her eyes and folding her palms in prayer began to call upon Bihari. "My life is empty, my heart is empty, all around me is nothing but emptiness—come into this emptiness, come even though for a minute only, come you must, I will not give you up."

Repeating these words with all the fervour of concentrated devotion, Binodini felt stronger. This must be the strength of love, she felt, the strength of meditation which could never be in vain. It was no use merely wanting, merely pouring out one's heart's blood to feed the roots of despair. It merely exhausted the heart. But if one gathered one's thoughts in a single-minded discipline of meditation and willed desire, one felt a fresh accession of strength. The desire concentrated becomes a mighty power in itself which bypassing everything else in the world singles out its object and draws it steadily and surely towards itself.

Lost in her meditation Binodini did not notice that the evening had fallen and the room remained unlighted in the darkness. Her mind and senses were filled with a deeper awareness in which were drowned as in a flood all thoughts of the village, the society, the world outside. Suddenly there was a knock at the door. Startled, Binodini hurriedly rose from the floor and rushed towards the door and threw it open, exclaiming in the ecstasy of her newborn faith, "Ah, you have come!" She was supremely confident that only one person in the whole wide world could have come to the door at that moment.

"Here I am, Binod," said Mahendra.

"Get out! Begone!" shouted Binodini overcome with disappointment and stung into contempt.

Mahendra was stunned.

"I say, Bindi, if your granny-in-law turns up tomorrow . . . ." the words froze on the lips of the matronly neighbour who had just walked up to the door. "Oh dear!" she exclaimed in shocked surprise and pulling the sari over her face fled precipitately.

37

The scandalised village was in an uproar. The elders gathered in the temple courtyard and said, "This is intolerable. We might wink at what happened in Calcutta, but this brazen audacity—writing letter after letter to Mahendra and bringing him right here—this scandalous shamelessness is the limit. We can't harbour such a harlot in our midst."

Binodini was sure that there would be a letter from Bihari the next morning. But none came. "What is Bihari's claim on me?" she asked herself. "What made me listen to him? Why need I have given him to understand that I should carry out his will loyally and abjectly? His only interest in me is to use me for the benefit of his beloved Asha. I have no rights of my own, no claim—not even to a two-line scribble. So insignificant I am, so contemptible!" Fierce flames of jealousy leapt within her breast. "I might have put up with this hell for anyone else's sake—but certainly not for Asha. What a fool I was to have accepted this abject poverty, this exile in the wilderness, this shame and ignominy, this unmitigated frustration—all this to oblige Asha! Why didn't I go through with my deadly designs? What a fool I was, what an imbecile! Why did I love Bihari?"

As she sat brooding in her room, hard and severe like a wooden image, her granny-in-law entered, having returned from her visit to her son-in-law's house.

"What is this I hear, you shameless hussy?" She barked.

"The truth," replied Binodini.

"Why need you have dragged this scandal into our midst?" shrieked the old woman. "Why did you have to come here at all?"

Deeply mortified Binodini remained silent. Granny went on, "Look here, child, you can't stay on here any longer. As ill luck would have it, I lost almost every one of my own, nevertheless I managed to survive all calamities. But this sort of disgrace—no, I can never put up with it. You will please clear out immediately."

"Yes, I'll go just now," said Binodini.

Just then Mahendra arrived on the scene, unwashed, unkempt, his eyes blood-shot for lack of sleep, his face parched and haggard for lack of food. He had originally determined to make one more attempt to take Binodini away while it was still half light at dawn, but recalling the rebuff he had had from her the previous day he was afflicted with doubts and hesitated. As the morning advanced and the time of the train's departure drew near, he at last emerged from the station waiting-room and expelling all doubts and fears from his mind got into a carriage and drove right up to the door of Binodini's cottage. Having made up his mind he was filled with a wild joy that comes when one has taken a desperate decision to cast all scruples to the wind and defy the world. An upsurge of reckless courage wiped away all his depression and doubts and the curious villagers gaping at him from the wayside seemed to his frenzied eyes like so many lifeless figures of clay.

Without looking this side or that, Mahendra strode right up to Binodini and said, "Binod, I am not such a cad as to leave you here to face alone the brunt of public calumny. You must now come away with me. Afterwards if you wish to discard me, you may do so. I shan't in the least stand in your way. I swear by you that your wish, whatever it be, shall be carried out. If you're kind to me, life will be worth living. If you're not, I shall efface myself from your life. I've been guilty of many faithless acts but today for once please trust me. We stand on the edge of a precipice and have no time for subterfuges."

"You may take me with you," replied Binodini very simply and calmly. "Have you brought a carriage?"

"I have."

The old Granny came out of her room and addressing Mahendra said, "Although you do not know me, Mahendra, you are no stranger to me. Your mother Rajlakshmi is from our village and used to call me Auntie. May I ask you what you mean by this behavior? You have a wife and mother at home and yet you go about acting in this shameless manner. How will you show your face in decent society?"

Mahendra felt suddenly deflated. It struck him for the first time that he had a mother and a wife and that there was such a thing as decent society. There was a time when it would have seemed unthinkable that he would one day have to listen to such words at the door of an unknown cottage of a far-away village, that he would add to his biography the lurid episode of seducing and absconding with a young, respectable widow in broad daylight and under the very eyes of the village. And yet all this had happened, despite his wife, his mother and the claims of decent society!

Seeing Mahendra dumb and rooted to the ground, the old lady hissed, "If you must go, then go immediately. Don't linger near my door but clear out—at once."

She shut the door in his face and bolted it from inside. Binodini got into the carriage as she was, unwashed, without changing her dress, empty-handed and on an empty stomach. As Mahendra was about to follow her she said, "No. The station is not far off. Please follow on foot."

"But that will merely expose me unnecessarily to the village stares," protested Mahendra.

"So you do have a little bit of shame left?"

She closed the carriage door and ordered the driver, "To the station."

"Won't the Babu come in?" asked the driver.

Mahendra hesitated but lacked the courage to get in. The carriage drove away. Avoiding the main road Mahendra took a detour through the fields and trudged towards the station, his head bent.

The young wives of the village had by then had their bath and morning meal. A few matrons could still be seen with towel and oil jar in hand, winding their way to the shady, secluded bathing-stairs of the village tank, fringed with mango trees in blossom.

38

Rajlakshmi was so distracted with panic at Mahendra's sudden departure that she could neither eat nor sleep. While Sadhucharan was scouring all possible and impossible spots in his search, Mahendra returned to Calcutta with Binodini and leaving her in a rented flat in Pataldanga came home at night. As he entered his mother's room he noticed that except for the dim light of a lantern from behind a screen the room was in darkness. Rajlakshmi lay in bed like a sick person and Asha sat by her feet gently rubbing them. After a long time the daughter-in-law had earned the privilege of sitting by her mother-in-law's feet.

Startled at Mahendra's entry Asha rose and left the room. Mahendra mustered all his courage and said, "I find it difficult to study at home, mother, and have therefore rented quarters near the College where I propose to stay."

"Sit down, Mahin," said Rajlakshmi pointing at one end of the bed.

Mahendra sat down feeling embarrassed. Rajlakshmi continued, "You may stay where you like, Mahin, but please don't put Bouma on the rack."

Mahendra was silent. Rajlakshmi went on, "It is my misfortune that I failed to recognise the worth of so admirable a daughter-in-law"—her voice grew hoarse with feeling—"but how could you, having known and loved her so well, expose her in the end to such sorrow?"

Rajlakshmi began to cry, unable to control her tears. Mahendra wished he could get up and run away but found it difficult to break the ordeal so abruptly. He remained silent and motionless, perched on an edge of his mother's bed. After a long pause Rajlakshmi asked, "You're staying the night at home?"

"No," mumbled Mahendra.

"When will you go?"

"Just now."

"Just now?" repeated Rajlakshmi trying painfully to sit up in the bed. "Won't you even talk to your wife for a while?"

Mahendra remained dumb. Rajlakshmi went on, "Can't you even understand what hell she has gone through during these last few days? Shameless boy, your callousness is breaking my heart!" She sank back on her pillow like a fallen branch from a tree.

Mahendra came out of the room and slowly and noiselessly crept up the steps to his bedroom, trying to avoid Asha. As soon as he reached upstairs he saw Asha lying on the floor in the covered terrace facing his room. She had not heard his footsteps and seeing him suddenly face to face hurriedly sat up pulling her sari around her. Had Mahendra called out, "Chuni" she would have flung herself at his feet as though she were the culprit begging forgiveness and, taking all his blame on her own shoulders, would have sobbed her heart out. But Mahendra failed to utter the dear name. He would have liked to, but the more he struggled the more painful became the utterance. It seemed to him that any loving gesture on his part would be a cruel mockery of Asha. What comfort could he give her with sweet, empty words when with his own hands he had just banged the door shutting out any possibility of his renouncing Binodini!

Asha sat petrified with shame and embarrassment. She could neither stand nor go away nor make any movement whatsoever. Mahendra said not a word and began to pace slowly up and down the terrace. The moon had not yet risen. In one corner of the terrace was a flower-tub with tuberoses, a couple of stalks in flower. In the moonless sky above shone the Great Bear and the Orion, the same constellations which had so often been mute witnesses of their love's drama enacted in the seclusion of the terrace on many an evening. Tonight too they were on watch as silently as before.

Mahendra wished he could wipe off with the black sponge of the overhanging darkness the tempestuous changes of the last few days and could recover the ease and simplicity of the old days and sit once again beside Asha on a mat spread on the open terrace. No questions to be asked, no explanations offered, the same old trustfulness, love and joy! But alas! there was no way left for a return to the old; he had forfeited his right to share the mat with Asha. Until now his relationship with Binodini had had a certain flexibility of freedom— the frenzied joy of love was there without its irrevocable bondage. But now having with his own hands uprooted Binodini from her place in society, there was nowhere she could go, no place left in society to which she could return. He was now her only shelter. Whether he liked it or not, he must now bear her full burden. He squirmed within himself as a realisation of what he was in for dawned on him. This little domestic nest on the terrace, the peace of wedded intimacy in the calm seclusion of the night—all this suddenly seemed very sweet to him. But this ready bliss which was his and his alone by right had now receded hopelessly beyond his reach. Henceforth there would be no respite for him from the lifelong burden which he had imposed on his own shoulders.

Heaving a deep sigh he glanced at Asha. She sat unmoving, her heart congealed with frozen tears, the darkness of the night wrapped round her shame and sorrow, like the loose end of a mother's sari over her child. Breaking his restless parade Mahendra suddenly came and stood before Asha as though to say something. All the blood in her veins seemed to rush up to her head, thumping against her ears. She closed her eyes, but Mahendra stood there stupefied, not knowing what it was he had meant to say. What indeed was there to say! And yet he could not turn away without saying something. He mumbled, "Where are the keys?"

The bunch of keys was under the bed mattress. Asha got up and went inside the room, Mahendra following her. Taking the keys Asha placed them on the bed: Mahendra picked them up and began to try them one by one on the almirah containing his clothes. Unable to contain herself any longer Asha whispered softly, "That particular key was not with me."

With whom it was she could not bring herself to say, but Mahendra understood. Asha hurriedly left the room afraid of breaking down before Mahendra and hid herself in the shadow of the wall at a far end of the terrace, her face towards the wall. Controlling with all her might the swelling tide of sobbing she stood there silently shedding tears. But not for long, for she suddenly remembered that it was time for Mahendra's dinner. She hurried downstairs.

"Where's Mahin, Bouma?" asked Rajlakshmi on seeing her.

"Upstairs."

"Then why have you come down?"

"His dinner . . . ."

"I'll see to it, Bouma. Please go and wash and change. Put on the new Dacca sari and come down. I'll do your hair."

It was impossible to disregard the loving injunction of her mother-in-law, though the idea of dressing up at this moment filled her with shame. Like Bhishma * welcoming death by offering his person to the shower of arrows, Asha submitted patiently to the elaborate ordeal of dressing up prescribed by Rajlakshmi.

Having dressed, Asha slowly and silently went upstairs and peeped into the terrace. Mahendra was not there. She crept up to the door of the room. Mahendra was not there either. The dinner was laid, untouched.

Having forced open the door of the almirah Mahendra had picked up a few necessary clothes and medical books and left the house.

The following day was Ekadashi. Rajlakshmi lay in bed, sick and in pain; outside the clouds had gathered presaging a

* The venerable hero of *Mahabharata*.

thunderstorm. Asha tiptoed into the room and gently seating herself at the foot of Rajlakshmi's bed and rubbing her feet said, "Mother, I've brought you milk and fruit.* Please get up and eat."

Touched by this unaccustomed solicitude on the part of her grief-stricken daughter-in-law, Rajlakshmi's dry eyes overflowed with tears. She sat up in bed and drawing Asha into her arms kissed her tear-soaked cheeks.

"What is Mahin doing, Bouma?" she asked.

"He's gone," murmured Asha overcome with shame.

"When did he leave? I didn't know he had left."

"Last night," replied Asha her head bent low.

All her upsurge of tenderness suddenly froze in Rajlakshmi at these words. Her hands caressing Asha stiffened as though emptied of all feeling. Asha sensed the dumb censure and slowly left the room her head sunk on her breast.

39

When on the first day of their arrival in Calcutta Mahendra left Binodini in his Pataldanga flat and went home to fetch his clothes and books, she sat alone and brooded on her fate, unmindful of the ceaseless din and bustle of the city life outside. Her life had all along been narrowly circumscribed, but even then there was enough room for her to turn on the other side when one side became sore. But now even the bare elbow-room had shrunk further. The little boat in which she was floating down the current was so precariously balanced that the slightest jolt might upset it, flinging her into the water. She must therefore be very alert and steady at the helm, not taking any risks. What woman's heart would not tremble at this prospect? Where was left the scope for the free play of love, the necessary latitude which a woman

* Invalids are allowed to take milk and fruit on Ekadashi.

must have to be able to retain her hold on a man's heart? She had no alternative now but the dreary prospect of a cooped-up existence with Mahendra, she staring at him and he at her, with this difference that while he could escape, she could not.

The more Binodini realised the helplessness of her position, the more she seemed to recover her strength of mind. She must find a way out. It was impossible to continue like this.

The defences of her self-possession had given way the day she had confessed her love to Bihari. The proffered kiss unclaimed by Bihari still weighed heavily on her, she could not unburden herself of it, like a gift meant for the gods which cannot be offered to anyone else on earth. Binodini was by nature spirited and hopeful and never gave up the helm under any circumstances. She kept on repeating to herself, "Bihari must—he shall—accept my offering!"

Her desperate need of love as well as of protection drew her towards Bihari who seemed her only refuge. She knew Mahendra only too well. He was weak and unreliable, with no backbone. He would run after you if you eluded him but would run away from you if you tried to hold him. The shoulder that a woman can lean on must be strong, reliable and firm. Such a shoulder was Bihari's. In no circumstances could Binodini do without Bihari.

On the day she left the village she had made Mahendra go to the post office adjoining the railway station and leave definite instructions for her letters to be redirected to their new Calcutta address. She refused to believe that Bihari would totally ignore her letters and said to herself, "I shall wait for his reply for seven days. After that we shall see."

Having said that she opened the window of her unlighted room and absent-mindedly began to look out on the gas-lit street. At this very moment of the twilight Bihari must be somewhere in the city. She has only to cross a few streets to reach the door of his house, then pass the little courtyard with its water-tap, up the stairs and into the familiar room, neat, tidy, well-lighted and quiet, where Bihari is sitting in his chair, alone in the peaceful silence of the evening! Maybe, the little Brahmin boy would also be there with his pretty, fair and round face and wide, innocent eyes, turning over the pages of a picture-book. Lingering on the scene with her mind's eye her limbs ached with the ecstasy of tenderness. Hugging the idea that she could go there straightaway if she wanted to, she began to play with it. In the old days she would have set out on her quest, but now there were so many things to consider. It was no longer a question of merely satisfying the longing. The object too had to be achieved. "Let me see what reply he sends," she said to herself. "Then I shall decide what path to take." She did not dare any longer to inflict herself on Bihari without first making sure how the ground lay.

Thus she sat thinking until it was nearly ten at night when Mahendra slowly climbed the stairs. He had stood the strain and sleeplessness of the last few days under the stimulus of excited nerves. Having achieved his object and brought back Binodini he was overcome by weariness and fatigue and had no strength left to carry on his fight against himself and society. The heavy load of future responsibilities seemed to be already crushing his back.

He stood outside the closed door too ashamed to knock. The frenzy which had enabled him to defy the whole world seemed to have ebbed out of him and he shrank before the casual looks of the unknown passers-by on the road.

The newly engaged servant having fallen asleep inside the flat, it took a lot of knocking and shouting before he woke up and opened the door. Mahendra's heart sank as he stepped into the dark corridor of the unfamiliar flat. The spoilt darling of his mother, he had all his life been used to an elaborate apparatus of luxury at home, to expensive furniture and fans and what not. Their absence in the new flat seemed even more dismal in the dim light. He would now have to refurnish the flat and bear the full burden of running a household. He had never had to look after his own or any one else's comfort, but from now on he would have to attend to all the harassing details of a new and improvised household. The shabby kerosene lamp on the landing giving out more smoke than light would have to be replaced by a decent one; the floor of the portico leading to the stairs was in a mess due to the overflow of water from the water-tap and needed to be re-cemented for which a mason would have to be called; the shoemaker had not yet vacated the two rooms opening on the road—it would be necessary to make an issue of it with the landlord. The idea that all this music he would have to face by himself nearly drove him to the end of his tether.

He paused on the landing to recover himself and tried to whip up the frenzy of his infatuation for Binodini. He recalled that this was the day of his supreme joy, that the object of his desire for which he had defied the whole world had been attained, that Binodini was now his, nothing standing between him and her. But the very lack of barrier was turning into a barrier, his own self had become his worst obstacle.

Binodini had noticed Mahendra's arrival from her window. Shaking off her reverie she got up and lighting a lamp sat down beside it, her head bent over a piece of sewing in her lap—like taking shelter behind a screen. Mahendra entered the room and said, "I am afraid, Binod, you must be greatly inconvenienced here."

"Not a bit," replied Binodini busy with her sewing.

"I'll get all the necessary furniture and utensils in a couple of days. Till then you'll have to put up with a little discomfort."

"Nonsense. You'll do nothing of the sort. There is enough and more—much that is superfluous already."

"Is this unfortunate fellow also a part of a superfluous?"

"You could do with a little less conceit. A bit of modesty won't do you harm."

The sight of Binodini self-possessed and bent over her work in the lonely lighted room immediately revived the ardour of his desire. Had they been in the old house he would have immediately flung himself at her feet but an awareness of the new setting, of the fact that Binodini was at his mercy held him back. It would be cowardly to take advantage of her helplessness.

"Why have you brought your clothes and books here?" asked Binodini.

"Because they are needed by me—they're not part of the superfluity."

"I know that. But why bring them here?"

"You're right," said Mahendra. "These prosaic necessaries are out of place here. Throw them out of the window, Binod. Here they are. I won't say a word—provided you don't throw me also out with them."

Taking advantage of the excuse he moved nearer to Binodini and placed the handbag containing books at her feet.

"Thakurpo, you can't stay here," said Binodini gravely, without raising her face from the sewing.

Nonplussed at this sudden rebuff to his excited anticipations, Mahendra broke out piteously, "Why, Binod, why are you thrusting me away? Is this my return for having sacrificed everything on your account?"

"I will not let you sacrifice everything on my account," said Binodini.

"That is no longer in your hands," cried Mahendra. "My entire world has crashed into bits around me. Binod! Binod. . . ."

He flung himself on the ground and clasping her feet violently began kissing them again and again.

Shaking herself free Binodini stood up and said sternly, "Mahendra, have you forgotten your pledge?"

Mahendra pulled himself together with a supreme effort and said, "No, I remember it. I had sworn that whatever you desired would be done and that I would never stand in the way. I shall honour the pledge. Tell me what is your wish."

"Go and stay at home."

"Am I the only object of your aversion, Binod?" cried Mahendra. "If that was so, why did you ever draw me to yourself? Where was the need of your hunting down what was of no use to you? Tell me truly, was it I who threw myself at you or was it you who seduced me deliberately? Must I suffer being made a plaything for your amusement? However, I shall keep my word and go back and stay in the house where I have trampled on my own rightful place shattering it to bits."

Binodini resumed her seat on the floor and her silent sewing. Mahendra stared at her fixedly for some time and then burst out again, "You are cruel, Binod—heartless! It's my terrible misfortune that I am in love with you."

Binodini made a slip in sewing and holding the piece of cloth under the light began very meticulously to unpick the thread. Mahendra wished he could grab her stony heart in his iron fist and crush it to bits. He itched to use his physical strength to break her silent callousness, her unrelenting smugness and to make them grovel in the dust.

He left the room but almost immediately came back and asked, "If I don't stay here, who will look after you?"

"You don't have to worry about that," answered Binodini. "Pishima has sacked Khemi. She came to see me here and I have engaged her from today. We two women will lock ourselves in the house and will be well able to look after ourselves."

The more angry Mahendra became the more irresistibly desirable Binodini seemed to him. How he wished he could break this cold, invulnerable woman against his heart in a titanic embrace! Frightened by the violence of his own desire Mahendra fled out of the room.

Wandering aimlessly on the road Mahendra swore to himself that he would repay Binodini's indifference with indifference. That she should dare to spurn him with such blunt, categorical and silent disdain and at a time when he was her sole refuge, was a humiliation such as no man had ever suffered at the hands of a woman! His pride, broken and crushed, yet refused to die and kept on wriggling in the dust. "Am I indeed so very worthless?" he asked himself. "How dare she treat me like a worm when all she has is myself!"

While he was thus fretting he suddenly remembered Bihari. For a moment his blood stood still as though congealed. So it is Bihari on whom she is depending—I am a mere tool, a ladder for her feet to rest upon and to kick! No wonder she despises me. He suspected that she was in correspondence with Bihari and had received some sort of an assurance from him.

He turned his steps towards Bihari's house. The night was far spent when he reached the house and knocked at the door. After a prolonged knocking the door was opened by a servant who said, "The master is away."

Mahendra gave a start. "While I was wandering on the road like a fool," he said to himself, "Bihari must have been with Binodini, taking advantage of my absence. That's why she repulsed me and drove me out of the house callously at so late an hour in the night and I too like a kicked ass came trotting away!"

He asked the servant who was known to him for long, "Bhaju, when did the master leave?"

"About four or five days ago, Sir. He's gone on a trip to the west." *

Mahendra heaved a sigh of relief. There was then no danger and he might as well have a little sleep. He was too tired to walk any more. He went up to Bihari's room and stretching himself on a sofa fell asleep immediately.

* Bengalees refer to the whole of North India to the west of Bengal as the west.

Bihari had left Calcutta the very next day after Mahendra had suddenly invaded his house and caused a scene. Not knowing where to go he went westwards. He was afraid that his continued presence in Calcutta might provoke his old friend to more ugly scenes leaving a lifelong regret in their trail.

When Mahendra woke up the next morning it was eleven o'clock. As soon as he got up his eye fell on an envelope addressed to Bihari in Binodini's hand resting under a stone paper-weight on a teapoy in front of him. He snatched up the envelope and found that it had not been opened and was still awaiting Bihari's return. With trembling fingers he opened the letter and read. It was the letter which Binodini had sent from her village and to which she had received no reply.

Each word of the letter was like a sting into his flesh. From their childhood Mahendra had been used to overshadowing Bihari, himself monopolising the lion's share of others' affection and solicitude, while Bihari received only the stale leavings. And yet today Binodini was wooing this uncouth Bihari despite his indifference and had jilted Mahendra who was a suppliant for her favours. He too had received letters from Binodini but compared to these they were fakes, mere baits to hoodwink a fool. He recalled Binodini's anxiety to register her change of address at the village post office and understood the reason of it. She was still waiting with passionate eagerness for Bihari's reply.

The servant was well trained and even in his master's absence brought Mahendra tea and some refreshments from a nearby confectionery. Mahendra forgot to bathe. He kept on perusing Binodini's letter wincing under its fiery, impassioned words like the feet of a traveller skipping on hot sands. He swore never to see Binodini again but immediately realised that after waiting for a day or two more for Bihari's reply Binodini was sure to come over to Bihari's house and find out for herself the real reason for the letter remaining unanswered. The idea that having discovered the truth she would feel relieved was anathema to Mahendra.

He put the letter in his pocket and presented himself at the Pataldanga flat shortly before sunset. Seeing his wan and haggared look Binodini felt a twinge of pity and suspected that he had perhaps spent the night sleeplessly trudging the roads.

"Didn't you go home last night?" she asked.

"No," replied Mahendra.

"Then you haven't eaten the whole day!" exclaimed Binodini greatly upset. Solicitous as ever she got up immediately to improvise a meal when Mahendra said, "Please don't bother. I've had my food."

"Where?"

"At Bihari's."

For a moment Binodini went pale and dumb. Then pulling herself together she asked, "I hope Bihari Thakurpo is all right?"

"Yes, he's all right and has left for the west," replied Mahendra in a tone implying that Bihari had left that very day.

Once again her face was drained of colour, but she soon recovered herself and said, "I never saw such a restless person. I suppose he knows all about us! Is he very angry?"

"Why otherwise would a person go west in this terrible heat? Certainly not for enjoyment."

"Did he say anything about me?"

"What is there to say? Here is the letter!"

He handed the letter to her, his eyes riveted on her face. Binodini eagerly took the letter, only to find that the envelope was already open and was addressed to Bihari in her own hand. She took the letter out and saw that it was the one she had sent. She turned it this way and that but could discover no note from Bihari by way of acknowledgment. She remained silent for a while and then asked, "Have you read the letter?" Frightened by the expression on her face, Mahendra glibly lied, "No."

Binodini tore the letter to pieces and tore each piece into tiny bits and threw them outside the window.

"I am going home," said Mahendra.

Binodini did not reply.

"I shall do as you have wished," went on Mahendra. "I shall stay at home for the next seven days and shall drop in here once every day on my way to the college to see that Khemi has no difficulty in running the house. I won't inflict myself on you and will spare you the inconvenience of seeing me."

Binodini made no reply and continued to gaze outside the window at the dark sky. It was doubtful if she heard what Mahendra said. Picking up his things Mahendra left the flat. Binodini sat for a long time rooted to her seat, motionless. Then as if to restore her own sensibility she tore open her blouse and began to beat herself on the breast. Hearing the sounds Khemi rushed into the room crying, "What *are* you doing, Bou-thakrun?"

"Get out of here!" thundered Binodini as she sprang up and shoved Khemi out of the room. Then banging the door and bolting it she flung herself on the floor and began to roll on the ground with clenched hands, moaning piteously like an animal mortally wounded. Thus having battered and wearied herself out she lay on the floor as in a faint the whole night under the open window.

Early in the morning as the first rays of the sun fell into the room she was suddenly struck by a doubt that perhaps Bihari had not left Calcutta at all and that Mahendra had lied to her to put her off. Immediately she called Khemi and said, "Please Khemi, go at once to Bihari Thakurpo's house and find out if all is well there."

Khemi returned after about an hour and reported, "The whole house is locked, all the windows closed. When I knocked at the door a servant shouted from inside that the master was not at home and had gone on a trip to the west."

There was no room for further doubt in Binodini's mind.

40

Rajlakshmi was very annoyed with Asha on hearing the news that Mahendra had left the house on the very night of his return. She suspected that Asha's reproaches had driven him out. She asked Asha, "Why did Mahendra go away last night?"

"I don't know, mother," replied Asha hanging down her head.

This sounded like peevishness to Rajlakshmi and only irritated her the more.

"Who would know if you don't?" she asked irritably. "Did you say anything to him?"

"No."

This was hard to believe for Rajlakshmi.

"What time did Mahin leave last night?" she asked.

"I don't know," replied Asha shrinking with fear.

"You know nothing, do you?" flared up Rajlakshmi. "An innocent babe indeed! Stuff and nonsense!"

Without mincing matters she made it bitterly plain to Asha that it was the fault of her nature and her foolish ways that Mahendra had left home. Asha listened to the tirade with bowed head and then went and cried in her room. "I don't know," she said to herself, "why my husband once loved me. Nor do I know how to win back his love." It is easy to please a lover since the heart itself shows the way, but how to win back the heart of a lost lover was an art of which Asha knew nothing. Moreover, how could she make the abominably shameful attempt to coax caresses from one who was in love with another?

The family astrologer and his sister had come in the evening, at Rajlakshmi's invitation, to avert the evil influences working against her son's domestic life. Rajlakshmi requested the astrologer to see her daughter-in-law's horoscope and hand and sent for Asha who came down, feeling painfully embarrassed at the idea of her private tragedy being discussed with strangers. As she reluctantly put out her hand for the astrologer to see, there was a sound of stealthy footsteps on the unlighted veranda outside Rajlakshmi's room as though some one was trying to pass unnoticed. Rajlakshmi called out, "Who's there?" At first there was no response but on her repeating the cry, Mahendra entered the room without uttering a word.

How could Asha rejoice at Mahendra's return when the shame of Mahendra's abjectness, the sight of him creeping stealthily like a thief in his own house, filled her with pity! The presence of the astrologer and his sister only aggravated the shame whose pain was stronger than the pain of her sorrow.

"Bouma dear," said Rajlakshmi, "please ask Parvati to bring up Mahendra's dinner."

"I'll fetch it myself, mother," replied Asha.

She was anxious to spare Mahendra the shame of facing the inquisitive looks of the servants.

Mahendra fumed with speechless rage at the sight of the astrologer and his sister in his mother's room. It was intolerable that his wife and mother should conspire shamelessly with ignorant and illiterate charlatans and resort to hocus-pocus to influence him. So when the astrologer's sister addressed him in a voice dripping with honey, "How are you, my son?" he could stand it no longer and without bothering to acknowledge the polite query merely said to his mother, "I'm going upstairs."

The mother, fondly imagining that her son was looking for an opportunity of intimate chat with his wife, was greatly pleased and readily agreed. She rushed into the kitchen and said to Asha, "Please go upstairs immediately—Mahendra wants something."

Asha hurried upstairs, her heart thumping with nervous anxiety. She understood from her mother-in-law's words that Mahendra had sent for her but when she reached the door of her room she could not bring herself to make a sudden entry. She paused in the shadow of the door and began to watch Mahendra.

He was reclining on the divan, his head propped up with a bolster, gazing vacantly at the wooden beams of the ceiling—the same Mahendra, in the same setting, and yet how different! This little room had once been turned by him into a love's paradise—today his presence seemed a desecration of that same room hallowed with happy memories. He had no right to lie in that divan with his heart loaded and scarred with misery and wrath. If lying there he was not haunted by those endless, unutterable whisperings of love on nights dark and heavy with passion, in afternoons still and languid, on rainy days inducing wild, vagabond desires, on spring evenings tremulous with the caress of the south wind—then what business had he to mock the sanctity of this little room of Asha's? There were plenty of other rooms for him in the house.

The more Asha watched Mahendra from where she stood screened by darkness, the more aware she became that he had just come from Binodini, that her touch still clung to his limbs, her image to his eyes, her voice to his ear, her desire to his heart, obsessing it. How could Asha yield her devotion to this Mahendra, how was she to say to him, "Come into my heart that has known no thoughts but yours, come and rest your feet on the hundred-petal lotus of my love, white, pure and undefiled!" The precepts of her aunt, the legends of the *Puranas*, the injunctions of the *Shastras*—no, she could no longer believe in them, she could no longer worship as a god the husband who had degraded the purity of married life.

She would now renounce the god she had worshipped so ardently and would consign its image to the turbid waters of

Binodini's dark passion as Hindu devotees consign the image of goddess Durga to the river. From the depth of her despair rose the trumpet-wail of renunciation, filling the dark, love-sick night, resounding in her ears, in her breast, in her head, in every limb and vein of her body, its echoes spreading from her little room on the terrace to the stars in the heavens above.

Binodini's Mahendra seemed a stranger to Asha—worse than a stranger. The sight of no other stranger could have filled her with such shame. She found it impossible to enter the room.

Gazing absently at the ceiling, Mahendra's eye strayed to the wall facing him. Following his gaze Asha noticed her own photograph on the wall hanging beside Mahendra's. She wished she could cover it up with a fold of her sari, wished she could snatch it away and tear it to bits. She was angry with herself for having failed to notice it before and for not having removed it from the wall—its very familiarity had blinded her to its incongruity. It seemed to her as if Mahendra were secretly laughing at her portrait, as if even the image of Binodini seated on the pedestal of his heart had raised its eyebrows in a mocking smile.

At last Mahendra shifted his harassed gaze from the photograph. Asha had of late taken seriously to reading and study to improve her mind and used to sit down at her task every evening, after finishing her household duties and attendance on her mother-in-law, and would continue till late in the night. Her books and notes were piled high in one corner of the room. Suddenly Mahendra stretched his listless hand and picking up one note-book began to turn over its pages. Asha felt like screaming and tearing the note-book out of his hand. The idea that his callous, heartless eyes were mocking at her childish, unformed handwriting was so unbearable that she could not stand and watch the scene a minute longer. She turned back and hurried downstairs, not caring even to deaden the sound of her footsteps.

Mahendra's dinner was long ready. Rajlakshmi deferred

serving it for fear of interrupting the couple's *tête-à-tête*. Seeing Asha come downstairs she had the dinner served and sent for Mahendra. The moment he entered the dining room Asha rushed into the room upstairs and snatching her photograph from the wall tore it into bits and threw them over the wall of the terrace and then removed her note-books from the room.

The dinner over, Mahendra came back and sat in his room. Rajlakshmi looked around for Asha but could see her nowhere. Finally she found her in the kitchen on the ground floor boiling milk for her mother-in-law—which wasn't necessary, for the maid who usually prepared the milk was also sitting by and was in fact protesting against Asha's unexplained enthusiasm which she had every reason to resent since it deprived her of her daily share which she was in the habit of pilfering for herself, replacing it by an equal quantity of water.

"Why are you here, Bouma?" protested Rajlakshmi. "Go upstairs, please hurry."

Asha went upstairs and took shelter in Rajlakshmi's room which only added to her mother-in-law's irritation who grumbled to herself, "Instead of taking advantage of Mahendra's lucid intervals of absence from Binodini, the silly girl is merely showing off her own wounded pride and resentment and almost driving Mahendra out of the house again. In fact, but for her silliness Mahendra would never have fallen into Binodini's clutches. Men are always prone to go astray and it is the duty of the wives to keep them to the straight path by hook or by crook." She turned to Asha and rebuked her severely. "What sort of behaviour is this, Bouma?" she snapped. "You should thank your stars that your husband has come back home. Why then must you go about with a long face moping and hiding in corners."

Heavy with the shame of her own inadequacy Asha went upstairs and without allowing herself time to pause and hesitate burst into the room. It was past ten. Mahendra was standing beside the bed, idly dusting and shaking the mosquito-net, looking sore and chafing within himself. Did Binodini look upon him as such a bondsman that she could send him back to Asha without the slightest fear? If he really went back to Asha and resumed his marital obligations seriously, where would Binodini be? Where would she find shelter? Was he such a worm as to be incapable of even a desire to redeem himself? Was that her final estimate of him? Cheated of love, degraded in her esteem, he was exposed only to her contempt! Standing before the mosquito-net he took a solemn vow to avenge Binodini's impertinence and to pay her back in the same coin by making it up with Asha.

As soon as Asha entered the room Mahendra stopped fiddling with the mosquito-net, unnerved by the immediate problem of how to begin conversation with her. Forcing an affected smile he blurted out the first words that came into his head. "So you too have become studious like me! Where are the note-books I saw here a little while ago?"

The remark was not only inept and fatuous, it mortified Asha. That the ignorant girl was trying to educate herself was a secret which, she was convinced, would expose her to ridicule if divulged. It was a secret to be hidden from all mocking eyes and in particular from Mahendra's. So when Mahendra made this secret the subject of his very first jocular remark, she winced like a sensitive child under a lash. She made no reply and turning her head stood leaning on the edge of a teapoy.

Mahendra too had immediately realised that his words were ill-chosen and ill-timed but much as he racked his brain he could think of no speech that would fit the occasion. After the recent upheaval nothing would sound simple and natural, the heart too was dumb and could find no new expression. Maybe, it'll be easier in the intimate proximity of the bed, hoped Mahendra. Encouraged by this hope, he began once again to dust and shake the hanging folds of the mosquito-net, ostensibly to beat the mosquitoes off but in reality to gain time to rehearse what he should say and do, like an actor about to make his maiden appearance on the stage nervously lingering behind the wings and repeating his lines to himself again and again. Startled by a soft rustling sound he turned his head to find that Asha was no longer in the room.

41

The next morning Mahendra said to his mother, "Mother, I need a quiet room to myself for my studies and propose to shift to Kakima's old room."

The mother was delighted. "It means he'll now stay at home," she said to herself. "He has made up with Bouma. No wonder. How can he ignore for long such a gem of a girl and run after that wicked sorceress?" She promptly replied, "An excellent idea, Mahin" and taking out her bunch of keys opened the room and set about having it aired and cleaned. "Bou, where are you?" she shouted and after considerable search discovered Asha sitting disconsolately in a corner. "Please bring me a clean bedspread. And look here, there's no table in this room. Get one put in. This light is no good. Send a table-lamp from upstairs." And so the two ladies fussed around and turned Annapurna's old den into a chamber fit for the lord of the house. Not bothering to show the slightest appreciation for all this solicitude and ignoring the ladies altogether, Mahendra took his seat in the room, looking grave and sombre, and without wasting any time busied himself with his books and papers.

In the evening he sat down again at his table after dinner, giving no indication where he proposed to sleep, in the new room or in the old. Rajlakshmi took infinite pains over Asha's dress and toilette and having succeeded in making her look like a prim, decorative doll, said to her, "Bouma dear, go and ask Mahendra if his bed should be made upstairs."

Asha's feet refused to move on such an errand. She stood still, dumb, her head hung down. Rajlakshmi began to chide and harangue her sharply. At last Asha slowly and painfully advanced towards Mahendra's room and paused at the threshold, unable to cross it. Rajlakshmi who was watching from the other end of the veranda was infuriated by her shilly-shallying and made impatient signs to egg her on. Asha desperately dragged her feet into the room. Hearing the foot-steps Mahendra, without lifting his eyes from the book, said, "I'll be late tonight and since I'll have to work again at dawn I'll sleep here."

Asha dripped with shame. Did Mahendra imagine she had come to coax him to sleep upstairs?

As soon as she came out of the room Rajlakshmi asked in a vexed tone, "What happened?"

"He is busy and will sleep downstairs," replied Asha and fled into her own room which stank of her humiliation. There was no comfort for her anywhere. The whole world seemed like a burning noon-day desert.

A little later in the night there was a knock at her door.

"Please open the door, Bouma!"

Asha immediately opened the door and found her mother-in-law breathing painfully, having climbed the stairs in her asthmatic condition. As soon as the door was opened she came in and sank down on the bed and then recovering her breath said in a panting, broken voice? "Why must you lock yourself up in your room like this, Bou? Is this the time to indulge in tantrums? Has all this suffering failed to din some sense in your brain? Come, go downstairs."

"He wants to be left alone," said Asha gently.

"What if he did say so? Because he said something in anger doesn't mean that you must run away and make a mountain out of a mole-hill. It doesn't pay to be so peevish. Come, hurry downstairs."

Schooled by suffering, the mother-in-law made no bones

any longer about propriety or modesty. She was ready to use whatever means were available to keep Mahendra at home.

Her excited speech again brought about a relapse of pain-ful breathing, and only with a great effort of will did she get up. Without any attempt to protest or hold herself back Asha helped her downstairs to her room and putting her in bed began to arrange the pillows and bolsters to make her sit in comfort. Rajlakshmi said, "That's enough, Bouma. Get Sudho here to do the rest. Please go and don't delay."

This time Asha did not hesitate but went straight to Ma-hendra's room. He was reclining in his chair, absorbed in a reverie, his head propped up by the back-rest, his feet resting on the table where lay an open book. Startled by the foot-steps he turned his head—as though hoping to see her of whom he was dreaming. Seeing Asha he recovered himself and hurriedly removing his feet from the table picked up the open book and placed it in his lap.

Mahendra was surprised to see Asha enter so boldly when of late his mere presence filled her with embarrassment and if by chance they ran into each other she would turn and go away. Her sudden presence in his room at this time of the night, without any sign of nervous hesitation, was something incredible. Without raising his eyes from the book he could feel that she was determined to draw his attention and would not go back without it. She was standing in front, still and solemn. It was impossible to keep up the pretence of reading any longer. Mahendra was obliged to raise his head and look at her. She said—clearly and firmly,—"Mother's asthma has taken a turn for the worse. It would be good if you could see her."

"Where is she?"

"In her bedroom. She can't go to sleep."

"Come, let's go to her."

After many days of strained silence this little dialogue helped considerably to lighten Mahendra's heart. The dark shadow of silence had stood between the husband and wife like an impregnable fortress wall against which he had no adequate weapon. Suddenly Asha came and opened a tiny gate.

He went inside his mother's room while Asha waited outside. Seeing Mahendra in her room at this untimely hour, Rajlakshmi was frightened that he had perhaps again quarrelled with Asha and come to inform his mother that he was going away. She asked nervously, "Haven't you yet gone to bed, Mahin?"

"Has your asthma got worse, mother?" asked Mahendra ignoring her question.

The belated inquiry after so many days only served to revive the mother's wounded pride. She understood that he had come to see her only on receipt of an alarming report from Asha. The recoil of hurt love made her breathing more painful and it was with great difficulty she was able to utter, "It's nothing. Go and sleep now."

"No, let me examine you, mother. The symptoms can't be ignored."

Mahendra knew that his mother's heart was weak and was worried by the ominous signs in her face.

"It's no use examining me," said the mother. "The trouble is past cure."

"Let me at least get you a sleeping draught," persisted Mahin. "Tomorrow we shall see what can be done."

"I've had enough of drugs," went on Rajlakshmi, "they do me no good. Please go to bed, Mahin, it's very late."

"I'll go as soon as you feel better," replied Mahendra.

The piqued mother then called out to the daughter-in-law screened behind the door, "Bou, why did you have to drag Mahendra here only to harass him?" The effort made her breathing more painful.

Asha entered the room and said to Mahendra in a gentle but firm voice, "Please go to bed. I'll stay with mother."

Mahendra called Asha aside and whispered, "I am sending for a medicine. There'll be two doses in the phial. Give her one and if it fails to bring sleep, repeat the dose. If she has any discomfort in the night, don't hesitate to call me."

He went into his own room wondering at this new Asha in action. In this new Asha there was no fear or inferiority complex, no helplessness. She had discovered her own rightful place and stood her ground firmly without having to lean abjectly on Mahendra. He could ignore her as his wife but could not help respecting her as the daughter-in-law of the house.

Rajlakshmi was secretly pleased that Asha out of concern for her had called Mahendra to her bed-side. Outwardly she repeated, "I sent you to bed, Bouma. What made you go and drag Mahendra here?"

Asha made no reply but busied herself with fanning the mother-in-law, sitting behind her.

"Please go to bed, Bouma," said Rajlakshmi.

"He has told me to stay by your side," replied Asha gently.

She knew that Rajlakshmi would be pleased by the knowledge that Mahendra had expressly instructed her to nurse his mother.

42

When Rajlakshmi realized that Asha was unable to win back Mahendra on her own, she said to herself, "If my illness could keep him at home it would be a welcome illness." She began actually to fear recovery and would throw away her medicine when Asha was not looking.

Though Mahendra, unobservant as usual, failed to notice the symptoms, Asha could see that Rajlakshmi instead of recovering was steadily getting worse. She suspected that Mahendra was not paying adequate attention to his mother's treatment owing to his preoccupation with his own infatuation. She was disgusted at his callousness which his own mother's suffering failed to pierce. Was his degeneration so all-embracing as to bring about a general moral collapse?

One day when Rajlakshmi was in great pain she suddenly thought of Bihari. It seemed so long since he last visited the house. She asked Asha, "Where is Bihari these days, Bouma?" Asha understood that extreme pain had made her mother-in-law recall that it was always Bihari who used to attend to her and look after her whenever she fell ill. Unfortunately this one solid, reliable friend who had never failed them so far had also drifted away. Had he been near, mother would have been well looked after in this crisis. Bihari could never be callous like Mahendra. Asha heaved a deep sigh.

"Has Mahin quarrelled with Bihari?" asked Rajlakshmi. "It's very wrong of Mahin, Bouma. He has no other friend like Bihari, so devoted and well-wishing."

Her eyes filled with tears as she spoke.

One by one a host of memories assailed Asha—how Bihari had tried in many ways to warn her in time of her danger and how his efforts had merely resulted in alienating her from him. Recalling her blind folly Asha was filled with bitter self-reproaches. Why should not Providence punish an ungrateful ninny who spurning her only well-wisher hugged her one enemy to her heart? Would not the sigh which escaped Bihari as he left this house, broken-hearted, hang over the house like a curse?

After a long pause of anguished silence Rajlakshmi resumed, "Bouma, had Bihari been here he could have helped us and staved off the worst."

Asha remained silent, plunged in thought. Rajlakshmi went on, heaving a sigh. "If he heard of my illness, he would never keep away."

Asha understood that her mother-in-law was anxious that the news of her illness should reach Bihari. She had come to a stage where she felt lost without him.

Having put out the light in his room, Mahendra was standing silently by the moonlit window. He was sick of reading. The home had become bleak and cheerless. Once the intimacy of affection with near and dear ones is strained, they can neither be thrown off easily like strangers nor ever again accepted as one's own—the intimacy, cold and indissoluable, weighs oppressively on the heart day and night. Mahendra was reluctant to visit his mother who as soon as she saw him approach would gaze at him with such alarmed anxiety as to unnerve him. If Asha came near him by any chance it was as difficult to talk to her as it was painful to remain silent. It was becoming increasingly hard to carry on like this. He had sworn not to see Binodini for a week. Two days still remained before he could see her—two days so difficult to spend.

He heard a footstep behind and knew that Asha had entered the room, but pretending not to have heard it he remained motionless as he was. Asha saw through it but nevertheless came forward and standing behind him said, "I want only a word with you and will leave as soon as I have done."

"Why need you leave?" said Mahendra turning around. "Do sit down."

Ignoring his courtesy Asha continued to stand and said, "We should inform Bihari Thakurpo of mother's illness."

Bihari's name pricked Mahendra in the sorest spot but pulling himself together he asked, "Why is it necessary? Don't you trust my treatment?"

Full as she was of resentment at Mahendra's indifferent treatment of his mother's illness Asha could not help blurting out, "As a matter of fact, instead of improving, mother's condition is getting worse day by day."

Mahendra felt the sting behind this blunt statement. He had never before had such a bitter and contemptuous reproach from Asha. Taken aback and smarting under this blow to his self-esteem he said with a sneer, "I suppose I must learn medicine from you!"

. This unexpected sneer provoked Asha's accumulated resentment and encouraged by the darkness of the room she burst out, "Not medicine but solicitude for your mother you may well learn from me."

Mahendra was dumbfounded by this unexpected rebuke from Asha. Rancour made him pitiless and he retorted, "You know very well why your Bihari Thakurpo has been forbidden this house. I suppose you are missing him?"

Asha turned and left the room as though a whirlwind of shame had swept her out of it. Not shame for herself but for the man who could utter such baseless infamy, himself sunk neck-deep in dishonour. What atonement could cover up such a stinking pit of infamy?

As soon as Asha had left Mahendra realised the fullness of his discomfiture. He had never imagined it possible that Asha could one day treat him with such utter contempt. The pedestal on which he had once been enthroned had been shattered into fragments. He was suddenly assailed by a fear lest Asha's wounded love should be wholly transmuted into a contempt for him.

On the other hand, the mention of Bihari's name revived his apprehensions regarding Binodini and nearly drove him crazy with anxiety. Who knew, Bihari might have returned from his journey or Binodini might have discovered his whereabouts! Very likely the two had already met! Mahendra found that it was impossible to observe the vow of not seeing her for a week.

At night Rajlakshmi's breathing trouble grew worse and she herself sent for Mahendra. Uttering the words slowly and with difficulty she said, "Mahin, I should like to see Bihari very much. He hasn't been here for a long time."

Asha continued to fan her mother-in-law, her head bent low.

"He's not here," replied Mahendra. "He's gone west."

"My heart says he's here," insisted Rajlakshmi. "He's merely keeping away from us out of hurt pride. Please go and see him tomorrow—for my sake."

"All right, I'll go," promised Mahendra.

Every one seemed to ask for Bihari. Mahendra felt himself forsaken by the whole world.

43

Early the next morning Mahendra called at Bihari's house and found the servants lifting the furniture and household goods into bullock carts waiting outside. He asked Bhaju, "What's the matter?"

"We're moving into a villa the master has bought on the Ganges near Bali," replied Bhaju.

"Is Babu at home?" inquired Mahendra.

"He was here for a couple of days but has since left for the villa."

The news filled Mahendra with apprehensions. He had no doubt left in his mind that Binodini and Bihari had managed to meet in his absence and almost fancied he could see bullock carts outside Binodini's flat too. He was convinced that that was why Binodini had kept him away from her flat. What a simpleton he had been!

He jumped into his carriage and ordered the coachman to drive fast and kept on shouting at him all the way that the horse was not moving fast enough. Arriving at his destination in the lane he found no signs of preparation for a journey. A fear seized him that perhaps Binodini had already left. He began pounding on the door. As soon as the aged servant opened the door from inside he asked, "Is all well in the house?"

"Yes, sir, all is well," replied the servant.

He went upstairs and was informed that Binodini was in her bath. Entering the empty bedroom he flung himself on the bed slept in by Binodini and not yet made and clasping the coverlet to his heart and to his lips he began to mutter, "Cruel! Cruel!"

Having indulged his heart's longing in this fashion he got up and began impatiently to await Binodini's arrival. Pacing up and down the room he noticed a newspaper lying open on the divan. Absent-mindedly he picked it up and to while away the time began to read where his eye fell. Curiously enough the paragraph he thus began to read had Bihari's name in it. Immediately his full attention was focussed on it. A correspondent had written that, among other things, in order to provide free medical treatment and nursing for low-paid clerks, Bihari had acquired a villa on the river where at any one time about five indoor patients would be admitted.

No doubt Binodini had read the news and was itching to run away there. Besides this apprehension Mahendra was assailed by anxiety lest the news had raised Bihari even higher in her esteem. "Humbug!" he muttered to himself, venting his hatred of Bihari. "Mere show and claptrap! He always was like that since boyhood—showing off his philanthropy." Complimenting himself on his own candour and honesty he said, "I hate this pretence of generosity and self-sacrifice to impress and delude the rabble." Unfortunately, the people and in particular one person was not likely to appreciate the magnificence of his own supremely artless honesty. Mahendra began to feel that here was another victory scored by Bihari against him.

Hearing Binodini's footsteps he hurriedly folded the newspaper and sat down over it. Looking up he was amazed at the incredible transformation in Binodini's face as she entered fresh from her bath. It was as though she had passed through a penance of fire. She had grown perceptibly thinner and her pale face was aglow with a light from within.

Binodini had given up all hope of hearing from Bihari. She

feared that his silence was a mark of his utter contempt of
her and this thought was like a flame wrapped round her,
silently consuming her day by day. She could see no way out
of this suffering. It seemed to her that Bihari had gone away
only to make obvious his censure of her, and she was now
powerless to reach him. By nature active and energetic, she
felt suffocated for lack of anything to do, cooped up in the
small flat, her pent-up energy tearing her up from within.
The bleak prospect of having to spend her whole life in this
loveless, joyless hole, tucked in a narrow lane without the
stimulus of any useful activity made her rebellious nature rise
in revolt, dashing its head in vain against the inexorable wall
of fate.

She was filled with a bitter and boundless loathing for
Mahendra whose insensate folly had hemmed her in on all
sides, closing all avenues of escape. She realised the impossi-
bility of keeping him at arm's length for long in the narrow
confines of that small apartment. Each day he would creep
closer to her, inch by inch, driven by an animal desire until
there would flare up in the bottom of the dark and muddy
pit of their aberrant lives a daily battle, bitter and gruesome,
between fascination and revulsion. How was she to extricate
herself from the coils of the slimy, repulsive, ravenous reptile
with its lolling tongue which she herself had unearthed from
the subsoil of Mahendra's heart? Binodini shuddered as she
thought of her plight—her anguished heart, the dismal,
cooped-up existence, and the pressure day and night of Mahendra's unrelenting siege.

Where would this all end? When would she be free from
it?

The sight of Binodini's pale, emaciated face inflamed Mahendra's jealousy. Was he utterly impotent to pull her out by
force from her obsession with Bihari? As an eagle swoops
down on a lamb and lifting it up in its talons in the twin-
kling of an eye carries it away to its inaccessible and impregnable nest in the mountain, was there no such spot cloud-
wrapped and lost to the world where he too could carry away

his lovely and tender prey and keep her securely locked up in his arms, nestling against his heart? Fanned by jealousy the fire of his desire hissed and leapt fiercely. No, he could not let Binodini out of his sight any longer, he dare not allow her a moment's respite, day and night he must mount guard to keep Bihari's spectre away.

He had read in Sanskrit poetry that a beautiful woman looks more beautiful when she is lovelorn. Today he saw it with his own eyes as he looked at Binodini and the more he saw it the more his heart was churned in a seething turmoil of pain and pleasure.

Binodini remained silent for a while. Then she asked, "Have you had your tea?"

"What if I have!" cried Mahendra. "You might still make me a cup with your own hands and not be stingy about it! —'Come, fill the cup,'" he quoted facetiously.

"Do you know where Bihari Thakurpo is now?" asked Binodini, snubbing his ebullience with perhaps deliberate harshness.

"But he's not in Calcutta," said Mahendra, immediately losing colour.

"What's his address?"

"He doesn't wish it to be known to any one."

"Isn't it possible to find out?"

"I see no desperate need of it."

"Is need everything and lifelong friendship nothing?"

"It is true Bihari is my lifelong friend, but you have known him only since the other day and yet the desperate need seems to be on your side."

"That itself should put you to shame. You couldn't learn the value of friendship from even such a friend as he!"

"I don't regret it much—but I do wish I had learnt from him the art of stealing a woman's heart. I would have found it useful."

"That art can hardly be acquired merely by wishing to learn it. You must have the right heart for it."

"If you know the great teacher's address please let me have

it so that I may receive the initiation from him—even at this age. The heart can then be put to the test."

"Don't you talk to me of your heart when you can't even trace your friend's address. After the way you have behaved with Bihari Thakurpo, who will ever trust you?"

"If you didn't trust me fully you wouldn't dare slight me like this. Were you less sure of my love I wouldn't have to endure this intolerable agony. Bihari knows the art of resisting. Had he taught that art to this unfortunate fellow, he would have been a friend indeed."

"Bihari happens to be a man. That's why he can't be tamed," snapped Binodini, as she continued standing by the window, her unmade hair streaming down her back.

Clenching his fists Mahendra jumped up from his seat and shouted angrily, "How dare you keep on insulting me? If you get away with it, is it due to your superior might or to my forbearance? If you insist on treating me as a beast, remember it is a beast of prey you are facing. I am not such a coward as not to know how to strike."

He stood transfixed gazing at her. After a while he suddenly pleaded, "Binod, let's get away from here, anywhere, to the west or to the hills, wherever you say. We can't survive here long, we're destroying each other."

"Let's go," said Binodini, "now, this very moment—west."

"Where in the west?"

"Nowhere in particular. We won't stay anywhere for long—always on the move."

"That's fine. Let's leave tonight."

Binodini nodded her assent and hurried to the kitchen to arrange for Mahendra's food.

Mahendra could see the news-item in the paper had not come to Binodini's notice. In fact, she was in no mood to read the newspapers. Nevertheless, Mahendra was on the alert the whole day to see that this particular report did not reach her.

44

Meanwhile the food was kept ready for Mahendra at home, in the hope that he would return with news of Bihari. When it grew late Rajlakshmi became fretful in her sickbed. Not having had any sleep the whole night she was already prostrate with exhaustion so that Asha, seeing her also fretting for Mahendra, sent to inquire and was informed that Mahendra's carriage had come back empty. The coachman supplied the news that Mahendra after visiting Bihari's house had gone on to the Pataldanga flat. Hearing this Rajlakshmi turned her face towards the wall and lay motionless. Asha sat by her head fanning her, her body rigid as a statue.

On other days Rajlakshmi would insist on Asha taking her meals at their proper times. Today she said nothing. When Mahendra, even after seeing her so ill the previous night, could still go running after Binodini, what was there left for Rajlakshmi to wish for, to try for, to live for in this world? She was aware that Mahendra did not take her illness seriously and thought that it was merely one of the usual indispositions that now and again recur and run their course and are cured. But this very unconcern of his was what rankled most—that his obsession with a love affair should so fill his mind as to leave no room whatsoever for any other care or concern or duty, that he should take so lightly his mother's illness and suffering, that scared of being tied to his mother's sickbed he should so shamelessly have run away to Binodini at the very first opportunity. Rajlakshmi lost all interest in her recovery. In her bitter resentment against Mahendra she wanted to remain ill so as to prove to him how wrong he had been in treating her condition so lightly.

At two in the afternoon Asha said, "Mother, it is time for

your medicine." Rajlakshmi did not reply. As Asha got up to fetch the medicine she said, "I don't need any medicine, Bouma. You go."

Asha understood the despair of wounded love in these words and as though infected by it the anguish of her own grief was intensified, and trying to hold back her tears she burst into sobs. Rajlakshmi slowly turned on her side towards Asha and patting her hand with affectionate tenderness said, "Bouma, you are young and have plenty of time and occasion yet for happiness. Don't trouble about me any more, my child. I've lived long enough. What is there now to look for?"

This only made Asha sob the more. She hid her face in a fold of her sari.

Thus the unhappy day dragged to its close in the sick woman's room. Even in their despair the two women held on to a faint hope that Mahendra would turn up at any moment. They held their breath at every sound and understood each other's suspense. Gradually the evening light faded. The twilight in the interior of Calcutta homes is nothing but dusk, it has neither the brightness of light nor the full veil of darkness, it makes pain more painful and despair more frozen, it saps energy and drives away solace and robs even repose and detachment of their peace. Asha got up and moving stealthily went and brought a lighted candle into the cheerless and gloomy sick room. Rajlakshmi said, "I don't like the light, Bouma. Please leave the candle outside."

Asha took the candle away and came and sat down. When it grew very dark she asked her mother-in-law softly, "Mother, shall I send word for him?"

"No, Bouma," replied Rajlakshmi severely, "you are not to send any word to Mahendra. This is my solemn injunction."

Asha remained silent, rooted to her seat. She lacked even the energy to cry.

The servant's voice could be heard reporting from outside the room, "The master has sent a letter."

Rajlakshmi, imagining that Mahendra had perhaps suddenly been taken ill and, unable to reach home, had dispatched a letter, was immediately overcome with penitence and said impatiently, "Please see what Mahin has written, Bouma."

Asha came out into the passage and opening the letter with trembling fingers read it by the light of the candle. Mahendra had written that as he had not been feeling well of late he had decided to take a trip to the west and though there was no cause for anxiety on account of mother's condition, he had asked Dr. Nabin to visit her regularly. He had also prescribed in the letter what was to be done or given to his mother in case of headache or sleeplessness. A couple of light tonics from a pharmacy were also sent with the letter. In a postscript he had added that news of his mother's health should be sent to him positively and without fail to an address at Giridih for the present.

Asha was stunned. She forgot her grief in an overwhelming nausea of disgust. How could she read out such a callous letter to her mother-in-law!

Seeing Asha take so much time Rajlakshmi grew more impatient and called out, "Bouma, come and tell me at once what Mahin has written." In her excitement she raised herself and sat up in the bed. Asha came in and slowly read out the whole letter. Rajlakshmi said, "Please read out again what he has said about his health."

Asha read out again: "I have not been feeling well of late and so—"

"Stop!" cried Rajlakshmi. "No need to read out any more. How could he possibly feel well—when the old mother refuses to die and merely plagues him with her illness? Why did you ever tell Mahin of my illness? He had settled down at home, was busy with his books in his own room without bothering anybody—what satisfaction did you derive from hounding him out of the house by raising the bug-bear of his mother's illness? What harm would it have done anyone if I had remained in my bed unobserved, cooped up in my own despair? Not even so much suffering has dinned a little bit of sense in your head!"

She sank back in her bed again.

There was a shuffling of feet outside the door. The servant announced that the doctor had come. As he came into the room, Asha hurriedly covered her head and face and went and stood on the further side of the bed. The doctor inquired, "Please tell me what exactly is your trouble."

"Trouble!" cried Rajlakshmi angrily. "What trouble is there! Won't you let a person die even? Is your medicine going to make me immortal?"

"I may not make you immortal," replied the doctor gently, "but I may be helpful in relieving the pain. . . ."

"Pain!" interrupted Rajlakshmi. "The best cure for pain was when the widow burnt herself on the husband's pyre. Now it is only a prolonged death. Please go away, doctor, and don't worry me any longer. I wish to be alone."

"Let me at least feel your pulse," said the doctor timidly, "and. . . ."

"I tell you, leave me alone," cried Rajlakshmi very irritably. "My pulse is all right. There's no hope that the wretched thing will cease to beat soon."

The doctor was at last obliged to leave the room. He sent for Asha and questioned her in detail about the patient's condition. Having heard everything he re-entered Rajlakshmi's room and said gravely, "Mahendra has specially requested me to look after you. If you don't let me do so, he will be hurt."

The idea of Mahendra being hurt on this account sounded like mockery to Rajlakshmi's ears. She said, "Don't worry about Mahin. No one can escape being hurt in this world, but I can assure you that Mahendra won't be unduly upset on this account. Please go now, doctor, and let me sleep a little."

The doctor realised that it wouldn't do any good exciting

the patient. He slowly retraced his steps and after giving necessary instructions to Asha left the house.

When Asha came back into the room, Rajlakshmi said, "Go and rest a little, my child. You've been sitting the whole day by this sick bed. Go and send Haru's mother * here and ask her to remain in the adjoining room."

Asha knew her mother-in-law and understood that this was not a mere gesture of affectionate solicitude but a command —not to be ignored. She went out and sending the maid in, went into her own room and lay down in darkness on the cool floor. She had not eaten the whole day and was weary and limp with pain and fatigue.

A wedding was being celebrated in a neighbouring house from where, now and again, snatches of music wafted in. Just at that moment the *sanai* could be heard again, the familiar notes of the wedding pipes seemed to crash through the darkness raising waves of agony which dashed against Asha's heart. Every little detail of her own wedding assumed a living shape before her eyes, filling the darkness of the sky with dream-images—the wedding lamps, the noise, the crowd, the auspicious garland and the sandal paste, the bridal dress and the fragrance of the incense burning, her own shyness, hesitation and fears tremulous with joy.

Assailed on all sides by poignant memories the pain in her heart redoubled and became almost unbearable. As a hungry, famine-stricken child keeps on striking the mother clamouring for food, so the revived memories of past happiness clamouring for their food pounded on Asha's heart until she could remain still no longer. She folded her palms to pray to God, and as she did so, the gentle, calm image of her aunt floated into her tear-soaked heart—the only visible image of the divine she had known in her life. She had sworn never again to call and drag back that austere devotee into the painful turmoil of her life, but today it seemed to her that there was no

---

* A common way of calling or referring to a married woman with children—in this case obviously a maid-servant.

other alternative, no other escape from the thickening fog
of suffering that was enveloping and choking her. Lighting a
lamp she sat down with a sheet of paper over a copy-book in
her lap and wiping her profuse tears began to to write:

"At your lotus feet—

"Mashima, I have no one but you left. Please come, I beg
you, and take this unhappy child once again in your lap. I
shan't survive if you don't. I don't know what else to say. I
bow at your feet a million times.

Your loving
Chuni."

45

Arrived back from Kashi, Annapurna entered the room with
soft steps and touching Rajlakshmi's feet lifted the hands to
her forehead in the customary salutation. Despite the intervening rupture and bitterness, Rajlakshmi felt on seeing Annapurna as though she had recovered a lost treasure. She
realised in a flash how much she had missed her sister-in-law
in the depth of her heart without being aware of it, how
much of her weariness of spirit, its pain and petulance, were
due to Annapurna's absence. Her anguished heart immediately opened its door to welcome and reclaim a lost friendship.

The two sisters-in-law had lived together in the same house
in friendly intimacy long before Mahendra was born, sharing
each other's joy and sorrow, participating in the same festivi-
ties, sacred and secular, and facing shoulder to shoulder their
common responsibilities and misfortunes. This old intimacy
was almost instantly restored in Rajlakshmi's heart. In her
dark hour of sorrow the old friend of her girlhood days, the
faithful companion in the early adventures of her life's journey, once more stood by her side—despite the many misun-

214

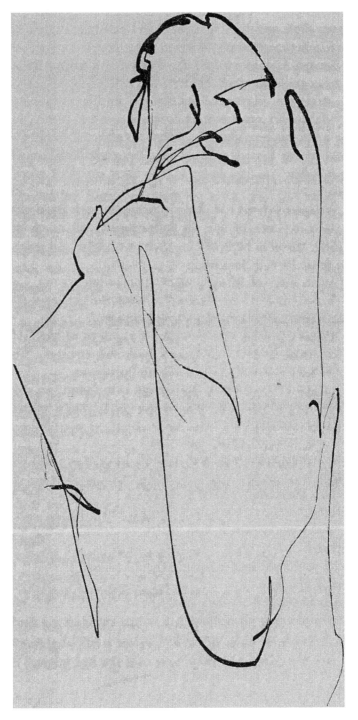

215

derstandings and estrangement of the intervening years. And he on whose account Rajlakshmi had treated her sister-in-law so shabbily and callously—where was he today?

Annapurna sat down by the sickbed and taking Rajlakshmi's right hand into her own said, "Didi!"

"Mejo-bou!" responded Rajlakshmi, unable to articulate any more, the tears streaming down her eyes and cheeks. The scene proved too painful for Asha who retreated to her own room where she lay down on the floor shedding copious tears.

Annapurna dared not discuss Mahendra with Rajlakshmi or Asha, so she sent for old Sadhucharan and asked him, "Uncle, where is Mahin?" Sadhucharan related the episode of Mahendra and Binodini.

"What news of Bihari?" asked Annapurna.

"I am afraid I don't know," replied Sadhucharan. "He hasn't been to this house for a long time now."

"Please go to his house and bring me news of him."

Sadhucharan did so and came back and reported, "He's not at home. He's staying in a villa on the Ganges."

Annapurna sent for Dr. Nabin and questioned him about the patient's condition. The doctor said, "She's suffering from dropsy as well as a weak heart. Anything may happen at any time. It is difficult to say."

In the evening when Rajlakshmi's discomfort was aggravated, Annapurna suggested, "Didi, let me send for Dr. Nabin."

"No, Mejo-bou," replied Rajlakshmi. "Dr. Nabin can do nothing."

"Then whom would you like to be called?" asked Annapurna.

"If you could send news to Bihari I should be glad," replied Rajlakshmi.

A pain stabbed at Annapurna's heart. She had not forgotten that evening when Bihari had waited outside her door, in the darkness, far away from home, and she had spurned and turned him away. Never again would he return to her door and she had little hope of ever being able to make amends in this life for the wrong she had done him.

She went up to the terrace and into Mahendra's room which had once overflowed with gaiety and joy. It lay in a cheerless disorder, bleak and dismal, the bed, furniture and every article in the room shabby and uncared-for, the plants dried up in their tubs on the terrace for lack of water.

Seeing her aunt go up to the roof-terrace, Asha slowly followed her. Annapurna took her in her arms and kissed her head. Asha bent down and clasping her aunt's feet touched her head against them repeatedly, crying, "Mashima, pour your blessing on me that I may gain strength. That a human being can endure so much suffering I had never before thought possible. Good Lord, how much longer must I suffer like this!"

Annapurna sat down on the floor where Asha lay sprawling at her feet. She raised Asha's head onto her lap and remained seated without uttering a word, praying inwardly, her palms joined together.

Her silent prayer charged with love seemed to flow like a blessing into the deeps of Asha's heart filling it with a peace long sought. Asha felt as if her own prayers were about to be answered—the gods may reject the petition of a silly girl like her but how could they fail to respond to Mashima's! After a long while she sat up and drew a long sigh, having regained solace and strength. She turned to Annapurna and said, "Mashima, won't you please send a letter to Bihari Thakurpo?"

"No, I won't send a letter," replied Annapurna.

"How then will you let him know?"

"I'll go and see him personally tomorrow."

46

During his wandering in the west Bihari came to realise that unless he absorbed himself in some occupation he would find no peace. Returning to Calcutta he devoted himself to the founding of a nursing home for poor clerks. Cooped up with their large families in cheerless tenements huddled in narrow lanes, the stunted lives of these clerks were spent like fish gasping for breath in the slimy bottom of a pond sucked almost dry by the summer drought. Bihari had long felt sorry for this community of pale, emaciated and harassed gentlefolk and decided that they should at least have the benefit, when ill, of a little sylvan shade and open air beside the Ganges.

Having acquired a garden he engaged Chinese carpenters to make small cottages in the grounds. But he failed to find the peace he had sought. As the day approached nearer when he would have to assume the full responsibility of running the nursing home, his heart shrank at the thought and murmured in protest, "There's no joy, no beauty, no fulfilment in this work—it's a mere dry burden of duty." The prospect of work had never before scared him as it did now.

There was a time when no special hankering ever troubled Bihari's mind. He could easily engage himself in whatever activity or problem presented itself. But now a nameless hunger was consuming him which unless quenched would not let him concentrate on any activity. Force of habit made him take up this or that, but as soon as he took it up he was seized by a longing to run away from it.

The life-force which had lain curled up in quiet repose within him had awakened at the touch of Binodini's golden wand and was now scouring the world for food, like a newborn Garuda, the fabulous bird on which the great god

218

Vishnu rides. Not having known this fabulous creature before, Bihari was at a loss to know what to do with himself. And what was the use of his bothering himself with the fate of the sickly, emaciated, short-lived clerks of Calcutta!

In front of him flowed the Ganges swollen with the rains. Now and again thick masses of clouds gathered and hung brooding over the dense foliage on the opposite bank; the surface on the water glistened like a sword of steel, now flashing darkly, now burning brightly like a flame. Whenever Bihari's eyes strayed to this pageantry of the rainy season, the door of his heart burst open and there appeared etched on the soothing canvas of the dark-blue sky a solitary figure, her dark hair, freshly washed, falling in thick, loose waves on her shoulders, her eyes fixed in a steadfast, mournful look on Bihari—a look tragic but luminous, as though all the scattered flashes of lightning in the clouds were gathered and concentrated in it.

All his previous life spent in ease and comfort now seemed to Bihari as so much of life wasted. How many such cloud-drunk evenings, how many nights of full moon had come to the door of his empty, vacant heart, loaded with flasks of nectar and had gone back with the flasks unemptied—unknown to him! Many such divine moments had come and gone—the music unplayed, the festival unfinished. All the memories of his previous years seemed pale and futile, made trivial by the passionate glow of Binodini's lips raised to his.

It seemed to him incredible that he should have spent the better part of his life as Mahendra's shadow. He had been deaf to the ravishing melody wrung from the very heart of earth and sky by the anguish of an awakened love. He could not even have imagined that such music was possible, that such beauty and enchantment existed until Binodini put her two arms around his neck and lifted him into another world. How could he ever forget Binodini who worked this miracle! Her ardent look and the longing in her eyes seemed to permeate the whole universe, her heavy, passionate breathing coursed through his blood raising waves of desire day and night, the warm feel of her soft flesh was wrapped round him coaxing his heart with thrills of ecstasy to unfold its petals.

Why then was he keeping so far away from Binodini? Was it because he could think of no earthly relationship which would preserve intact the rapturous experience of beauty in which Binodini had initiated him? When the lotus is plucked, the slime is stirred and raised. How and where to place her so that the beautiful should not turn odious? Moreover, the idea that his relationship with Binodini should become a bone of contention between him and Mahendra was revolting. It made the whole thing too sordid for words. And so he had isolated himself on the bank of the Ganges and was content to adore the image of his beloved in the beauty and wonder of nature, burning his own heart like incense at the altar of love. He had not even written to Binodini for fear of receiving news which might tear asunder the web of lovely dreams he had woven for himself.

One early morning Bihari was lying under a *jam* tree in a southern nook of his garden, watching idly under a cloudy sky the boats plying to and from a neighbouring factory. Slowly the day advanced. The servant came to inquire if the morning meal * might be served. "Not yet," replied Bihari. The head-mason came to take him to see a construction on which his advice was needed. Bihari answered, "Later on."

Suddenly he saw standing before him Annapurna. Bihari sprang to his feet in confusion and respectfully greeted her in the orthodox fashion by kneeling on the ground and touching her feet with his forehead. Annapurna placed her right hand affectionately on his head and said in a voice thick with tears, "Bihari, you looked so pulled down—why?"

"To win back your affection, Kakima," replied Bihari.

The tears began to stream down Annapurna's eyes.

---

* In an average Indian home, "morning meal" serves for both breakfast and lunch.

"You haven't had your meal, have you, Kakima?" inquired Bihari anxiously.

"No, it's not time yet."

"Come, let me arrange for your cooking * here. At least I'll have once more the luxury of tasting your cooking and partaking of your *prasad*."

Bihari refrained from asking for news of Asha or Mahendra, his hurt pride would not let him broach a subject which was closed to him since the day when Annapurna had so callously banged the door in his face.

The meal over, Annapurna said, "The boat is waiting at the landing, Bihari. Come with me to the town."

"Why need I come to Calcutta?" asked Bihari.

"Didi is very ill and wants to see you." Bihari was startled. "Where's Mahinda?" he asked.

"He's not in town. He's gone west."

Bihari went pale. He said nothing.

"Don't you know the whole story?" asked Annapurna.

"Some of it. Not the later part."

Annapurna told him of Mahendra's elopement with Binodini. All the beauty and wonder of the earth and the sky suddenly vanished, the honey gathered and stored by his fancy turned bitter as gall. So the enchantress was merely playing with him on that evening, fooling him with her mock surrender! She has left the village home and run away with Mahendra to the west! Shameless creature! More shame on him, the fool who allowed himself to be taken in by her!

Nothing seemed beautiful any more—not the cloud-drunk sky of July nor the cloudless nights of full moon. The bubble of enchantment had burst.

* Orthodox Hindu widows cook their own food.

47

Bihari wondered, how can I face the unhappy Asha? As he passed the portico he felt oppressed by a sense of desolation and gloom that hung over the house deserted by its master. So overcome was he by shame at his friend's conduct that he found it difficult to look the durwan and the servants in the face and hung down his head, not daring to greet the servants pleasantly as was his wont. His feet dragged heavily as though unwilling to enter the inner apartments. How could he bear the sight of Asha loaded with sorrow and shrinking in shame, exposed in the utter nakedness of a public humiliation, deprived of a woman's dearest pride, discarded and thrown by Mahendra on the dung-hill of others' pity and curiosity!

But he was given no time to indulge in these doubts and fears. The moment he entered the apartments Asha hurried up to him and said, "Come in, quick, Thakurpo. Mother is in great pain."

This was the first time that Asha had ever spoken directly to Bihari. When the wind of misfortune blows, a mere gust is enough to tear away the veil of reserve. The flood huddles together on the same narrow strip of bank all those who had drifted apart.

This sudden lack of reserve in Asha shocked and pained Bihari. In itself a little thing, it seemed to him symbolic of the great havoc caused by Mahendra. As the neglected, unkempt appearance of the house bore witness to a family catastrophe, so its mistress had shed all delicacy and fastidiousness of deportment and had not had even the time to regret the loss.

Bihari entered Rajlakshmi's room. She had just recovered from a sudden fit of asthmatic choking and though still very pale was feeling much better. As Bihari bent down and touched her feet she motioned him to sit down by her and said very slowly, "How are you, Bihari? It's so long since I saw you."

"Why didn't you let me know of your illness earlier?" asked Bihari. "I would have been here in no time."

"Don't I know it, my son?" said Rajlakshmi in a faint voice. "I did not bear you in my womb and yet no one in this world is more my own than you."

As she spoke, the tears fell from her eyes. Deeply moved Bihari hurriedly rose and turned towards the niche in the wall, pretending to examine the phials and pots of medicine to give himself time to recover. Having pulled himself together he turned back to Rajlakshmi and tried to feel her pulse.

"Don't bother about my pulse, Bihari," said Rajlakshmi. "Rather tell me, why have you grown so thin?"

She raised her emaciated hand and passed it over his neck caressingly.

"These bones of mine will never put on flesh," replied Bihari, "until fed again with fish curry made by your own hands. So please get well soon. In the meanwhile, I'll keep the fire ready."

"Yes, do keep the fire ready, my son," said Rajlakshmi smiling wanly, "But not for cooking."

Taking Bihari's hand in her own and pressing it she continued, "Get yourself a wife, Bihari—there's no one to look after you at home." Then turning to Annapurna she said, "Mejo-bou, you must look out for a bride for Bihari. Don't you see what a skeleton he has become!"

"Get well soon, Didi," replied Annapurna. "Giving him in marriage is your privilege—we'll all join in the festivity."

"My time is up, Mejo-bou. I entrust this responsibility to you all. See that Bihari is made happy. I could not repay my debt to him—may God's blessings be on him!"

She put her right hand on Bihari's head. Asha could bear

the sight no longer and went out of the room crying. Annapurna looked affectionately at Bihari through tear-dimmed
eyes.

As though recalling something, Rajlakshmi called out,
"Bouma! Bouma!!" On Asha hurrying back into the room
she said, "I hope you have made arrangements for Bihari's
dinner?"

"Don't you worry, mother," interposed Bihari. "They all
know about this greedy son of yours. As soon as I entered the
house I saw Bami * hurrying in with a basket loaded with a
huge *koi* † with its roe—unmistakable evidence that my reputation in this house is still intact."

He laughed and glanced up at Asha who no longer shrank
in shyness. She responded to his pleasantry with an affectionate smile. She had never understood till now how much
Bihari mattered to this household—she had often resented
his presence as an unwelcome visitor and had made no secret
of her displeasure. Recalling this she was filled with shame
and remorse and made amends by her unreserved expression
of esteem and affection.

"Mejo-bou," said Rajlakshmi, "please see to the cooking
yourself—the cook won't know how to make the dishes hot
and spicy enough for this East-Bengal provincial ‡ son of
ours."

"What!" protested Bihari. "Your mother hailed from Vikrampur and yet you dare call a Nadia boy an East Bengal
provincial!"

Many pleasantries were exchanged on this issue and after a
long time the oppressive gloom which had hung over the
house was relieved. No one spoke of Mahendra, although for-

* Name of a maid-servant.
† Name of a fish much loved by Bengalees.
‡ West Bengal people make fun of the East Bengal people, much as
the English do of the Scots. Vikrampur is right in the heart of East
Bengal, while Nadia is on the border between the two parts.

merly he was almost the sole topic of conversation whenever Rajlakshmi discussed anything with Bihari. In fact Mahendra used to tease his mother about this obsession of hers. Today the same Rajlakshmi did not once utter Mahendra's name. Bihari was secretly amazed.

Seeing Rajlakshmi droop and doze off with fatigue, Bihari came out of the room and said to Annapurna, "Mother's illness is a serious one."

"That is obvious," replied Annapurna sitting down by the window. She remained silent a long time and then suddenly said, "Won't you fetch Mahendra back, Bihari? There is no time to lose."

Bihari was silent. Then he replied, "I shall do as you command. Does anyone know his address?"

"I am afraid not. You'll have to find out.—One more thing, Bihari. Just look at Asha's face—she looks like one who is mortally wounded. I don't think she will survive if you don't rescue Mahendra from Binodini's clutches."

"Rescuing indeed!" thought Bihari with a bitter laugh. "Good Lord, who will rescue me?"

Outwardly he replied, "What magic can I command, Kakima, that will protect Mahendra against Binodini's charms forever! His mother's illness may hold him in check for a few days, but how can one guarantee that he won't run away again?"

Just then Asha entered the room, her face half veiled, and slowly came and sat down by her aunt's feet. She thought they were discussing Rajlakshmi's illness and was anxious to listen to what they were saying. Looking at the face of the devoted wife ennobled by silent suffering, Bihari was filled with admiration for her. Bathed in the sacred waters of penance her young face shone with the undying grandeur of the heroines of old, she was no longer a mere young girl, the baptism of sorrow had made her ageless like the paragons of chaste womanhood of which the legends speak.

Bihari discussed with Asha the treatment prescribed for Rajlakshmi. When Asha had left he heaved a deep sigh and said to Annapurna, "I shall save Mahendra."

He proceeded to Mahendra's bank and discovered that of late he had been drawing on his account through the Allahabad branch of the bank.

48

On reaching the station Binodini straightaway got into an Intermediate compartment reserved for ladies and took her seat.

"What's this?" protested Mahendra. "I'll get a second class ticket for you."

"Not necessary," replied Binodini. "I shall be quite comfortable here."

Mahendra was surprised. He knew that Binodini was no ascetic and normally shrank from poverty and discomfort and used, in fact, to be ashamed of her straitened circumstances. He was aware that Binodini had once been attracted to him on account of the reputation of his family for wealth and good living and had been excited at the prospect of what might have been, had she been the mistress of so much wealth and luxury. Why then was she now spurning this wealth and luxury which was hers for the taking and clinging so haughtily to the discomfort and shame of privation?

It was obvious that she was straining her utmost to reduce her dependence on Mahendra to the barest minimum. She would take nothing from him—who in his infatuation had dragged her down forever from her rightful place in society —which might seem a price for her degradation. When she was staying with Rajlakshmi in Mahendra's house she did not particularly observe all the taboos enjoined on a Hindu widow but now, after all this time, she denied herself

226

every comfort and luxury. She took only one meal a day, wore a coarse cotton sari and no longer indulged her fertile gift of wit and repartee. She had become so reserved, withdrawn, aloof and severe that Mahendra was afraid to address any words to her, even the most commonplace. He was astonished, impatient and furious at this change and kept on saying to himself, "Having taken such pains to bring me down like a rare fruit from the topmost branch of the tree, what does she mean by throwing the fruit away in the dust without so much as smelling it even?"

"For where shall I get the tickets?" asked Mahendra.

"Anywhere to the west. Wherever the train stops tomorrow morning, we'll get down."

This kind of aimless wandering was not to Mahendra's taste. In his case any lack of comfort spoiled everything and he felt at ease only in a big town where comfortable lodgings could be had. He was not smart or resourceful enough to fend and improvise for himself. It was therefore in a grumpy, bilious mood that he got into his carriage. On top of it he was on tenterhooks lest Binodini give him the slip and get down at some wayside station.

Thus Binodini wandered from place to place, Mahendra hanging on to her at a prescribed distance like a satellite to a baleful planet.

Binodini had the knack of winning affection and making friends; she would in no time get into friendly conversation with the other women in her compartment and would find out all about the places she intended to visit. She put up at the travellers' rest-house and was never in want of obliging female companions to show her round the various places and sights. She had little use for Mahendra who, in fact, soon discovered that he had nothing to do save purchase a ticket for her when necessary. He smarted under a sense of his own superfluousness which, he felt, was making him seem more and more insignificant in Binodini's eyes. He sat moping the whole day and wrestling with his futile longings. In the beginning he had tried to trudge behind Binodini when she went out sight-seeing with her female-companions, but he soon got weary of it and preferred to spend the day in a prolonged siesta after meals, while Binodini wandered around. Who could have imagined that this pampered darling of a fond mother would land himself in such a plight!

One day while they were at the Allahabad railway station waiting for a train that happened to be late, Binodini to while away the time went about watching other trains come and go. Throughout her wanderings she had behaved as though she was perpetually on the look-out for someone. At any rate she derived more peace and comfort from this constant seeking amid the hustle and bustle of the crowded highway than from her idle existence in the dingy and lonely flat in Calcutta where she had constantly to suppress and kill herself.

Suddenly her eye fell on a postal notice-board in a glass case on the wall where undelivered letters were hung up for the benefit of whom it may concern. She noticed one envelope among them addressed to 'Biharilal.' It is not an uncommon name and there was no reason whatsoever for Binodini to assume that this was the Bihari she was looking for. Nevertheless, she did so assume; and having committed to memory the address on the envelope, she walked back to where Mahendra was seated on a bench looking disconsolate and said, "I'll stay on a few more days in Allahabad."

The humiliating consciousness that he was, as it were, held in leash and led by Binodini wherever she willed—without even a sop being thrown to him to assuage the hunger gnawing at the bowels of his desire—had been rankling in his mind, goading his masculine pride and making it rebellious. And so—although he would have loved nothing better than to prolong his stay in Allahabad where he could rest in comfort—he revolted at the thought that he must submit to every passing whim of Binodini and flared up, "No, we can't turn back now. Having set out we must go on."

228

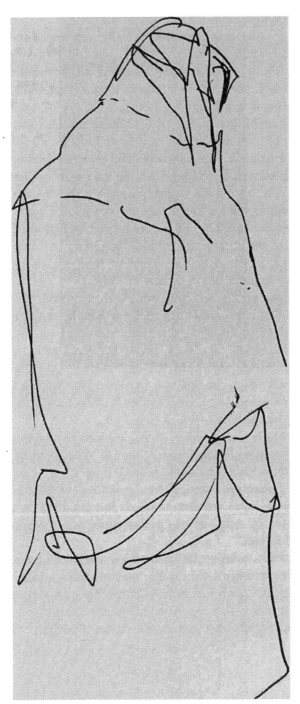

229

"I won't go," rejoined Binodini firmly.

"Very well then, you stay on by yourself. I'm going ahead."

"It suits me fine," said Binodini and without wasting another word motioned to a porter to carry her things and walked out of the station.

Hugging his manly dignity, Mahendra remained seated on the bench frowning darkly. As long as Binodini was in sight he remained stiff and motionless. But when she disappeared without even once looking back, he sprang to his feet and hurriedly thrusting his luggage on a porter's head ran after her. Coming out he found that she was already seated in a carriage. Without uttering a word he had his luggage thrown on top of the carriage and himself jumped on the coach-box, preferring to sit with the driver to facing Binodini after having swallowed the ignominy of defeat.

The carriage drove on and on. An hour passed, the town and its dwellings were left behind, and still the carriage drove on, with tilled fields on both sides. Mahendra was ashamed to inquire from the driver where they were going, lest he think that the lady inside was the mistress and he a mere hanger-on whom she had not even taken the trouble to tell where they were to go. He therefore kept his mouth shut and sat on the coach-box glum and frowning.

At last the carriage drew up at a secluded villa on the bank of the Jumuna. Mahendra was stunned. Whose was the villa and how had Binodini come to know of it?

The house was closed. After a good deal of shouting and calling an aged caretaker emerged muttering, "The owner lives not far away—if you get his permission I'll open the house for you."

Binodini looked at Mahendra who, overjoyed at the prospect of staying at the lovely, romantic villa, readily said, "Come, let's go to the owner's house. You can wait outside in the carriage while I go in and fix up everything."

"I can't gad about any more," replied Binodini. "I'll rest

here while you go and fix up everything. The place seems safe enough and there's nothing to be afraid of."

Mahendra went away in the carriage. Binodini engaged the aged Brahmin in conversation, inquiring about his sons and grandchildren, how many and what they were, how the boys were faring and where the girls had been married. Learning that his wife was dead, she showered him with her sympathy and expressed great concern that there was no one to look after him. And then while talking of this and that, she casually asked, "Wasn't Bihari Babu staying here?"

"Yes, he was here for a few days," replied the old man. "Does the lady know him?"

"He's a relation of ours," said Binodini.

The old man's description of Bihari and his ways left no room for doubt in Binodini's mind. She made him open all the rooms and learnt which was the one in which Bihari used to sleep and which was the sitting room. As the house had been closed since his departure it seemed to her that his unseen presence still hung about the rooms and had not been blown away by the passing wind. She breathed in and filled her heart with the still air heavy with Bihari's breath and felt it wrap round her limbs.

The old man could give no news of Bihari's present whereabouts. It might be that he would return to the villa. He consoled Binodini with an assurance that he would ask the owner of the villa if he knew anything and would report to her.

49

For endless years the Himalayas have fed the waters of the Jamuna from their perennial snows. Perennial too are the romantic associations which endless generations of poets have woven round its banks. Its murmurs are resonant with a thousand rhythms and beats and in the play of its ripples and waves are reflected the heavings of a million hearts.

When in the evening Mahendra came and sat on the river bank, the highly charged atmosphere of romance stirred the waves of desire in his blood, his nerves tingled, his eyes burned and his breathing became heavy with passion. The golden *vina* of the setting sun seemed to vibrate with the exquisite melody of pain.

Gradually the long stretch of sand on the deserted bank ceased to glow with the many colours of the twilight and was veiled in darkness. Mahendra sat with eyes half closed and felt himself in Brindaban where he could see the cows returning in the evening from their pasture grounds, raising clouds of dust, and could hear their lowing as they entered their familiar sheds.

It was the season of rains and very soon the sky was overcast with clouds. The darkness of night in an unfamiliar spot is something more than a mere black veil; it seems to hide many mysteries underneath. The vague shapes and shadows discernible seem to whisper in a language strange and inarticulate. The pale glimmer of the receding sands on the opposite bank, the blue-black stillness of the unruffled waters, the dense foliage of the overspreading *neem* trees in the garden, the curving outlines of the dusty-grey banks—all these seemed like so many mysterious presences surrounding Mahendra on this dark, cloudy evening of July.

He recalled the familiar Vaishnav lyrics which sing of just such a night as this, dark and tense with clouds, when the love-lorn maiden slips out of the house to keep her tryst with the lover on that very bank of the Jamuna. There she lingers on the bank wondering how to cross the swollen river. "Please, O boatman, ferry me across!"—this cry resounding through the ages raised an echo in Mahendra's heart— "Please, O boatman, ferry me across!"

There she was on the other bank, far away—and yet Mahendra could see her clearly. Ageless, timeless, the eternal cowherd maiden—Mahendra recognised her immediately. She was Binodini, the eternal feminine, trudging through the ages in quest of her lover, weary with pain, distracted with longing, bursting with the throb of desire, trudging through poetry, through song, until there she stands on the other shore crying, "Ferry me across, O boatman!" How long will she stand there in darkness, waiting for the ferry!

Through a rift in the clouds smiled the three-day-old moon casting its unearthly spell over the river and the sky and dissolving the barriers of time and space. The past with its cargo of memories, the future with its burden of consequences alike vanished and what remained was only the present, the Jamuna flowing with its silver specks and Mahendra waiting on this bank and Binodini on that, all else obliterated.

An ecstasy of desire possessed Mahendra. On such a night as this Binodini could not reject him, into such an exclusive paradise she could not help but walk. He jumped up and headed straight for Binodini's room.

The room was filled with the sweet smell of flowers. Through the open window the light of the moon fell on the white bedsheet on which Binodini lay, decked with flowers— flowers in her hair, on her neck, a girdle of flowers round her waist—like a creeper in spring laden and bent with blossoms. The sight made Mahendra delirious with excitement.

"Binod," he cried out in a voice choked with passion, "I was waiting for you on the Jamuna bank. The moon came up and whispered that you were waiting for me here. So here I am!"

He moved forward to sit on the bed. Binodini, startled, hurriedly sat up and stretching out her right arm to ward him off cried, "Go away, get out of here—don't you dare to sit on the bed!"

Mahendra was stunned—suddenly arrested with a jolt like

an overloaded boat stuck in a sand-bank. He stared dumbly unable to utter a sound. Afraid of his trespassing on the bed Binodini jumped down and came and stood before him.

"Why then are you decked like this?" broke out Mahendra at last. "Whom are you waiting for?"

"For him," replied Binodini clutching at her heart, "who is here, right within me."

"Who is he? Bihari?"

"Don't you dare utter his name with your tongue."

"Is it for him that you're wandering in the west?"

"For him."

"Is it for him you are waiting here?"

"For him."

"Do you know where he is?"

"No—but I shall know."

"I shan't let you know."

"Even if you don't, you can't dislodge him from my heart."

She closed her eyes as though to reassure herself that he was there, within.

Repulsed in his violent attraction to this love-sick lady wreathed in flowers, Mahendra was wild with rage. Clenching his fists he shouted, "I'll slash him out of your breast with my knife."

"I'd rather have your knife in my breast than your love," replied Binodini calmly.

"Why don't you fear me at least?" cried Mahendra. "Who's there to protect you here?"

"You," replied Binodini. "You will protect me from yourself."

"So you still have that much faith, that much trust in me?"

"If I didn't have that, I would have put an end to my life long ago and not come out with you."

"Why didn't you put an end to your life?" cried Mahendra. "Why need you have put this noose of trust round my neck and dragged me out of my own home? How much good your dying would have done—just think of it!"

"I know that—but while the hope of seeing Bihari lives within me, I can't even die."

"And until you die, my hope of having you too will not die—and there's no release from this bondage for me. From now on I shall pray for your death with all my heart. May you be—neither mine nor Bihari's! May you just cease to be and so give me my freedom! My mother is wailing, my wife is weeping, their tears are like red hot iron on my soul. I can't even wipe their tears until you cease to be, until you are out of my reach, out of everyone's reach on this earth!"

He rushed out of the room tearing into bits the dreamweb which Binodini had woven round herself. She stood there dumbly, gazing outside at the sky where the moonlight seemed emptied of all its enchantment. The garden with its flower-beds and beyond it the expanse of sand and the dark water and beyond it the shadowy obscurity of the other bank —all these seemed like a mere pencil-sketch on a sheet of blank paper, lifeless and meaningless.

A fever of unrest seized her as she realised how fatal was the spell she had cast on Mahendra, how like a tempest she had wrung and torn him out of his soil, root and branch. If such was her power, why could it not drag Bihari to her door as it did the moonstruck Mahendra? Why only this wail of futile, unwanted longing always pounding at her door day and night? Why only this howl of pain intruding on her heart from the outside, giving it no time to weep out its own sorrow? All this ceaseless turmoil churned up within her breast, how could she bear with it all her life? Where was the charm with which to quieten it?

She tore into bits the garlands of flowers with which she had earlier wreathed herself. Mahendra's infatuated gaze had fallen on them, polluting them. All her power, her striving, her very life were in vain—and vain and futile too were this garden, this moonlight, this Jamuna bank and all the beauty of this earth!

And yet despite this gigantic futility everything remained as it was, there was nowhere the least aberration from the normal—tomorrow the sun would rise as it did yesterday and nature would not forget to perform its pettiest operation and Bihari would remain immobile and as far away as he was, still teaching the Brahmin brat his new lesson from the primer!

The tears rolled down Binodini's cheeks. Why was her strength and her suffering being wasted in trying to move a block of granite? Her heart might dissolve in a pool of blood but the stone would not move even by a hair's breadth.

50

Mahendra could not sleep the whole night. Weary and tired he dozed off in the early dawn. He woke at about nine and hurriedly sat up, immediately aware of the stab of pain at his heart which even in sleep must have vaguely troubled him. Gradually the events of the previous evening passed before his mind, vivid and blatant, casting their melancholy shadow on his spirit already weary with lack of adequate sleep. The morning sun, the earth and his own life, they all seemed bleak and cheerless. Why had he bent his back with all this load—the shame of home-forsaking, the bitter reproach of moral transgression, all the turbulence of a warped existence? What for? In the pitiless light of the morning sun he stared at his own heart and found that he did not really love Binodini.

He looked at the road outside and saw the bustle of the human hive at work after the night's rest. That he alone should squirm abjectly in futile devotion at the feet of a woman whose face was turned away from him and let his self-respect be sunk in the mire, seemed to him utter folly. The frenzy of excitement had brought its inevitable reaction, the spirit wearied and listless wanted to turn away from its recent object of desire. The receding tide leaves behind its slime on the mind's shore and what had seemed desirable suddenly becomes repulsive. He now found it difficult to understand what had made him grovel in this indignity. "I am superior to Binodini in every respect," he said. "Why then should I trail behind her like a despicable beggar, wallowing day and night in abject humiliation? What devil planted this strange imbecility in my brain?"

Suddenly Binodini seemed a mere woman, like any other woman—her uniqueness, the wonder of her beauty in which had met all the enchantment of poetry, the loveliness of this earth and the glamour of romance vanished like a mirage. The spell was broken and Mahendra was now seized with a desire to return home—back to the peace, comfort and affection of home which now seemed infinitely sweet. "How foolish we are," he said to himself, "to mistake peace for dullness and depth for stagnation and to run breathlessly chasing false delights that bring no enduring joy! I'll return home this very day, making arrangement for Binodini to stay where she likes. I'll be free."

"I'll be free"—no sooner was this resolve put into words than a thrill of delight passed through his frame and the oppressive weight of indecision which had so long lain heavy on him was lightened. All these days he had been on the rack, unable to make up his mind to a Yes or No, recoiling one moment, pursuing the next, gagging his conscience and rushing headlong into what he knew was an aberration—but now the moment he said "I'll be free" his storm-tossed heart found its bearings and he heaved a sigh of grateful relief.

He jumped up from his bed and hurrying through a wash went straight to Binodini. Her door was locked. He knocked.

"Are you sleeping?"

"No," came the reply from within. "Please go away."

"I've something important to say. I won't take long."

"I am sick of listening to you. Please go away and don't pester me any more. I want to be alone."

Formerly such a rebuff would have served merely to inflame Mahendra's passion. Today it filled him with extreme disgust. "What a worm I have reduced myself to that this woman assumes the right to insult and spurn me at her sweet will! She has no inherent right over me, it is I who have allowed her this right and made her so insolent." Having said so to himself he tried to make up for the rebuff by imagining how much superior he was to Binodini in every respect. "I shall break these fetters," he said, "and go away. I shall win in the end."

After lunch he went to the bank to cash a cheque and having got the money went round to the Allahabad shops to buy gifts for his mother and Asha.

Once again there was a knock on Binodini's door. Out of sheer vexation she did not answer the knock at first, but when it was repeated persistently she flew into a rage and opening the door abruptly, rapped out, "Why must you pester me again and again?" Before she could complete the sentence she was aware of Bihari standing before her.

Bihari looked into the room to see if Mahendra was there or not. His eye fell on the bed on which lay a heap of broken garlands and dried petals. A storm of anger and disgust swept over him. It was not that he had no misgivings regarding Binodini's relations with Mahendra during all these days; a suspicion had all along lurked in his mind but it had been overshadowed by the image of Binodini's loveliness with which his imagination was constantly at play. His heart, as he entered the garden, was in a flutter of fear lest the image he wrought by his fancy receive a rude shock and tumble down. Which is exactly what happened as soon as Binodini opened the door.

Bihari had once fondly imagined that the overflow of his love would wash away with its pure and holy water all the stains from Binodini's life. But now as he stood face to face with her he found that his heart had shrunk, the upsurge of righteous anger had squeezed out all pity from it. Binodini now seemed to him too unclean. He abruptly turned away and began to call aloud, "Mahinda! Mahinda!"

Swallowing her pride Binodini said gently, "Mahendra is not in. He's gone to town." Seeing Bihari turn to leave she added, "Bihari Thakurpo, please wait a while, I beg of you."

Bihari had determined not to listen to any pleas and to break away immediately from this shameful sight, but there was something so sad in Binodini's voice that his feet were arrested and he found himself unable to move. He turned towards Binodini and said, "Why must you try to drag me into your life, Binodini? What have I done to you? I have never stood in your way, I've never tried to interfere with your life."

"How much you mean to me, I have once before confessed to you," replied Binodini. "You did not believe me then—nevertheless, I shall say it again, despite your indifference and despite your denying me the woman's privilege of saying it without words, of revealing myself through modesty. You have spurned me—and yet I cling to your feet and I say I love —"

"Don't you dare utter words," interrupted Bihari, "which are impossible to believe."

"Maybe, the world will not believe them—but you will. That's why I want you to listen."

"What does it matter whether I believe them or not—since your life will continue to be what it is?"

"I know it matters little to you, one way or the other," replied Binodini. "It is my ill luck that I have no right, no means of standing by your side with my head held high. I must for ever keep away from you. I have only one small favour to beg of you—that you may think of me with a little charity, a little sweetness, wherever I may be. I know that once you did have a little regard for me—let it remain as my only treasure in this life. That's why you must at least listen to what I have to say. I beg of you, Thakurpo, please sit down for a while."

"All right, let's go," said Bihari, making a move to look around for some other room.

"Thakurpo," said Binodini, "what you suspect is not so. This room has not been defiled. You had once lived here—to that memory I have dedicated this room. These dead flowers which you see are the relics of my worship of that memory. It is here, in this room that you must sit."

Bihari's heart swelled with joy at these words. He entered the room and sat down on the bed to which Binodini pointed with both hands. She seated herself on the floor near his feet and seeing Bihari about to rise in protest said, "Please be seated, Thakurpo. Do not get up, I beg of you. I am not fit to sit by your feet even—it's your kindness to let me do so. I shall cling to this little right, even when you are far away."

She remained silent for a while and then suddenly started and asked, "Have you had your meal, Thakurpo?"

"Yes, at the station."

"I had sent you a letter from my village," said Binodini. "You sent it back to me with Mahendra, opened and without a word of acknowledgement. Why?"

"I never saw the letter," replied Bihari.

"Did you see Mahendra in Calcutta this time?"

"The only time I saw him was on the day following your departure for the village," replied Bihari. "Immediately after that I left Calcutta and was wandering around these parts. I have not seen Mahendra since."

"What about the earlier letter which too you sent back to me unread?" asked Binodini.

"I have never done any such thing," replied Bihari.

Binodini was stunned and remained speechless. After a

while she sighed deeply and said, "Now I understand. Let me also tell you everything. If you believe it I shall consider myself fortunate. If you don't, I won't blame you. It's not easy to believe me."

Bihari's heart had melted. He now found it impossible to spurn such humble and genuine heart-felt devotion. He said, "You don't have to tell me anything, Bouthan. Without hearing a word more, I believe you fully. I shall never despise you. Please say no more."

The tears rolled down Binodini's cheeks. Bending down she touched Bihari's feet with her hand and passed the hand on her forehead. She said, "I shall die of suffocation if I don't speak out. Please have a little patience and listen. I had willingly accepted the sentence of exile you had passed on me. Although you did not write even a line to me, I would have continued to put up with my lot in exile, put up with all the calumny and jeers which the village folks had heaped on me—let me have, I said, if not your love, your punishment—but fate denied even that to me. The sin I had provoked pursued me even in exile. Mahendra came to the village, came to the door of my cottage and covered me with disgrace in the eyes of all the people of the village. It was impossible for me to stay on there any longer. I looked for you everywhere to seek your guidance once again but could find you nowhere. Mahendra deceived me by bringing back my letter from your house, opened, and flinging it at my face. I was made to understand that you had given me up, spurned me, altogether. After that I could have gone to the dogs but—how wonderful is your influence, it works even from a distance!—I didn't. Because your thought was in my heart I remained chaste. Your image, hard and severe, ordering me into exile—this image I have carried in my heart, hard and severe like burnished gold, like a precious stone, making my life, worthless before, infinitely valuable. I swear to you, my angel, I touch your feet and swear that nothing has happened to destroy this value."

Bihari remained silent. Binodini too said nothing more. Gradually the afternoon light faded into dusk. Suddenly Mahendra arrived on the scene and was startled by Bihari's presence in the room, his newly acquired detachment reeling and tottering under the impact of reawakened jealousy. The sight of Binodini sitting like a statue at Bihari's feet was a challenge and a blow to his own manly pride. No doubt was left in his mind that these two had been corresponding on the sly and had arranged this rendezvous. Binodini was difficult enough when Bihari had turned away from her, but now that he had walked into her parlour, who could restrain her! No, Mahendra could not give up Binodini. He could, provided no one else got her. But not like this! Smarting with frustration he turned to Binodini and said in a bitter, mocking tone, "So the stage is set for a new scene—Exit Mahendra, Enter Bihari! What a charming scene! One feels like clapping. Let's hope it is the final act—the last affair."

Binodini flushed crimson. Having been obliged to accept Mahendra's protection, she had no retort against this insult. She looked at Bihari, helpless with pain and shame. Bihari rose from his seat and stepping forward said, "Don't insult Binodini like a coward, Mahendra! If your good breeding cannot restrain you, let me tell you, I have the right to do so."

"Indeed!" laughed Mahendra. "The right is only too obvious. Let's give you a new name from now on—Binod-Bihari." *

Seeing Mahendra bent on creating a scene, Bihari caught hold of his hand and said, "Mahendra, let me tell you that I propose to marry Binodini. So please keep a hold on your tongue."

Mahendra was stupefied. Binodini started, the rush of blood causing a tumult in her breast.

"There's one more piece of news for you," continued Bihari. "Your mother is lying seriously ill, there's little hope of

* Pun on the compound word which also means, one who enjoys Binod.

her surviving. I'm returning to Calcutta by tonight's train and Binodini is coming with me."

"Pishima ill!" exclaimed Binodini startled.

"Seriously," replied Bihari. "Little hope of recovery."

Mahendra left the room without another word.

"How could you say what you said just now?" asked Binodini turning to Bihari. "What a mockery!"

"No mockery," replied Bihari. "Believe me, I wish to marry you."

"To redeem this sinner?"

"No, but because I love you, because I respect you."

"Then let that be my final reward. I want nothing more than what you have just affirmed. If I took more it wouldn't last. Religion and society would never tolerate it."

"Why not?" asked Bihari.

"The very thought of it is shameful," said Binodini. "I am a widow and, besides, a woman in disgrace. I can never allow you to lose caste on my account. Please, don't ever again utter such words."

"You will cut me off then?" asked Bihari.

"That I can't. Nor have I the right to do so. You have many secret philanthropic missions in hand. Entrust me with some work in one of them so that I may make my life useful in your service. But marry a widow! What a shameful thing to do! You may be generous enough to court such a disaster, but if I let you do it, if I exposed you to social calumny, I should never be able to lift my head up again."

"But, Binodini, I love you," cried Bihari.

"In the pride of that love let me today commit a little impertinence," said Binodini as she bent herself prostrate on the ground and kissed Bihari's toes; then sitting up by his feet again she continued, "I shall pray and do penance that I may have you as mine in our next life—in this life I dare not hope for more, I do not deserve it. I have caused much suffering, have borne much suffering and have learnt a great lesson. Dare I forget that lesson and drag you into the mire, myself sinking lower! If I have not done so, if I am able to raise my head once more, it is because you stood above me and helped me to rise. This pillar, this refuge, I will not destroy."

Bihari remained silent, looking grave. Binodini continued, her palms held together in entreaty, "Do not deceive yourself. You will never be happy if you marry me. You will lose your pride and self-respect and I shall lose mine. Live your life as you have always lived it, detached and serene—and let me remain at a distance, engaged in your work. May happiness and peace be ever yours!"

51

As Mahendra was about to enter his mother's room, Asha hurriedly came out and said, "Don't go in yet, please."

"Why?" asked Mahendra.

"The doctor has warned us that any kind of shock, pleasant or unpleasant, may prove fatal for her."

"Let me tiptoe stealthily behind her and have a look at her—she won't know it," said Mahendra.

"She starts at the slightest sound," insisted Asha. "She's sure to wake up as soon as you enter the room."

"What then do you propose to do?" asked Mahendra.

"Let Bihari Thakurpo come and see her first. Whatever he advises shall be done."

Just then Bihari arrived. Asha sent for him.

"Did you send for me, Bouthan?" asked Bihari. "I hope mother is better?"

Asha seemed relieved at the sight of Bihari and replied, "She has been more restless since you left. The very first day she inquired, not seeing you, 'Where's Bihari gone?' I replied, 'He's been called on urgent work and should be back by Thursday.' Since then she wakes up now and then with a start—as if she is expecting someone, though outwardly she says nothing. Yesterday when your telegram arrived I told her you'd be coming today and so she has ordered special dishes to be made for you, all your favourites, and has directed that the cooking be done in the veranda facing her room so that she can personally supervise it. She simply wouldn't listen to the doctor. Only a little while ago she called me and said, 'Bouma, you must cook every dish with your own hands. I'll seat Bihari in front of me and see that he eats.' "

The tears filled Bihari's eyes. He asked, "How is she?"

"You had better see her for yourself," replied Asha. "I am afraid she is worse."

Bihari went inside. Mahendra, stupefied, remained standing outside the door, lost in amazement at the ease with which Asha held the reins of the household in her hands. How naturally and simply, without timidity and without resentment, she forbade Mahendra to enter the room! And he—how ineffectual he had become in his own house, standing mutely like a culprit outside his mother's room, lacking the courage to enter!

No less amazing was the sight of Asha talking freely and without embarrassment to Bihari, consulting him as though he was the sole guardian of the house, beloved and trusted by all. It was he and not Mahendra who now had free access to every room, whose word was listened to by all. Mahendra discovered on his return that his status in his own home was no longer what it had been.

As soon as Bihari entered the room Rajlakshmi looked up at him tenderly and said, "You've come back, Bihari?"

"Yes, mother, I'm back."

"Your work done?" she asked looking at him steadily.

"Yes, mother," replied Bihari beaming, "my mission is completed. I've no anxiety any more."

"Bouma will cook your meal with her own hands today.

I'll tell her what to do from here. The doctor says, don't do this! don't do that!—but of what use, my son? Can't I even watch you people eat before I depart?"

"There's no sense in what the doctor says, mother," rejoined Bihari. "How can we carry on without you? Since childhood we've been used to enjoying dishes cooked by your hands—and Mahendra, poor chap, he's sick of eating *dal-roti* * and is longing for your fish curry. Today we two brothers shall once again sit down to eat together, as we used to do as children, vying with each other, gobbling away the choicest tid-bits. Let's see if your Bouma's cooking will suffice."

Although Rajlakshmi had guessed that Bihari had brought Mahendra along with him, her heart trembled at the sound of his name and her breathing became painful. When she had recovered, Bihari continued, "Mahinda's health has improved very much by his trip to the west—although he looks tired after the journey. He'll be all right after bath and lunch."

Finding that Rajlakshmi did not even then respond, Bihari went on, "Mahinda is waiting at the door, mother. He can't come unless you call him in."

Rajlakshmi looked towards the door, without saying anything. Seeing her look Bihari called out, "Come in, Mahinda!"

Mahendra came in, slowly. Afraid of a violent shock to her heart, Rajlakshmi refrained from looking at him and half-closed her eyes. Mahendra looked at the bed and gave a start as though someone had struck him. He bent down, his head on his mother's feet, his hands clutching them. A trembling shook Rajlakshmi's heart and limbs.

After a while Annapurna said softly, "Didi, please ask Mahin to get up. He won't otherwise."

* *Lit.* lentils and bread. Reference is to the food habits of people to the west of Bengal who take plenty of wheat, while Bengalees love rice and fish.

246

"Get up, Mahin," mumbled Rajlakshmi articulating each word painfully.

After a long drought the tears rolled down her cheeks in a profuse flow, as soon as she had uttered her son's name. The oppression in her heart eased. Raising himself Mahendra came over to his mother's side and knelt on the floor, bending over her. With a painful effort she turned on her side and holding Mahendra's head in her hands drew it towards her face and kissed his forehead.

"Mother," pleaded Mahendra in a broken voice, "I've brought you much suffering. Please forgive me."

Pulling herself together Rajlakshmi said, "Say no more, Mahin. How can I live without forgiving you!—Bouma! Bouma!! Where are you?"

Asha was in the next room preparing the invalid's diet. Annapurna sent for her. When she came, Rajlakshmi motioned to Mahendra to rise from the floor and sit beside her on the bed and then addressed Asha, "Bouma, you sit here— I want to see you two seated side by side today—then only will my suffering cease. Don't be shy, Bouma, sit down here and wipe away all resentment against Mahin from your mind. My little mother, fill my eyes with peace."

Lightning Source UK Ltd.
Milton Keynes UK
UKHW022141060223
416587UK00005B/116